H.M. Sandlin

ISBN:9781661801984

One who is wise though their years are few
Will awaken the elements to when they were true
And the worlds in between will awaken soon
After the power is bestowed on you

If they choose dark, the world will be destroyed
But if light is chosen the world won't fall into void
Many will fall to dark's endless ways
But a few will stay strong for the coming days

Under the land on an isle green
The water sprites help if they are seen
Above the clouds where cold winds blow
The sylphs are waiting to help those below

Where fire touches a sky so blue
The drakos are waiting to save a few
But underground bad dryads wait
Except for one who seals alls fate

Friends will help though may be lost
Look around, or you'll pay the cost
All powers together will fight the dark
And seal him away in void's pure mark

CHAPTER ONE

The baby dragon looked at me sleepily. It was curled up on my bed. Its golden scales glistened as the light reflected off of them, each movement causing the dragon scales to sparkle and glitter in new ways. Mauevene, a water sprite, flew around the dragon, flinching when its tongue snaked out, trying to grab her.

"Bad baby dragon," I said, giving it a hard look. Its black eyes locked on mine before it looked down. I wasn't sure what to do with it. I didn't know dragons even existed before this one showed up. I sat on the other side of my bed, and it scooted closer to me, trying to snuggle against my leg. I sighed and lifted it up, placing it in my lap while Mauevene flew around us. I could feel a rumble coming from the baby dragon, almost like a cat's purr. It lifted one eyelid to look at me as I shifted my weight.

"I'm not going anywhere," I said, running my hand over the scales. I thought a dragon would feel similar to a snake, but its scales were rock hard. Only its belly was a soft silky texture. Even the ridges around its eyes were hard.

It settled back down as I studied it. I was going to have to come up with a name. I couldn't keep calling it the baby dragon. I remembered reading a book about a dragon where it told the person its name. I reached my hand out and placed it on the dragon's head. When no name came to me, I let out a little huff. Too bad, that would've made this so much easier, I thought.

I looked to Mauevene for help, but she disappeared as soon as she saw me glance at her. She probably saw the pleading look in my eyes. She didn't want anything to do with this responsibility. Maybe my friends could help me. I didn't even know what to feed it. I heard a grumbling noise from the dragon. It sounded like laughter.

"Are you laughing at me? You made the same sound when I caught you in my room. You better not be laughing at me, or I won't help you."

The grumbling grew louder. It was definitely laughter. I tried to stand up and put the baby dragon on the bed, but it clung to me, its body wrapping around my arm. It clawed its way up my sleeve until it settled around my neck.

I looked in the mirror and watched as the dragon disappeared. I could feel him against me, but I couldn't see him. I walked to my door, telling him to stay invisible while I tried to find my friends.

Abby was across the hall in her room. She opened her door and told me to come in when I knocked. After stepping into her room, I looked around in shock. We had only been back a short time, yet she had managed to take all the clothes in her suitcase and spread them everywhere in her room.

"What are you doing?"

"I'm looking for a coin I took with me when we went on our trip," she said, talking about the school field trip we just got back from. It was a dangerous trip for us. While the other students were doing school stuff, my group snuck away to go help the air elementals in their realm at the top of the mountain. We managed to save them from the creatures guarding them. In return, they promised to help me when the time came for me to face the darkness that was moving closer and closer to earth, trying to take over.

The darkness was already influencing members of the council. Now it was causing trouble at the school too. Mrs. Sullivan, our headmistress, told us the Pulhu on the council were trying to get her fired and replace her with one of their own members. Most elementals didn't realize how bad things were getting. The Pulhu made sure to cover their tracks. No one could tie them to anything. A lot more elementals were starting to believe the lies they were spreading. They thought they should rule the world, and that nonmagical people should be beneath them.

I still couldn't believe people actually felt that way. To me, everyone was equal. That's why I was best friends with Tider, the son of the scariest family in the Pulhu. It was said they ran most of the Pulhu except for a small side group. I didn't care though. Tider was a sweet, caring person who didn't want to hurt anyone unless he had to. He had been tricking his family for years, pretending to believe the lies they spread while never doing anything terrible himself. It was the only way he could get by. If they knew how he really felt, they would have cursed him or killed him long ago.

I convinced Abby to look for the coin later. I wanted to talk to everyone about my baby dragon problem. I mentally reached out to Richard, asking him to find the other guys and meet us in the cafeteria. I felt him respond through our link. They would be there soon. Abby and I beat them to the cafeteria and put our stuff on a table. I grabbed a granola bar and some juice before heading back to our spot.

The guys came in soon after, and we all ate quietly for a few minutes before I told them about my baby dragon.

"You have a what?" exclaimed Adam, the newest member of our group.

We had helped him escape from the water elemental realm when they caught him sneaking around their palace. Ever since then, he had stuck with us.

"It was on my bed when we got back. There was a note telling me it would help guide us and to hurry. I think the first thing we need to do is name it," I told them when no one said anything.

Abby immediately started throwing names out like Cuddles and Mr. Spitfire. My baby dragon hissed in my ear at each one.

"I don't think it likes those," I told her.

"Wait, it's with you?"

I nodded and explained how it had become invisible and wrapped itself around my neck. My friends wanted to see the dragon, so we decided to meet that night in the south wing. It was the only place we could all talk privately. The south wing was spelled to keep everyone out. It hadn't been used for a long time.

Most of the students and teachers thought a fire destroyed the south wing, and it was never rebuilt. I found out a spell was placed on it to keep anyone from entering. I broke the spell for my friends so we could use it as a hiding place.

Someone else knew about it too. We didn't know who though. They wore a black cloak, but I could tell it was a female and either a teacher or someone who worked or went to the school. We saw her in the south wing meeting with someone last term. We made sure to keep our eyes out for her when we were there, but we hadn't seen her since.

I snuck a few handfuls of extra food to feed to the baby dragon when I got back to my room. When I tried to feed it to him, he turned up his nose, disgusted. I shrugged and turned away from him. I hadn't figured anything else out about dragons. From the books I looked at, dragons were rare to see, even when the elementals were allowed to roam the human realm freely.

My friends were going to see if they could learn anything to help me before I met with them in the south wing. Maybe one of them could tell me what to feed it.

That night I snuck down to the south wing with Abby to meet the guys. As we neared the door, I heard voices around the corner. I grabbed Abby's hand, dragging her into the corridor with me. We watched as the new teacher, Mr. Burwel, walked past with Sean. I couldn't hear what they were saying. I went to take a step closer, but Abby stopped me.

"You can't walk out there. They will see you." We were only five feet from them, but the spell on the south wing kept them from being able to see us. Even if they looked directly toward us, all they would see was a closed door. I watched as they said goodbye, and Sean headed toward the boy's wing. Mr. Burwel turned and walked back toward the classrooms. I wanted to follow him. There was no reason to go that way in the middle of the night, but I had to worry about the baby dragon first.

I turned away and walked farther into the south wing, finding the classroom where we all met up. The guys were already waiting. I told them what I saw, and they agreed we would have to keep an eye on the new teacher. Especially since Mrs. Sullivan thought he was part of the Pulhu.

No one had learned anything about dragons. We were going to have to guess how to raise it. Mauevene hadn't known either.

"Is he here?" Abby asked excitedly.

"Yes," I told her. "Baby dragon, you can show yourself to my friends. They won't hurt you." The dragon slowly became visible wrapped around the back of my neck, his tail coming around the front and trailing over my shoulder.

"Oh, my goodness. He is adorable. Can I pet him?" Abby asked.

My baby dragon puffed up his chest and let out a small growl.

"I think that's a no," I said.

Abby looked sad but perked back up when Richard asked about names.

"I still don't know. I'm not even sure if it's a boy or girl."

"He seems to know what we are saying. Let's give him or her a bunch of names to choose from," Richard said.

Everyone started saying different names as the dragon snorted at each one. He didn't seem happy with any of the choices. I felt him bump his snout to my face, and a name came to me.

"His name is Sievroth," I told my friends. At their questioning looks, I explained how I knew his name now. I asked Sievroth why he didn't tell me his name sooner, but he didn't respond. We stayed for another thirty minutes, talking about the new teacher and what Mrs. Sullivan said. If she wasn't here to protect us, the Pulhu would be able to get to us in no time. We decided to start figuring out a backup plan in case the council sent her away.

Back in my room, I watched as Sievroth unfurled from my neck and gently flew around the room, stretching his wings. Mauevene appeared, and he immediately tried to snatch her up. I grabbed him and leaned into his face, scolding him. Hot smoke blew from his nostrils, and I leaned back, startled.

"You better not breathe fire in this room, Sievroth," I told him. "I don't want to try and explain why my room has scorch marks all over it. If you need to breathe fire, you go outside and do it where no one will see you. Or better yet, control it, so you don't have to do it at all."

Sievroth turned his head to the side and started shaking it.

"I mean it, Sievroth," I began to say. The baby dragon let out a small sneeze, and a ball of fire hit my wall, burning the poster I had up. I used air to put the fire out as quickly as I could, but it still left a few marks that would be hard to explain. Dragon fire must be incredibly hot to be able to burn the wall so fast. I looked at the ashes of my poster. I would need to ask my mom and dad to send another one. Sievroth glided over to the bed and landed softly, looking up at me with his large orange eyes. They were tilted downward, and he hung his head.

"It's ok, Sievroth. I know you didn't do it on purpose. You are still a baby and learning how to control yourself." I sighed and picked him up for a cuddle, laying on my bed while I watched Mauevene flit back and forth across the room.

I had the weekend off and spent my time in the common room with my friends. Most of the other students looked at me oddly when they saw me, and a few even came up to say they were glad I wasn't killed during the avalanche. I said thanks to them, but I felt terrible for making so many people worry. They thought we had been trapped on the mountain by a series of avalanches. We couldn't tell them we were in the air elemental realm.

I went to class with Richard and Tider on Monday so we could all work on our air powers together. Richard brought the book from the air elemental queen that she gave him, and Mr. Connor looked through it for the first half of class. He could only look at it when one of us was with him, or it would disappear. It had been enchanted by the air elemental queen to keep it safe. Mr. Connor had us start practicing the forms, and he even joined in to practice with us.

After we knew a few forms, Mr. Connor had us use air magic during each form the way the book taught. We all felt a boost in magic. The air wanted to work with us. It felt like we had been forcing it without the forms. Mr. Connor was ecstatic and couldn't wait to start teaching the other students. He looked upset when we told him he couldn't teach the other students until after the Pulhu and the darkness were defeated. The last thing we needed was for the Pulhu to be more powerful.

As Mr. Connor was fixing Tider's form, I heard a noise near the door of the dome. I stood up and looked over as the door opened. Mr. Burwel was standing there. I quickly cleared my throat, causing the others to stand up and look where I pointed.

"Excuse me, Mr. Burwel," Mr. Connor said. "This is a private masters class. What can I do for you?"

"I am here to watch the students in your classes. The council wants me to observe what is taught in each class. That includes masters classes."

"Masters classes are private for a reason, as you know," Mr. Connor said, irritated at Mr. Burwel. "No one is to watch until the final tests. You missed those by a few weeks and will have to wait until next year's test. Or you can view the videos of it. I'm sure Mrs. Sullivan has copies, or you can ask the council. They should already have copies since each school is required to send in masters test videos."

"I have seen them, and your students do a good job, but the council wants me watching all the classes." Mr. Burwel's mouth tightened. "You may check with the council if you need to, but I will be watching whenever I want."

Mr. Connor turned away from Mr. Burwel and addressed us. "Class is dismissed for the day. I will let you know when your next class is. Until then, remember, don't practice anything you learn here outside of the dome." He stared straight at me, making sure I understood what he was trying to say. The Pulhu were watching. Even the domes were no longer safe. Mr. Connor would try to take care of the problem, but I had a feeling Mr. Burwel would be watching everything I did.

"Ok, Mr. Connor," I said. "We'll see you next time. Nice to see you again," I said to Mr. Burwel. Tider grabbed the book and threw it in his book bag on the way out so Mr. Burwel wouldn't see it. Good thing I had worked so hard on my magic the last two semesters. I wasn't going to get much of a chance this semester. I could use my water and air magic, but not the other elements since the Pulhu didn't know I had them all. If they did, they would kill me. At least right now, most of them wanted to turn me to their side. It gave me a fighting chance.

I heard Mr. Burwel saying something to Mr. Connor as we left and stopped before I walked out the door to listen. "You can't cancel classes forever. Eventually, I will find out what you are hiding, and then I will let the council deal with all of you."

I quickly closed the dome door and turned to Tider and Richard. "We have a big problem," I said, telling them what I heard. "He is going to cause problems here. We can't let that happen."

"We won't," Richard said. I wanted to believe him but knew it was going to be hard to stop him.

Nothing else happened until the next day when I went to my masters class with Mr. Merrem. When I walked into the dome, Mr. Burwel was already there arguing with Mr. Merrem.

"You will not be allowed to stay in this class until I have a signed letter from the head of the council telling me it is ok. It is a violation of all our rules to have someone else watching masters classes without the student's permission. I doubt you got their permission."

"I don't need it," Mr. Burwel said.

"I'm afraid you do, or you need that paper," Mr. Merrem said. He grabbed Mr. Burwel's arm and started leading him out of the dome. Mr. Burwel resisted, and Mr. Merrem smirked, "We can do this the hard way then." Mr. Burwel let out a distressed noise.

"Fine, I'm leaving, but I will be back," he said as Mr. Merrem led him to the door. I could smell burnt hair and skin as they passed. When Mr. Merrem let go of Mr. Burwel's arm, I could see a handprint burned into his skin. When Mr. Burwel was gone, I laughed.

"You handled him better than Mr. Connor did. Now I can practice."

"You can practice today, but he will have that paper tomorrow. We can't keep him out of here if the council wants him monitoring classes. I've already talked to Mr. Connor. We will try slipping you or one of your friends a note with a time and location to practice where it is safe. We will have to be very careful not to be followed."

I frowned. I thought about telling him we could practice in the south wing, but that was my fall back plan if the teachers couldn't figure anything out. For now, I would let them find a safe place, and if we needed to, I would tell them my plan.

"I want to show you a few more defensive spells that we don't usually use. I have a feeling you are going to need them." He went over a few defensive techniques that I could use if the Pulhu got to close to me again.

He also taught me to use my invisibility to hide other things instead of myself. I could lay a trap and make it invisible until someone triggered it. Since the trap wasn't moving, this was easy for me. I had to make sure it was a small trap because it would continue pulling small amounts of energy from me. I also couldn't be too far away from it. With practice, I would be able to go farther and make the trap bigger.

Mr. Merrem walked me back to the school, not wanting to leave me alone with Mr. Burwel on campus. After telling me to stay close to my friends, he left me at the common room and headed toward Mrs. Sullivan's office. I was sure they were going to be trying to figure out a way to get Mr. Burwel sent back to the council.

CHAPTER TWO

I didn't know what to do with myself each afternoon without the extra classes. I made Abby or Tider come with me to the library to study more about the fire elementals since I needed to find them next. Sievroth stayed wrapped around my shoulders whenever I wasn't in class. I had no idea where he went during class. I overheard one girl say she saw a fireball out in the woods the other day and figured he was out there doing his own practicing.

He still hadn't eaten anything, but he didn't seem concerned. I had seen him drink some water from the creek out in the garden the other day, so I knew he was taking care of himself. Mauevene didn't come out when he was around anymore. He was getting too fast and almost grabbed her with his tongue the other day. I didn't want to see Sievroth eat my friend, so I didn't ask for her help with some of my questions. No matter how many times I told him not to eat her, he didn't listen to me. She was safer being away from me for now.

We were all sitting in the common room when a few men in suits walked past with Mr. Burwel. I slouched in my seat so he wouldn't see me. I recognized one of the men from the last time the council had been at the school. He had been a jerk to Mrs. Sullivan. He was definitely a Pulhu supporter. I wasn't sure which side of the Pulhu though. Hopefully, the side that didn't want to kill me.

Abby grabbed my hand as soon as they passed, and we headed for her room. I couldn't go to mine. Last time they were here, one of the council had snuck into my room and tried to hit me with a spell. I was in Abby's room after a warning from Richard had gotten me out of bed, and I watched the whole thing from her peephole.

As long as they were here, I wasn't safe. I broke out in a sweat and quickened my pace, glancing back over and over until we arrived at Abby's room. We slipped inside, and I used air to seal the door shut. I had been practicing that and was able to use minimal energy to make sure the door didn't open. No one was getting in without burning the door down.

I reached out to connect with Richard telepathically. "Is everything ok?" I asked him.

"So far. I'm watching from the end of the hallway. They went into Mrs. Sullivan's office, so I can't hear anything they are saying. We will have to wait until they come out and see if we overhear anything. Tider and Adam are also nearby in different parts of the hall to see if they hear anything. I'll let you know as soon as they leave."

"Thanks, Richard," I said, pulling out of his mind.

I repeated what he said to Abby, and she pulled out a book. "We might as well keep working on this since we can't leave for a while," she said. It was an old book about gods associated with fire.

"Where did you get this?"

"At the library. It was stuffed between some other books on volcanoes. It wasn't with the fire elemental books, but I figured it might be worth a try.

"Myths about fire gods," I read out loud. I tried not to sound skeptical.

"Yeah, I know, but maybe the fire gods are the true fire elementals. You never know. They were worshipped as gods a long time ago." She had a point. "You read that one. I'm going to read this one," she said, holding up a book on fire elemental magic. "I don't know a lot about the fire elementals. It might be smart to know a little more since we will be trying to find them."

I agreed and grabbed the book she handed to me. I sat on her floor, leaning against the bed as I opened it. The first few pages talked about humans making up gods to help themselves understand the world they lived in better. Whoever wrote the book didn't believe any of the fire gods were real.

I had to admit I wasn't sure either. Especially after reading about the first few gods. They sounded more like hellish creatures that were made up to scare children. There was one who supposedly ate people. Another one could only be seen and heard if you sacrificed the correct items on the correct day. Almost all of the sacrifices required killing animals. I thought about putting the book down, but I hadn't been able to find anything else on fire elementals, so I didn't stop.

I continued reading, looking up occasionally to see how Abby was doing and make sure the door was still sealed. Surprisingly, I learned a lot about older cultures. They needed to believe in a god for everything they did to understand the world.

Toward the back of the book, I found something promising. There was one fire god named Gibi, who could shoot fire from his hands. He was also able to withstand any fire. He had even taught this magic to many of his followers. He ruled for many years until he got in a fight with another god who smothered his flames with water.

A different fire god took his place, but very few followed him willingly. He was a cruel and vicious leader who brought destruction everywhere he went. Eventually, another powerful god defeated him. After that, no one heard from the fire gods or their followers.

That could have been when the shadow king destroyed all the elemental cities and sent them to live in their own realms. The shadow king had destroyed almost all of their followers after the elementals taught them to use magic. A lot of true elementals were also killed. They used their magic to fight other elementals and caused massive devastation to the human population and the earth. Eventually, the elementals were forgotten, and so was magic as generations of humans lived without any sign of elemental powers. The few that were born with magic kept it hidden for fear of prosecution.

At the back of the book was a map showing where each fire god lived. I looked for Gibi, the fire god that seemed the most promising. The map showed him in Italy. I pulled out my phone and looked up different volcanoes in that area. I couldn't believe my luck, Mount Etna was in Italy, and it was one of the oldest volcanoes. It would have been around when the fire elementals were still living in the human realm. I got Abby's attention and told her what I learned.

"It seems a little too easy, doesn't it?" Abby asked.

I hesitated. "Yes, but we don't have very long to find them. We are going to have to hope that this is really the spot."

"We need to tell Mrs. Sullivan. She will help us get there. Remember, she said she would help as much as possible before the council finds a reason to fire her," Abby said.

As soon as the guys said it was safe, we headed to Mrs. Sullivan's office. They hadn't been able to hear anything going on, so they decided to wait for us by her office and ask what the council wanted. Once we were all there and seated around Mrs. Sullivan's desk, I told her what I learned and said that I wanted to go and see if the fire elementals were there.

"I'm not sure that's a good idea, Sally," Mrs. Sullivan said. "How sure are you? Did you find any other information?"

"No, we haven't been able to find any other information. We need to go check this out. You know we don't have much time."

Mrs. Sullivan was still concerned, but after a few more minutes of us trying to convince her, she agreed. She would call Jordan to transport us there over the weekend to look around. We were not to go into the fire elemental realm. We were only going to see if it was the correct place. We would need a plan before we went to their realm. We couldn't disappear for almost a week again, or the Pulhu would figure out what we were doing.

"What will we tell the rest of the students while we are checking the area out?" I asked.

"We will tell them that you went on break with Abby to see her father if anyone asks," Mrs. Sullivan said. "You will only be gone for a weekend. We don't want to risk anyone realizing you aren't with Abby's dad."

"What about us?" Tider asked.

"You will stay here. We can't have all of you missing with the Pulhu watching the school. I'm sure Abby and Sally can handle this on their own."

"They can't go by themselves. What if something happens?" Richard didn't look happy that Mrs. Sullivan was going to let me go without him and the other guys.

"We are going to have to take that chance. I know you have more of the invisibility potion left. You can use that so no one sees you. If you see anything suspicious, hide until Jordan comes to get you. You will be meeting him in the same place that he drops you off. He will make sure you know exactly where that is so you can get back to him."

"I don't think it's a good idea," Richard said.

"It's a good thing it isn't your choice then," Mrs. Sullivan said. "This is a good opportunity to see if you can talk to each other telepathically when you are far away."

Richard grumbled something under his breath but didn't argue with Mrs. Sullivan anymore.

"Jordan will transport you back Sunday night. That gives you two days to look around. Come right to my office when you get back so we can discuss what you find out," she said.

We talked for a few more minutes about the plan, and then Mrs. Sullivan dismissed us. As I was getting up from my seat, she stopped me. "Sally, I don't think I need to tell you this, but I will anyway. Your extra classes are canceled until further notice. Mr. Burwel has already received the paperwork from the council so he can watch you. That's what they were doing here today. Richard and Tider, continue taking your masters classes but don't show him how much power you actually have."

"Yes, Mrs. Sullivan," they said.

We went to the library instead of the common room. We couldn't go out to the garden for privacy since it was raining again. It made it harder to talk when we couldn't go out. The library was the next best place. Barely anyone came in unless it was close to finals. Then the library was full of students studying.

I was more careful when we met in the library ever since Sean attacked us, so it was harder to concentrate. I almost expected Sean and his friends to jump out from around one of the aisles and throw potions at us. So far, he hadn't bothered us too much this semester, but I wasn't going to be able to fully enjoy the library in the school again. I pushed thoughts of Sean and his gang from my mind and tuned in to my friend's conversation.

Richard said he wanted to start meeting in the south wing so I could continue to practice. He would have Mr. Connor and Mr. Merrem tell him what I should practice, and he would teach it to me after everyone went to bed. I agreed. I needed to know everything I could if I was going to win against the Pulhu and the darkness.

"I think I can help you out with the location of the true fire elementals. I talked to my grandfather, and he reminded me about something I read once," Adam said. He was a fire elemental, and his grandfather was an archaeologist. He had been studying the fire elementals for a long time.

"I would look for any area that could open up into a cave. There is probably a rock nearby that you can put your hand on while it's bathed in fire to open the pathway to their realm. That was how they used to open their doors. If you weren't a fire elemental, you wouldn't be able to get in."

Adam also told us that fire elementals were said to have short tempers but could be very forgiving. They didn't like to be bothered by the other elementals. From the texts he read on them, they lived around a volcano. One of the books he read said they may even live underground. They had many caverns that opened to the surface. The heat didn't bother them. That's why they lived under the ground near the volcano. They were protected from the other elementals. He didn't know how much was true, but the book he read it in was very old.

"Thanks, Adam," I said. "We will try to find the area, and then we will come back to get you guys."

The days leading up to the weekend took forever. I couldn't wait. I wanted to find the fire elementals quickly. I still had to find the earth elementals, and no one knew what I had to do for void magic. And this all had to happen before the end of summer.

When Abby knocked on my door Saturday morning, I was ready. Sievroth was wrapped around my neck like usual, and I had a backpack slung over my shoulder. It held mostly food and a couple of potions. I didn't think we would need much for this trip. We were only gathering information.

I felt Richard in the back of my mind and reached out telepathically, giving him what would feel like a slap on the back of his head.

"Ow," he said in my head.

"I told you not to sneak up on me." I could feel his amusement, and I smiled. "What's up?"

"Make sure you are careful and try to contact me as soon as you get there. I want to know that we can get in touch with each other."

"I will," I told him seriously. I felt his worry bleed through our connection. He could tell I was worried too. I didn't like our group separating. We worked better together, but the fewer people, the better our chances of not getting caught. I still couldn't believe Mrs. Sullivan was letting me go. She must be anxious about the Pulhu coming to the school.

Jordan was waiting at Mrs. Sullivan's office. After she gave me a few warnings, she let us leave. We walked out the front door and to the gates.

We needed to be off school property to transport. Otherwise, the protections stopped us.

I grabbed Abby with one hand and Jordan with the other. I watched as Abby grabbed Jordan too.

"Let's hope this time we don't have anyone trying to rip you out of the transport," Jordan said, referring to the last time he took us somewhere. The Pulhu were able to interrupt the transport and force us to appear in a trap. We barely made it back to the school. We still didn't know how they did it. Transports usually couldn't be interrupted. Jordan said he was working on figuring out how they did it with a few of his friends, but no one was getting any closer to an answer.

"I hope they don't try that again," I told him.

"They don't know we are going anywhere, so we should be safe."

Jordan closed his eyes. So did I. The world dropped out from under me. The wind began spinning around me, catching at my hair and clothes before my feet landed on solid ground again. I opened my eyes to see Abby was standing too. Transporting was hard the first few times. We were starting to get used to it and didn't fall when we stopped anymore, though my stomach still hurt for a few minutes after we landed.

I could hear voices in the distance but didn't see anyone. We were hidden in a clump of trees near the base of the volcano. Behind us, I could see a bustling village. It would be nice to stay and visit. I turned back to the volcano. There wasn't time to play tourist for the day.

"How long does it take to reach the top?" asked Abby.

"It says about four hours with a guided hike," I replied, looking at my phone. "But you take a cable car part of the way."

"We are already above that, and that's on the other side. We are on the north side. There are fewer tourists on this side. Only guided hikes are allowed this high up, and there usually aren't too many over here. Everyone wants to go to the south side," Jordan said. "It shouldn't take more than three hours if you are going directly to the top, but I doubt that's the case. Whenever I have to transport you somewhere, you get in trouble with the Pulhu, so I'm guessing you are here looking for something that they want. Right?"

I looked around nervously. I didn't want anyone else to know that I might be the one from the prophecy. The Pulhu had spies everywhere. So far, they thought I was a powerful elemental. An enigma since my powers hadn't emerged until this year. Almost an adult. This barely ever occurred, and they wanted answers. They also wanted me under their thumb, which wasn't going to happen.

"It's ok, Sally," Jordan said, seeing my look. "You don't have to tell me it all. Besides, I think I have it almost figured out. I will keep your secrets. You know I'm not a friend of the Pulhu."

"Thanks, Jordan," I replied.

"I'll be back here in two days. Mark this exact spot on your phones so you don't get lost. It would be difficult to find you up here. It's a huge area, and there are many places to fall and get hurt where no one will find you."

Jordan said his goodbyes after his warning and disappeared. I reached out with my mind until I was able to contact Richard. I could tell he was very far away. I had trouble hearing him when he responded, but I could feel his emotions. I sent calm feelings to him so he would know I was ok. He sent a wave of calmness back to me. I dropped the connection now that he knew I was fine.

Abby and I walked out of the trees and over to a small path. We headed up toward the top of the mountain, deciding not to take our invisibility potions until we had to. As we rounded a bend, we saw people ahead of us. A man at the front was talking and pointing toward the peak of Mount Etna. We slowed our pace as we looked around for a different route. I didn't want to be stuck behind them, and we couldn't pass them. I quietly led Abby off the path.

"There are not many places to hide up here," she said. "People are going to see us."

"I know. I want to make sure they don't see us doing anything they shouldn't see. Adam told us to look for any areas that could open into caves. Do you see anything like that?"

"Not yet." I looked around the mountain, noticing that the higher we got, the steeper the climb would become.

"What about up there? Maybe there is a cave opening in one of the craters."

"I don't know," Abby said. "They wouldn't want anyone being able to accidentally see them coming in or out of their realm. It could cause the shadow king to destroy them all."

"Where do you think we should look first?" I asked.

"What about one of the areas off the path. Maybe there is a crater most people don't see. Something small and overlooked."

"We could try hiking straight up instead of following the path. The other hikers won't notice us if we are quick. They have a long hike if they follow the trail," I said. "We can easily get ahead of them while they hike around the mountain."

"We will need to be careful going this way. There is a lot of loose rock," Abby said, looking up.

"We can do it."

We started up the side of Mount Etna, being careful not to lose our footing. A few times, my foot slipped, and only a gentle push with my air powers kept me from falling. I had to boost Abby up a few times too, but we made it. I looked down the path and couldn't see the group that had been in front of us. They were a reasonable distance behind us now, and we could start searching for the fire elementals.

I wanted to go right up to the craters to try to find them. It seemed like the most obvious choice, but Abby still thought we needed to look somewhere else.

We compromised. We would look at all the smaller areas on the way up to the crater.

CHAPTER THREE

We were almost to the top and still didn't see any sign of the fire elementals. I couldn't even feel any magic from them. We had no idea where we were going. When I was looking for the air elementals, a dream showed me where I needed to go. This time I was on my own. We were almost to the largest crater when I heard voices again. I looked down the path, expecting to see the tour that had been behind us, but there was no one there. The voices were coming from ahead of us.

I put an invisibility shield around us as we walked closer. As long as I didn't use it for too long, it wouldn't take too much energy. We laid on our bellies behind a few large boulders. Walking out of the crater and around it were a few men and women. They weren't dressed in the usual hiking gear. They didn't even have backpacks with them. I felt a shiver crawl down my spine and pulled Abby back while digging in my pack. I pulled the potions out.

"Here. Take this. I think those are the Pulhu. We need to get in there, and I don't want anyone sensing my magic."

"How would they know about this place?" Abby asked.

"I have no idea, but they aren't tourists."

We both drank our potions and waited a few minutes to make sure they were working.

"What do we do?" Abby asked.

"We need to know what they are doing. The potion should last a few hours. We need to go down there and listen in to their conversations before it wears off."

"Are you sure that's a good idea?"

"No, but we need to know if they found the fire elementals and why they are looking for them."

We slowly walked around the rim of the crater, making sure not to disturb any loose stones on our way to the path leading down into it. When we came to the path, a large, burly man was standing in front of it. He stood as still as a statue. The scowl on his face scared me even though I knew he couldn't see me. We would need to get past him. I carefully stepped to the side of the path taking small steps on the loose rock.

We were almost around him when Abby accidentally kicked a stone. It went tumbling into the crater, and the man spun to look at it, dropping into a crouch. The other members of the Pulhu stopped and watched, waiting for something. Someone walked forward with their hands up. I got a glimpse of his face, and my heart froze. It was the creepy guy, Mr. Damon. I hadn't seen him since our fight a few months ago.

He was able to destroy my shields easily and would have captured me if not for Tider and Richard. I was terrified of him. I looked at Abby. She wasn't even breathing. He used Abby to get information about me, telling her he would hurt her and her dad if she didn't cooperate. I slowly reached out and grabbed her hand, squeezing it. She squeezed back and took a small breath.

After another tense minute, Mr. Damon put his hands down, "There is no one here," he barked. "Continue your work."

We took a few cautious steps forward, being extra careful not to disturb anything. Once we were all the way into the crater, I looked around. The Pulhu had equipment set up everywhere. I made my way over to a machine with a couple of guys in front of it. I was pretty sure I had seen something like this on TV once. It was supposed to read activity in the ground.

"This is a stupid mission," the younger guy said. "We aren't going to find them. I doubt they even exist anymore."

"I wouldn't say that too loudly," the other guy replied. "We do what we are told. You know that. If he wants us taking readings to search for an anomaly to find the fire elementals, then that's what we do."

"But why? What does he want with them if they are alive? I doubt they will be happy to see us."

"He said they will join us because the darkness has promised to let them live freely. They won't have to stay hidden from humans anymore."

"Yeah, and what about us. I doubt they will want to take orders from us," he pouted.

"If you want to go tell him you think this is a bad idea, be my guest. Before you go, what do you want to be written on your headstone, because he's going to kill you."

I listened to them argue for a few more minutes but didn't learn anything new, so I moved on. I kept an eye on Mr. Damon. I didn't want to get too close to him. A woman was talking to two men, and I snuck as close to them as I could.

"I'm sure they are here. I can't figure out how to get into their realm though," she was saying.

"Didn't the book tell you how?" one of the men asked.

"No. It only told us the location. It's on Mount Etna. We have to find out where, but the readings aren't helping. It's as if their magic doesn't exist up here. We were able to pick up trace amounts further down the slope heading this way, but then it disappears."

"Maybe the entrance to their realm is down there."

"We searched that whole area. There was nothing there. We even tried burning everything around that spot."

"You don't want to burn the portal," the guy said, scowling at the woman.

"We will burn everything down if we have to. And if the fire elementals won't join us, we will destroy them too," she said vehemently.

I felt Sievroth move against my neck. His body started to heat up. He didn't like hearing the Pulhu talk about destroying his home. I reached up and pet his body, trying to calm him. The last thing we needed was a loose baby dragon breathing fire everywhere. The Pulhu would try to capture him. As soon as he calmed down, I moved further away from the lady. I didn't want her saying something to rile Sievroth back up.

Abby moved in closer to me. "What now?" she asked.

I looked on the far side of the crater near Mr. Damon. "We need to go over there. I need to see the equipment they have so we can figure out what they know."

Abby visibly shook. "I can't, Sally."

"It's ok, Abby. He can't see or hear us." She was still as pale as a ghost. I put my hand on her arm. "You stay here. I will go check it out and then meet you back here. Ok?"

"Ok," she said quietly. Mr. Damon was terrifying to me, and I was never questioned by him. I couldn't imagine what Abby must be feeling.

I slowly crept forward, careful to keep from kicking the stones as I moved closer. The potion kept us from being seen or heard, but if we kicked something away from us, everyone would hear it. Mr. Damon was standing next to a woman with a frown on her face.

"We are not getting the results I expected," she said. "You told us this is where their entrance would be, but I have not found any traces of ancient magic."

"It is here," Mr. Damon said menacingly.

The woman frowned even more. "If it is here, we aren't doing something right. Have we checked the other craters?"

"Yes. I have teams at each one. So far, there is nothing. You will find their entrance, Noreda. Do you understand me?" He lifted his hand and let a small flame emerge from his fingers. "Or you will face my wrath."

Noreda paled. "I will find it," she said.

"Good."

Mr. Damon walked away from her, moving to another set of equipment.

I walked closer to Noreda. She was mumbling under her breath. She was saying something about magic not being able to find them, so why would technology be able to do it.

They must have been searching for weeks before we showed up. I got a good look at the equipment before heading back to Abby but didn't learn anything new. We made our way back to the path to leave the crater, but we needed to get past the guard again. Thankfully, the tour group was coming. The guard saw them too and stepped a few feet away from the rim, holding his hand up to stop the tour.

"No one may pass."

"I have the proper paperwork," the guide said.

"No one is coming into the crater. We are in the middle of a scientific study that cannot be disturbed. You will turn back now," I heard him say as we moved past him and the guide, dodging between the other people on the tour. I stopped a few feet from the back of the group. I couldn't leave without making sure the Pulhu didn't try to hurt any of the innocent people.

His nasty demeanor must have convinced the tour guide that it wasn't worth arguing because he shrugged and turned back to the other people.

"That's as far as we can go," he said. "Scientists are here to take measurements, and we can't disturb them." Some of the people complained, but when the Pulhu guard cleared his throat, they all turned and walked away. No one wanted to mess with him.

Once I was sure all the people on the tour would leave, I grabbed Abby's hand and hurried down the path in front of them. We quickly pulled ahead and slowed down.

"What do we do now?" she asked. "We still have a few hours until nighttime. Should we head back to where Jordan dropped us off?"

"Not yet. I want to check out the rest of the craters. Something isn't right here. I'm sure the entrance is on this mountain, but I can't figure out where. I didn't see any rocks where I could use a fire handprint to open it like Adam told us."

"What if it's not all the way up here?" Abby asked. "The Pulhu are all over the craters and haven't found anything. Think about the spot Jordan dropped us off. It didn't have any caves, but there were some trees and large boulders that could easily have a place for a handprint. There didn't look like there was anything like that at the top of the mountain."

"I think you're right, Abby. They are looking in the wrong place." My shoulders fell. "That leaves a ton of places to search. I don't think we will be able to do it in one weekend."

We headed down until we reached an area where more boulders started to show up. We stepped off of the path, walking from boulder to boulder. We didn't find anything that resembled a cave and didn't see any boulders with a handprint on it. We made pretty good progress, but it would take months to search everywhere. We didn't have that kind of time.

We headed to a cluster of trees when night fell. We couldn't have a fire since the Pulhu were on the mountain too, but we did have a blanket to sleep with. I took the first watch. We wouldn't be invisible for much longer, and it wouldn't be good if the Pulhu stumbled over us in the dark. I watched as Abby laid down.

I reached out for Richard, feeling the connection between us. I tried to tell him everything that happened so far. He sent waves of worry to me, so I knew he heard some of what I said. The connection would get stronger the more we used it while we were so far apart. He knew that the Pulhu were here, and I was sure he would tell Mrs. Sullivan. Maybe they could figure out how the Pulhu found out where to look.

I dropped the connection after a few more minutes, and I watched the stars, thinking about how different my life had become in such a short time. Looking back, I wouldn't change it. I would rather the Pulhu not be after my family or me, but I didn't want to go back to living an ordinary life. I loved having my powers. I would have to find a way to stop the Pulhu and the darkness before it hurt anyone else.

I felt Sievroth move against me. "Hey," I said when he appeared in front of me. "Aren't you supposed to help me figure out where the fire elementals live?"

I felt him grumble against my neck.

"This isn't funny. We need to reach the fire elementals before the Pulhu hurt them." Sievroth unfurled his wings as I spoke and hissed, a small stream of flame coming out of his mouth, lighting up the darkness. "Sievroth, no," I said. "They will see us." Sievroth shook his head and pushed his face against mine, making small mewling noises. I stroked his back until he curled up in my lap. "Don't worry, Sievroth. We will find a way to get to the fire elementals first and maybe find your parents too."

I woke Abby up halfway through the night and took my turn lying down. Everything was silent. I hadn't seen or heard anyone else. I figured the Pulhu probably left for the night. I closed my eyes and fell into a nightmare. I was standing at the top of a volcano as it burped noxious black smoke into the air. Giant balls of fire were being thrown from the crater, landing far down the mountain, some hitting a town in the distance. Ash covered the ground and continued falling through the sky.

I knew immediately that I was in a dream. It was the same as the other two dreams I had when I was looking for the air and water elementals. It would help me find the way to the fire elementals.

I could feel the ground beneath my feet trembling as the smoke became even thicker. I turned to run down the mountain, hoping to get away before it completely blew. Instead, as I started down the path, a massive boom shook the mountain and lava was thrown into the air. It shot from the top of the volcano and ran down the sides in rivers. I looked around, trying to find a way to escape, but everything was blocked. The path was gone. I could hear screams coming from the town as the lava moved closer.

I turned back to the crater, watching it fill with lava and spill over the sides. The craters in the distance erupted too, and more ash was thrown into the air. Below me, the townspeople ran and panicked.

They would never make it out in time. There had to be something I could do. I pulled my fire magic to me, trying to think of something that might help, but fighting fire with fire would only make it worse. Instead, I tried using water, but I couldn't get enough to help cool the lava before it hit the town.

The heat from the volcano sucked all the moisture out of the air. There was nothing for me to work with. There were no lakes or rivers nearby. Because of the volcano, there was no river of water underground that I could pull on. I yelled in despair, knowing that I couldn't do anything. I watched as the lava surrounded me.

I didn't know if it would hurt me or not. Because of my fire element, I could walk through my own fire without being hurt, but I had never tried getting close to lava. I didn't really want to try now, but there wasn't anywhere to go. As the lava crept closer, I could feel the heat from it singeing my eyes. It looked like I wouldn't be able to withstand the temperature after all.

A noise above me caught my attention, and I glanced up. Flying toward me with a great burst of speed, was a large bird. It reminded me of a huge eagle. It lowered its legs and gripped me by the shoulders. I could feel one of its claws rip through my shirt and tear my skin. It carried me away from Mount Etna, skimming across trees that were now covered in fire.

When we landed, we were at the base of the mountain on the other side, away from any towns. We were in a clearing surrounded by trees. The eagle turned and put his beak to my chest. Immediately, images bombarded me. Behind the eagle was the cave I was looking for, the boulder off to the side and another boulder covering it so no one could see the palm print.

"Hurry," the eagle yelled into my mind. "You must hurry."

Before I had a chance to reply, a group of people with their hands up and ready to throw magic, emerged from the trees. The eagle slid in front of me protectively, as the leader of the people shouted, "You will serve the Pulhu."

They drew their magic to them and shot it at the eagle, hoping to take him down quickly. Right before the magic hit, my eyes opened. I was staring at the stars, Sievroth on my chest, gently head-butting me.

"Are you ok?" Abby asked.

"Yes, and I know where we need to go." I looked around. "At least I know the general area where we need to go. I saw it from the sky."

"The sky?" Abby asked.

"Yes, a giant eagle was carrying me."

"You have the weirdest dreams," Abby said, "but they do help us when we need it."

I agreed. We would need as much help as we could get. Usually, only the darkness came after me in my dreams, and the animals helping me were calm. This dream was different. The eagle wasn't expecting the Pulhu to show up. They were getting too close and somehow changed the dream. At least that's what I thought.

I looked down when I felt pain shoot through my chest. Blood was slowly seeping through my shirt. I moved it to the side to see what was wrong. I could see the puncture marks left by the eagle, but this time it wasn't healing as quickly. Usually, I recovered in seconds unless it was a horrible wound.

Even if this had been really bad, a few minutes had passed. I should have been completely healed. One of the positives of having magic was that we healed fast, and I healed quickly, even for an elemental. I called Abby over to look at it. She laid her hands on me, and her soft yellow magic slid around the wound, stitching the skin back together. I wiped the blood away. If not for the blood, I wouldn't be able to tell I had been wounded at all.

"Good job, Abby. You are getting much better at healing in non-life-threatening situations." Abby was a great healer, but she doubted herself too much. When it was an emergency, and she didn't have time to think, she could heal some of the worst injuries, but when it wasn't life-threatening, she had a tendency to doubt herself.

"I've been practicing a lot. I'm glad I was able to help you."

"I knew you would be able to heal it. I'm surprised it didn't heal on its own though. It wasn't too bad."

"Maybe it was worse than you thought," she said. "Or maybe your ability to heal is still glitchy." Most of the time, my body healed itself quickly, but every once in a while, it didn't. There was no reason for it, no pattern that I had noticed. Sometimes I just didn't heal.

"Maybe," I said. "Thankfully, I have you here with me."

CHAPTER FOUR

The sun was already starting to rise, so I stood up and wiped my jeans off before wrapping up my blanket. I looked at the plants around us, covered in a light layer of frost. I was glad we had our warmers. I pulled the small square out of my pocket. Gary had given them to us when we were on Gangkhar Puensum looking for the air elementals. They kept us warm no matter what the temperature was. Without them, we wouldn't have been able to stay here without a fire.

We hiked toward the area I thought the eagle had taken me. Everything looked different from the ground. We came to a few different clearings. Each time I thought it was the right one, but we couldn't find the handprint. As we neared the next clearing, I heard voices. We crouched behind the trees, trying to listen to what they were saying.

I couldn't understand them, so I crept forward, moving from tree to tree. Abby followed. When we were close enough, my heart plummeted. It was the Pulhu. They had noticed several different energies coming from this area. I moved closer until I could peek into the clearing. I immediately knew this was the place. I could even see the boulder I needed to place my hand on. I backed away until they wouldn't be able to hear us and told Abby.

"What do we do?" she asked. "We can't let them get into the fire elemental realm."

"We need to get them away from this area," I said.

"How?"

"We need them to think the portal is in a different spot. We will have to trick them. We can use the invisibility potion so they don't see us, and I can use a small amount of fire magic to draw their attention. If I spread it out enough, they won't know where the magic is coming from."

"Let's do it. We only have a few hours left."

We moved to a small area that we checked yesterday. The Pulhu hadn't bothered with this area, so it was perfect for our plan. I took a potion and handed the last one to Abby. As soon as we thought we were invisible, I let out a small burst of fire. The flame hit the ground and burned for a few seconds before going out.

I stopped and listened, waiting for the Pulhu to sense it, but they didn't come. I tried again, this time with a bigger flame. They still didn't notice.

"They should be able to sense my fire," I told Abby. "I'm not sure why they aren't coming?"

"They probably think it's their own people using fire magic."

"Oh yeah. I didn't think about that. They have been burning a lot of the craters. I don't think this is going to work after all."

I felt Sievroth uncurl from my neck. He leaned over my shoulder and blew a stream of fire onto a small group of rocks. As his fire faded, I glanced at the rocks. They were glowing a deep red and had slightly melted together. Shouts came from further up the path and from the trees behind us.

We quickly ran down the path and off to the side as the Pulhu came running in from everywhere.

"What is it?" one of them asked.

"That was it, what we've been looking for. That was a fire elemental."

"Are you sure? I didn't see anything."

"I'm sure, and look at those rocks. One of them was definitely here. Spread out and find him. You three stay here and figure out where he came from," a lady said, pointing at the group that had been near the portal. I breathed a sigh of relief. We stopped them from looking too closely at the portal. Hopefully, this would keep them busy for a few weeks. At least long enough for me to get into the fire elemental realm and get their help.

After they all separated, I headed back to our pickup point with Abby. We weren't there long when Jordan materialized in front of us.

"Are you ready to go?" he asked.

"Yes," I told him.

"Did you find what you were looking for?"

"Not quite, but we are close." I didn't want him to know what we had found.

"Let's get out of here then. The Pulhu are all over this mountain. I hope you stopped them from finding whatever they are after. It must be important."

"It is," I said as we grabbed hands, and the world fell away. As soon as we landed on solid ground, I opened my eyes and stepped onto school property. As we walked to Mrs. Sullivan's office, I reached out to Richard and told him to meet us there.

We were already seated in her office, and she was thanking Jordan when Richard, Tider, and Adam walked in. After Jordan left, I explained what happened at Mount Etna with Abby jumping in to explain some of the things I forgot. When we told them Mr. Damon was there, Mrs. Sullivan's lips thinned in anger.

"This is bad," she said. "I've called a few contacts in the council to see if they know why the Pulhu are searching for the true fire elementals. There have been rumors that they are searching for the true elementals to get them to join their side willingly or with force."

"How do they plan on forcing them? The true elementals are extremely powerful."

"You beat them," Adam said to me.

"Yes, but only five water elementals were fighting us, and it was still hard."

"Sally almost died," Abby said.

"I remember," Richard said, "but if we could do it, the Pulhu probably can too."

"The rumors say Mr. Damon has a secret weapon that can make a group of elementals powerless. Supposedly he can drain their magic."

My friends gasped, but I thought back to when I was fighting him. He put his hand on my shield, and it immediately started to turn gray and disintegrate. "I bet he was draining my shield's magic, and that's why it failed so fast in our last fight," I said.

"That would make sense. But he wasn't able to steal your energy."

"Maybe he found a way."

"You need to stay far away from him," Mrs. Sullivan said. "If he can make you powerless, we won't have a chance to defeat the Pulhu."

"I plan on staying away from him," I assured her.

We headed back to the common room for dinner before heading to bed. Once I was in my room, I touched one of the marbles on my desk and said, "Seal." Immediately a sheet of air sealed my door shut. I had spent a lot of time putting this spell into about twenty marbles. Every night I sealed my door to keep everyone out.

I wasn't taking chances. Mr. Merrem had told me to use a spell instead of sealing the door every night with my own energy after he found out what happened. It didn't use any of my energy. If anything did happen, I would be at full strength instead of weak from sustaining a shield all night.

Fluttering noises around my ear and shrieks woke me up, causing me to jump out of bed. Sievroth was flying around the room, trying to catch Mauevene.

"Stop it," I yelled, grabbing Sievroth. "You can't eat her. How many times do I have to tell you that?"

I held him closely as Mauevene fluttered over to my desk to land.

"Is everything ok?" I asked her. She never woke me up in the middle of the night.

"Yes, but we need to go to the south wing. Send Sievroth to the forest, or he can stay in your room. I don't want him trying to eat me."

"Why are we going to the south wing?" I asked.

"It's time for you to learn how to do a few things that only true water elementals can do."

"Then how can I do them? I'm not a true elemental."

"When the king gave you some of his power, you became a true elemental in a sense. You should be able to do anything that the true elementals are capable of. With Mr. Damon after the fire elementals, you need to learn some new defensive magic that I can teach you."

We snuck down to the south wing, making sure not to wake anyone. Mauevene flew around the room, chanting in the ancient language. She spoke too fast for me to understand. When she stopped, a light glow covered the whole room.

"What did you do?" I asked.

"I put up something similar to the domes outside that you practice in. Now you can practice without anyone sensing you. It also blocks all sound, so no one will hear you. It will only stay up for an hour. I don't have the strength to hold it any longer."

"Can you teach me how to do that?"

"I will, but that's not important right now. We are here for you to learn how to save yourself if Mr. Damon gets to you. You can already win against most of the Pulhu as long as they don't overpower you, and you have your friends with you. The two spells I'm going to teach you require a lot of effort and even more energy. You have enough to do them, but you will need to practice a lot. We are going to start small."

She held her hand out, and a ladybug appeared in it. She put it gently down on a desk and wove a small box of water, caging it.

"This seems like a simple spell, but look closer at the box," Mauevene said.

I closed my eyes and concentrated on the box so I could see the magic clearly. It was a water box, but woven throughout it were bars of deep blue magic. They held everything together. I reached out a finger to touch the box, but Mauevene flew over and pushed my hand away. My eyes flew open.

"Don't touch it. This is a tiny box, so it won't hurt you, but it will take a lot of your energy."

"Wait. The cage steals energy."

"Yes, it's why very few can escape it. It starts stealing their energy as soon as they are trapped. The cage releases once all of their energy is gone. It won't kill them, but whoever is inside of it will be powerless for days afterward."

"Wow. This is awesome. I could use this on the Pulhu, and they wouldn't be able to hurt me. Thanks for teaching me, Mauevene."

She laughed. "You still have to learn it. I bet Mr. Damon has figured out how to do something like this. It would explain how he can steal energy."

Mauevene said something, and the cage disappeared. The ladybug didn't look hurt at all. I smiled. I was going to like this new spell. Mauevene explained that all true elementals could use their element as pure magic if they were strong enough. Many learned only a few spells because of how hard they were to use.

"You need to find pure water magic inside you," Mauevene explained. When I didn't understand what she was talking about, she tried again. "You need to look deep inside yourself and open yourself up to the magic. Follow the path of the water magic until you reach pure magic. Pure magic for an elemental is stronger and possibly brighter in color to you. It will feel incredibly powerful, like holding a live wire."

I concentrated on my water magic and tried to find pure magic, but I wasn't having any luck. After twenty minutes, Mauevene called a halt. She looked at me questioningly.

"Can you feel the king's power still?" she asked.

"Yes."

"Let that magic out. Follow that magic to its center."

I still wasn't sure what she meant by following the magic. I could call on water magic and see the color of the magic in my hands, but there was nothing else. It was just there. It didn't connect to anything.

I called on the king's magic and felt my chest swell. The power was incredible. The king had given it to me when I saved him from a curse. Now I could call on him whenever I needed, and if anything hurt him, I would know and could help.

I closed my eyes, watching his magic swirl down my arm as I called a small ball of water into my hands. I gasped in surprise. I could see a trail of magic snaking its way to my chest. I looked closer. The magic was buried deep in my chest in a swirling ball. I could see threads of the pure magic spinning in it. I told Mauevene what I found, and she smiled at me.

"Use those threads to create the water trap."

Keeping my eyes closed, I pulled gently on one of the threads, weaving it through my regular water magic. I struggled with it. It wanted to stay tucked into the ball of magic. Every time I started to get control of it, it would slip away. Eventually, I gave up, panting.

"I don't know if I can do this, Mauevene. It doesn't want to work with me."

"That is normal. It takes a lot of practice to use pure magic. You will need to work on it often until you can control it. It will be difficult, but it may save your life one day."

I promised her I would continue to work on it. I knew I needed to learn as much as I could if I was going to fight Mr. Damon and the darkness. After practicing for another thirty minutes without much progress, Mauevene had me stop for the night. We made our way back to my room silently. It was going to take me a while to figure this new magic out.

When we got to my room, Mauevene reminded me not to tell anyone what she was teaching me, not even my friends. I didn't like it, but I agreed. We spent the next two nights working on it with little success. Mauevene told me to take a few nights off, and then we would try again.

During lunch the next day, we tried to decide what we needed to do before going into the fire elemental realm. We would have to leave soon, or the Pulhu would find their way in first. Mrs. Sullivan had a few people taking turns watching the Pulhu on Mount Etna. So far, they were still working in the same area where Sievroth melted the rocks, but they were starting to get agitated and spread out more.

We needed to find more information on the fire elemental realm before we could go. It was too dangerous to go through the portal with such a small amount of knowledge. So far, the water elementals had lived surrounded by water, and the air elementals had lived in a valley on a mountain covered in snow. You had to fly to get down to their palace. We knew the fire elementals entrance was on a volcano. The chance of their realm having a lot of heat and even fire wasn't too far fetched.

We needed to be prepared for it. Not to mention, we needed to find out if it was guarded by anything like the air elementals were. There was very little information in the books we found on the library shelves. It was mostly about what they could do, not where they lived. By the end of lunch, we decided we would need to go back into the south wing and look around more. Each time we went in there to look around, we found something that could help us.

We met up a few nights later in the common room to sneak into the south wing. I wanted to look at the room where we saw light coming from under the door. Once we made sure nobody was watching, we snuck through the door and into the dark hallway. Immediately, I turned my phone on for light. Everyone else did the same.

"What are we looking for?" Abby asked.

"Anything that looks out of place," I told her. "There must be a reason why the south wing was shut down magically. We need to find out what."

"Let's head down the hall to the room that had the light on the other night," Richard said.

"We need to be quiet until we make sure no one else is in here with us."

We crept along the hallway, listening for any sign that someone else was here, but I didn't hear anything. I remembered exactly where the door was and led us to it quickly. There was no light coming from beneath the door, but it was shut. I put my hand against the door first and closed my eyes. I didn't sense any magic, so I gripped the doorknob and slowly turned it.

I pushed the door open a few inches, listening for sounds inside the room. When I didn't hear anything, I pushed the door open the rest of the way and stepped inside. There was nothing unusual in the room at first glance. It was set up like an office with a desk and multiple chairs on one side and one large chair on the other.

In the corner, across the room, was a small fireplace with a table in front of it. I stepped closer to it, trying to see what was sitting on the top. A pad of paper and a pen were neatly set up. Next to them was a cork coaster. I slowly dragged my finger along the surface of the table.

"No dust," I murmured.

"What did you say?" Tider asked.

"There's no dust. This table has been used recently." I looked down at the pen and pad again.

"Isn't there a way to find out what was written on this last?" I asked.

"Here, let me," Adam said, grabbing the pad of paper. He grabbed a pencil out of his backpack and started to lightly color the paper. I could see letters forming.

"I've done this with my grandpa at some of the ancient sites. Usually on a rock, but even on paper, an impression is left behind."

We watched as words formed. When Adam finished, we waited impatiently for him to read it out loud. He cleared his throat before speaking.

"Beware the chosen and the imposter. Both sides are equal. Do not interfere until a side has been picked. If the imposter wins, protect yourself. Only the true chosen can defeat Helerium."

"What's Helerium?" Richard asked.

"I don't know, but it's capitalized, so maybe a name of someone or something. It must be important."

"Who is the imposter? What does it mean?"

"I have no idea, but it sounds like more trouble for us."

"Maybe we need to talk to the cloaked figure and find out what this means exactly. We could use more help," I said.

"I don't think so. They obviously don't want us knowing who they are. If we try to force them to talk, they might cause trouble for us. Right now, it looks like they may help us at some point as long as they don't think you are the imposter," Tider said, looking at me. After a minute, I nodded. For now we would leave the cloaked figure alone.

What if I was the imposter, and there was a different chosen out there? I voiced my concerns to my friends, but none of them agreed with me. They all thought I was the chosen, which meant someone out there was going to pretend to be the one in the prophecy, or maybe they were told they were the chosen one and believed it. When we met this other person, we would have to figure out what to do and if they were really the enemy.

CHAPTER FIVE

The next day classes started out fine. By period three, kids were whispering to each other in hushed voices. I looked at Abby, but she shrugged. She didn't know what was going on either. I looked over at Richard as he took a quick peek at his phone. His eyes widened, and I felt him reaching out for me through our connection.

"Mr. Mitchel is back. There is a rumor going around that Mrs. Sullivan is being placed on temporary leave. Mr. Mitchel is taking over for her until the council can find out what is going on at this school. Another student has claimed that Mrs. Sullivan allows students to learn dark magic here."

"No way. Mrs. Sullivan would never allow that."

"We know that, but someone has convinced a few of the students to lie to the council to get rid of Mrs. Sullivan. Remember, she told us evidence of someone using dark magic was planted at the school last time the council was here. This is the third student to say that she allows it. The council may think they are doing the right thing."

"There are too many Pulhu on the council. They probably got the other members to agree to it through scare tactics," I said.

"Maybe," Richard said doubtfully. "I think they planted evidence against Mrs. Sullivan and maybe bribed a few council members. It wouldn't take much, and we know some of the students here have parents involved with the Pulhu. I'm sure they are the ones saying she allows dark magic."

"What are we going to do? You know Mr. Mitchel will want to test my magic as soon as he can if it's true."

"I know. I don't know how to stop him. You may need to take his tests and try to hide your magic."

"What if he finds out anyway?"

"You've done a good job hiding the fact that you can use all the elements from everyone else. I'm sure you can hide it from him too. It will be a little bit trickier though. Don't worry. We will figure it out."

I couldn't wait for class to be over so I could talk to my friends about what we should do. When we finally got to the cafeteria and sat down, Abby exploded.

"This is horrible. How can this be happening? Mrs. Sullivan needs to be here."

"There is nothing we can do, Abby. The council decided this was the best thing to do for now."

"Yeah, but we know it's not. They are going to ruin the school. What about all the kids here. What if Mr. Mitchel decides they are too powerful. We all know what happens to anyone he doesn't like. They go missing," Abby said, panicked.

"It will be ok, Abby. Only two kids have gone missing, and it would be hard for him to get rid of any of us. We are not new students."

"I'm still fairly new," I said.

"Not really. Besides, everyone here knows you. He won't be able to say you are a problem. No one would believe him."

"That's not true," Tider said. "He could easily blame Sally for the dark magic at the school and say his niece found out about it and was trying to curse Sally so she would admit to it. Mr. Mitchel will always find a way to get what he wants. For now, we need to stay on his good side and listen to him. I will talk to my father and see if he can control Mr. Mitchel."

"Thanks, Tider, but let's not take any chances. I don't want your father to force you to go home."

Tider hesitated before agreeing. It wasn't worth upsetting his father. We would figure it out on our own. If they took Tider home, they would force him to do dark magic. The Tider I loved like a brother would be gone. I wasn't going to let that happen.

Before we could discuss anything else, someone came up to our table. "Sally, please go to the front of the school and bring your friends. Mrs. Sullivan asked me to get you," the kid stammered and turned bright red.

"For what?" I asked.

"Nothing. Something. I don't know," the kid mumbled and walked away quickly.

"That was weird," Adam said.

"Yeah. Something's going on. Let's hurry up."

We grabbed our stuff and quickly walked toward the front of the school. I was worried about Mrs. Sullivan, and it took me a minute to realize she wouldn't have sent a random student to come get us. I slowed down, watching everything, worried it was Mr. Mitchel calling for us and not Mrs. Sullivan. As we got closer, I stopped my friends. I reached out for Mrs. Sullivan trying to connect with her, so I could see if she really called for us. I felt her mind ahead of us and slipped through her defenses.

"Mrs. Sullivan, did you send someone to come get me?"

"No," she replied. "Sally, you must be careful. Mr. Mitchel will have tests and traps placed everywhere to try and get you to slip up and show all of your magic. You must not let him know that you have power over all the elements."

"I don't know how to keep him from finding out. I need you here," I begged her.

"I can't stay, Sally. The council can't be trusted. Don't trust anyone except your friends." Her voice became faster until I could no longer feel the connection between us. She must have transported away from the school. I turned to my friends and told them what she said.

"What should we do?" Abby asked.

"I think we should go back to the cafeteria. We can't get in trouble. We were told Mrs. Sullivan was waiting for us, but she's no longer in the school. We can say we ran into someone who told us Mrs. Sullivan already left," Tider said.

"I agree," Richard said. We turned around and headed back to the cafeteria. We were almost there when the same kid came up to us and asked why we hadn't gone to see Mrs. Sullivan.

"We ran into another student who said she already left. I was surprised she left without waiting for us, but I suppose the council made sure she left right away. There probably wasn't any time to wait for us," Richard told the kid.

We walked past the kid who had nothing to say and went into the cafeteria.

"This is going to be harder than I thought if Mr. Mitchel already has students doing his dirty work for him. What do you want to bet that he forced Tim to say that somehow? Tim is a good kid," Richard said.

"I bet Mr. Mitchel told him he would fail if he didn't do it or something worse."

"It wouldn't surprise me. Mrs. Sullivan was right. We can't trust anyone but our group. Everyone else can be forced into doing something that might hurt us."

"Do we have to stay here?" I asked.

"For now, yes. If we leave, the Pulhu will know you are hiding something. Right now they only suspect it, we can't give them proof. It's already going to be hard to get into the fire elemental realm. If the Pulhu are actively tracking you, it will be much harder. We need them to stop looking so closely at you. Hopefully, you can fail whatever test Mr. Mitchel gives you so he leaves you alone."

"I hope so," I responded.

We spent the rest of the day on edge, but nothing else happened. Before bed that night, Mr. Mitchel's voice came over the loudspeaker, saying we were all required to go to the auditorium in the morning to go over some new rules at the school.

When I got to the cafeteria with Abby, we immediately tried to find the guys, but Mr. Burwel stopped us.

"Sorry, girls, but you have been assigned a seat alphabetically. Sally Abeneb, you are up front," he said, looking at a clipboard. "Go find your seat." He turned to Abby, "What is your name?"

I heard her answer as I walked toward the front row. It didn't look like any of my friends would be sitting with me. Mr. Mitchel had figured out a way to keep me away from all of my friends without using any magic. I craned my neck, trying to spot them. I saw Adam and Richard a few rows back, but I didn't see Tider anywhere. Abby was making her way to her seat at the very back of the auditorium.

I looked forward as I heard someone clear their throat. Mr. Mitchel stood on the stage directly in front of me. His eyes met mine, and I shivered involuntarily. I could tell he had plans for me, and I doubted any of them would be good. He smiled when he saw me shiver. He knew I was scared of him.

That could work in my favor. Maybe if I seemed weak and scared, he would leave me alone. I dropped my gaze, not wanting him to continue looking at me. I couldn't let him realize I was going to fight back. I wasn't as scared as he believed, and he wasn't as powerful as he made himself out to be. I would find a way to win against him, but for now, I would let him think he had me cornered.

I used my connection to tell Richard my plan before Mr. Mitchel started speaking.

"Good morning, students," Mr. Mitchel began. "I will be the head of this school from now on. Mrs. Sullivan is under investigation for using dark magic. The council has chosen me to take over and make sure all students are behaving the way they should." He looked over at me again, but I put my head down.

"There will be a few new rules now that I am here. Things that should have been done much sooner. Every student will have to undergo a test, which I will administer to see where your powers are at and how strong or weak they are. Then you will be placed in the appropriate classes. Age will no longer matter in class. No one is to use magic unless specifically approved by me. That includes masters classes. No one will be doing those classes unless I have seen their powers and agree that they are strong enough to be in masters classes."

"How will we practice?" I sent to Richard as other kids gasped.

"We will find a way. Let's see what else he has to say."

I slipped out of Richard's head and listened to Mr. Mitchel.

"You will also be given weekly tests on your magic to see if you have improved. If you have not improved as much as I think you should have, you will be placed in a lower-level class. There will be rewards for whoever is in upper-level classes and is doing the best. Those rewards will be set by me. Teachers will send in daily reports of student's activities during class, and you will be monitored throughout the day by all the teachers. There will be no more roaming the halls or sleeping in another student's room." He looked my way again.

I was going to have to make sure my air seal was strong enough to keep him out. Maybe I could do another spell too, just to be safe. I wasn't going to take any chances with Mr. Mitchel having access to the school.

He finished his lecture, telling us that he would be calling each student to his office. We would go one at a time over the next few days in alphabetical order. I looked to my left and sighed. Lucky me. I was going to be the first student tested. When we were all dismissed, I heard my name being called and turned back to the stage. Mr. Merrem was standing there looking at me. I walked over to him.

"Sally, be careful. He will be calling you up to his office shortly. There is nothing I can do to stop him. You must be ready for anything. I don't think he is going to test your powers too hard today. I'm sure there will be a trap or two waiting for you, and he will probably try to test your air and water elements. He doesn't know about the others, so I doubt he will try to test you for them."

"I will try to be careful, Mr. Merrem, but what if I have to show him how strong I am?"

"He won't use too much power on you in his office. The council has access to it during these tests, and he won't want them to think he is going too far, or they may pull him from his position here. As long as you are in his office, you will be safe. The teachers had a meeting with the council earlier about this. If he tries to test you somewhere else though, that could be trouble. For now, work on getting through this test. Connect with me if things get out of control. I will come as fast as I can."

"Thanks, Mr. Merrem," I told him gratefully. Knowing Mr. Mitchel was being watched by the council during the tests made me feel a lot better about the situation. Even though a lot of the council sided with him against Mrs. Sullivan, I didn't think they were all part of the Pulhu. They were tricked into believing Mrs. Sullivan was doing a lousy job.

I headed down to Mrs. Sullivan's office, now Mr. Mitchel's office, I thought with distaste. I kept all my senses alert and even worked on seeing different magical signatures while I was walking. It wasn't hard for me to do, but I needed to concentrate a lot more. I didn't see anything off until I got to the front hallway. In the center of the hall, magic was seeping from the ceiling onto the floor. A trap had been laid, but I wasn't sure what it was.

I looked around but didn't see anyone watching me. I pretended to stop and tie my shoe while I figured out a plan. I didn't want to walk into the trap, but I didn't have a reason to walk so closely to the sides of the hall. If someone was watching, they would realize I knew where the trap was. An idea came to me, and I carefully took my ring off, concealing it in my hand.

As I stood up, I reached into my bookbag, grabbing something out. When I pretended to pull my phone out, I accidentally dropped my pencil pouch. Pencils spilled out, and since I was facing the side of the hallway, they rolled all the way to the edge. I placed my ring by my foot when I bent down, and now I kicked it so it would roll along the side of the hall. It came to a stop a few feet past the trap.

I walked over to grab my pencils and then walked along the edge of the hall, pretending to search for my ring. When I finally found it, I held it up to look at, so anyone watching would see that I was actually looking for something. I thought I did a great job of getting past the trap without letting anyone know I could see it. I stepped up to Mr. Mitchel's door as I was putting my ring back on and knocked.

"Come in," he called sharply.

I walked into the office and tried to hide my gasp. He completely changed the office. All of Mrs. Sullivan's stuff was gone, even the furniture. Now only a few wooden chairs sat in the room in front of a large black desk and chair that looked more suited to a throne room.

"I see you noticed the change in furniture. Did you come to Mrs. Sullivan's office a lot?" he asked. "You seem like a decent kid, why would you be sent here enough to worry about the furniture?"

"You know I've only been here a few months," I said stiffly. "I spent more time here than the other students because I have been trying to adjust to this life, and when I had a question, I would ask Mrs. Sullivan."

"What kind of questions did you need to ask her?" he pried.

"Nothing important," I said carefully. "I asked about the school or schedules and basic information that any new student would need."

He looked stymied for a minute. I guess he thought I would give him more information. "You know why you're here. I'm going to test your powers. Mrs. Sullivan never let you be tested, and I want to find out why."

"I didn't realize everyone here was tested," I said icily, knowing it wasn't usual for the council to test students.

"You are a special case, not receiving your powers until you were older. We need to know what you are capable of and why they didn't emerge earlier."

"I don't know what to tell you," I said when he looked at me for an answer. "Maybe they didn't emerge because I was never really hurt before. When I broke my ankle, they showed up. If I hadn't broken my ankle, maybe they never would have emerged."

He looked thoughtful. "Maybe, but since you are here now, you must be tested. Let's begin."

I started to ask what he wanted me to do, but he threw his hand up, and a streak of power flew at me. Immediately I threw a shield up and watched as the power bounced off of it.

"Interesting. You have very quick reflexes. Now drop the shield so we can see what you can do. I'm told you have power over water and air. Is this correct?"

I hesitated. "Yes," I finally said. There wasn't anything I could do. He already knew the answer, now he wanted to know how powerful they were.

"Good, let's start with air. I want you to stop me from getting to you." Before he finished his sentence, he was moving forward. I immediately constructed a whirlwind in front of me that pushed the air toward Mr. Mitchel, keeping him away from me. It was an intermediate skill that I should know since I took those classes last term.

He was still moving forward but slower than before. I didn't want to add much more power to my whirlwind. Most of the kids wouldn't be able to hold this for much longer, and they definitely wouldn't be able to make it more powerful.

I let the power slowly start to fade away as he got closer, but I put up a small wall of air in front of me. It was advanced magic, but we had been practicing it in class the past couple of weeks. When he slammed into it, his smile grew.

"Enough," he said as I let the magic falter, my wall of air flickering. He walked back to his desk and turned around. "Now for water. Stop me."

He moved forward again. This time I used water from the bowl in the corner of the room to push at him like I had done with air. It was the same spell, but I made it a lot weaker, and he moved forward faster. When he was almost to me, I let the water form coils and wrapped them around his arms and legs, holding him in place for a few seconds before he broke through them. I bent down, pretending to pant, and he stopped.

He watched me for a few minutes before walking back to his desk. Without turning around, he threw his arm up, and power blasted straight toward me. I put my shield up without thinking, and he smiled again as he faced me.

"You are more powerful than we originally thought," he said. "You will not be able to hide it from me. We are done for today, but we will be doing more tests to see how strong your power truly is. I got everything the council needed to see today. Go back to your classes."

I walked out of his office, shaking slightly at the thought of more tests with him. He had managed to get me to put my shield up when I shouldn't have had enough power left to do it. This would be more challenging than I thought. The trap was no longer in the center of the hall, so I was able to walk away without trying to get around it.

I reached out to Richard, letting him know what happened and to be very careful. Richard was hiding a lot of power too. I got through the rest of my morning classes and went to the cafeteria with my friends. Students had been leaving classes all day as they were called to Mr. Mitchel's office. Some of them didn't return. We found out that he was already sending students he didn't feel were strong enough to the lower classes.

Our class continued to shrink as the lower-level class became bigger. Mr. Mitchel didn't think many of us could do advanced magic. The next day most of my friends took their test and came back looking as shaken as I felt. Abby never came back to class, and when I reached out to check on her, she told me she was sent to the lower-level class. I could feel her anger and sadness over the way Mr. Mitchel had treated her.

"Don't worry, Abby. He doesn't know how good you are at healing, or he would have you in advanced classes, but that's a good thing. We don't want him to know that you can heal us. Now he won't pay as much attention to you." Abby perked up after that and promised she would become the best healer and prove that she didn't belong in lower-level classes, even if she could only prove it to us right now.

I smiled as I let her get back to class. My friends were the best. The smile fell as I thought of Mr. Mitchel. He was going to make our lives difficult. Our class had shrunk down to less than eight people. Richard was still with me, and Tider had been forced into the classroom, which surprised everyone.

He never took classes with the rest of us because of his family name and how much power he was supposed to have. Sean and Sasha were also in the class. There were two other guys in the class, but I didn't know them. They didn't sit near Sean and Sasha, so I figured they weren't on their side either.

CHAPTER SIX

The rest of the week went by slowly as students struggled with their new class schedules. Other things in the school were changing too. There was a somber mood everywhere I went. No one was happy with Mr. Mitchel being in charge. Two kids were caught trying to practice their magic and were suspended immediately. A rumor was going around the school that the kids weren't suspended for practicing magic but for not having Mr. Mitchel's permission.

There was no way for me to practice my magic now that Mr. Mitchel was keeping such a close eye on everyone. I didn't even sneak down to the south wing to practice with Mauevene since Mr. Mitchel took over. I was worried he would somehow know I was out of bed.

Mauevene didn't come out of hiding either. She must be as worried as me. I talked to Richard every night, but we still hadn't found a solution. I needed to practice my magic, or the Pulhu would be able to defeat us, but there wasn't any chance. The longer we waited to go to the fire elemental realm, the higher the chance the Pulhu would find the entrance.

Finally, I decided I wasn't going to keep playing by Mr. Mitchel's rules. He thought he could keep track of me, but I would show him. I used my invisibility shield that night and slowly walked down the hallway. It took a long time, but I finally made it into the south wing and dropped my shield when I was sure no one else was in there.

Immediately, Mauevene appeared. "I've been waiting for you to come here. That man has a special spell on the school to track all magic. I can't come out of hiding unless you come in here."

"Are you sure it's safe in here?"

"Yes. He is affected by the south wing spell like everyone else and barely notices it's here."

"What am I supposed to do?"

"You need to keep practicing, and we need to get to the fire realm. I wouldn't wait more than a few weeks. They will find the entrance if you wait longer than that."

"How am I supposed to get there? Mrs. Sullivan always sent for Jordan to take us."

Mauevene disappeared from sight as Sievroth came racing toward me. I was worried about him and where he was every day. Ever since Mr. Mitchel arrived, Sievroth had been missing. He flew directly into my arms and rubbed against my chest like a cat. I laughed and pet him until he calmed down.

"What do you think, Sievroth? What are we supposed to do?"

He bumped his head against my hand, and I saw my friends standing outside the school, holding hands. I was standing with them, and so was Jordan. I blinked, and we were gone. It had been very early in the morning or really late at night. I couldn't tell which one, but it was dark out with only a hint of light. "Soon," I heard the voice in my head say.

"How will I know when it's the right time?" I asked him, but he wouldn't give me any more information and curled around my neck.

I sighed, knowing I wouldn't get any more out of him. "Mauevene, come back out. Sievroth is resting," I called.

Mauevene appeared and scowled at Sievroth as he lifted an eyelid lazily and flicked his tongue out. Mauevene moved farther away from me before landing on a table. I felt her magic encircle the room, and I let out a sigh. I would be able to practice here as long as Mauevene kept the spell up. She immediately had me start working on using pure magic again.

I was improving slightly, but I would need to practice every night. I was going to be using a lot of energy over the next few weeks. When I got back to my bed, I fell asleep immediately and was almost late for breakfast. As I ate, I listened to the stilted conversations going on around us. No one wanted to talk because we all thought Mr. Mitchel had a way of listening in. Thankfully, he didn't know I could speak to all my friends telepathically.

It was a pain to have to relay everything to everyone though. I still wasn't able to connect my friends together. We managed to work out a plan that would hopefully help us. The guys would keep looking up information on the fire elementals, and Abby and I would try to contact Jordan. We were going to leave in three weeks with whatever information we had. We couldn't wait any longer, and if we couldn't contact Jordan, we would find another way.

My friends weren't able to get to the south wing to practice with me, but I went every night. My grades weren't doing well since I was so tired from practicing at night, but I figured it didn't really matter anyway.

At the beginning of the second week with Mr. Mitchel as the head of the school, he announced all the students who would be taking masters classes. Richard, Tider, and Sean were called, which we all expected, but when he said my name, I looked around in shock. I couldn't take masters classes. He would find out my power level. Sasha was also called and seemed pleased with herself.

We would all be taking the class together everyday after regular classes. Mr. Mitchel decided it would be better for all of us to learn about our powers together. I was pretty sure he wanted to force us to reveal how powerful we were. Why else would he have us all together?

We were told to report to the East dome immediately after class. I let Abby know I wouldn't be able to meet her and Adam until later that evening before trudging down the path to the dome. Richard and Tider argued the whole way over until I finally yelled at them. Sean and Sasha laughed as they walked behind us, listening to us fight.

I had a smirk on my face as Sean helped Sasha get past the barrier around the dome. It was meant to keep everyone out, and if you walked through it, you felt an urgency to turn around, or something awful would happen to you. My first time had been hard too, but I got used to it. It wouldn't take Sasha long to get over it. She glared at me as she stalked into the dome.

Inside, Mr. Burwel was standing near a table placed in the center of the dome. There were various weapons on the table, and I looked at Richard, confused. We had never used weapons before.

Mr. Burwel saw my confused look and spoke. "You are all here to take masters classes. Therefore you should be able to defend yourselves against each other." We turned to look at each other. Sean and Sasha were grinning. They liked the idea of us fighting.

"Why are we fighting each other?" Richard asked.

"To test your skills," Mr. Burwel replied.

"What if one of us gets hurt?" Tider asked.

"Then you learn from your mistakes, or you don't belong in masters classes. Mr. Mitchel assured me you are all more than capable of completing this lesson without harming yourselves or anyone else badly."

"This sounds more like a gladiators ring than a class," I said quietly to Richard and Tider.

"What was that, Sally?" Mr. Burwel asked.

"I was wondering if we are using the weapons or magic?"

"You will be using both. I will teach you how to create one of these weapons out of your element, and then you will use it on your opponent. You will have the next three days to learn how to make the weapon, and then you will fight each other. Mr. Mitchel will be here to watch and decide the winner."

"What does the winner get?" Sean asked.

"A trip to town," Mr. Burwel said. "I'm sure each of you would like to get some time away from school." He turned to me. "Have you ever been allowed to go to the town? They have a very nice beach there."

"I'm sure they do," I replied. Mr. Mitchel was trying to force me to win first place so I could go to town. Luckily I didn't care all that much. "There will be many rewards for those of you that do well. That goes for the entire school. The students that work the hardest will be given extra privileges, so you should all do your best."

We all nodded as Mr. Burwel turned back to the weapons. "Sean you will be working on making an ax, Sasha will be making daggers, Richard will create a great sword, Tider will make a chakram and Sally will make a short sword. Now everyone, get your weapon and spread out, but make sure you can see me."

I walked to the table and picked up a short sword. I flinched as Sasha grabbed it from my hands, scowling. "You don't even know what a short sword is, do you? This is a dagger, what I'm going to be making. That is a short sword," she said, pointing to a longer weapon further down the table.

I shrugged. How was I supposed to know what each weapon was? I had never seen half of these items before. I turned the short sword over in my hands, trying to get a feel for it as I walked away from the table to give myself some space. I looked at Tider, wondering what a chakram was. It looked like a circular blade with a handle in the middle that could be thrown.

"Now I want everyone to try their weapon out. Pretend you are fighting someone and feel how the weapon moves in your hands."

I watched as everyone else swung their weapons around. I tried swinging mine around my head and nearly dropped it on my foot. I looked down at my sword, there was no way I could beat them if we ever had to actually use the weapons. I tried again with very little luck. If I kept this up, I was going to hurt myself. I was much better at magic.

"Sally, hold your weapon firmly, stop being so scared of it. It isn't going to bite."

"It will if I accidentally let go of it while I'm swinging it around," I mumbled, but I grabbed onto it firmly and tried moving it in front of me. This time I almost sliced my own arm as I moved the sword around. I ignored Mr. Burwel and moved the short sword in tiny little motions trying not to hurt myself. I was starting to get the hang of it when Mr. Burwel called for us to stop.

"It's time to use your magic now. Put your weapons down and call your magic to you, trying to form the same basic shape as your weapon. Move it around like you did with the real weapons. I will walk around and give you pointers. If you have questions, shout them out."

Mr. Burwel was a surprisingly good teacher. Even though I knew he was trying to force me to show all my magic, I could learn a few things from him. He came over by me first and shook his head. "What are you doing?"

"I don't know," I answered honestly. I was trying to force my air magic to create the shape of the short sword, but it wasn't working.

"Look at your sword. Picture its length and its weight in your mind. Then let your magic take the picture and create the sword."

I tried to do as he said and watched in awe as the sword started to form in my hand before it blew away. "What am I doing wrong?" I asked, frustrated. It seemed like an easy task that I should be able to do.

"You are focusing too hard on it. You need to let go and let your imagination work."

"You too," I groaned. "Everyone says I have no imagination."

Mr. Burwel looked at me thoughtfully. "I know you have enough power to do this, but you will need to learn how to let go. Haven't your teachers been working with you?"

"Yes, but they say I lack imagination because I was taught to believe in science and human rules. I have trouble creating new things because of it."

"That makes sense. I never thought of that before. Continue practicing. I'm sure if you keep at it, you will get it. You have two more days."

Great, I thought to myself, I'm supposed to fight someone in two days with a sword I can't create. That's going to go well.

I felt Richard's mind brush against mine. "Relax, you will figure it out. Besides, it's good that you are having trouble. You know he will report it back to Mr. Mitchel. Maybe if they realize you are struggling, they will leave you alone."

"I doubt it, but thanks for trying to make me feel better." I felt Richard leave me and focused on my magic again. Mr. Burwel had walked away to go help the other students. I could see him talking to Sean as Sean swung his ax around. He had made an almost perfect water replica of it without any trouble. I looked down at my empty hands, worried. I tried again to make a short sword, but I couldn't make it work.

By the end of class, everyone was swinging their elemental weapons around except me. I still wasn't able to create my short sword. Mr. Burwel told us we would be practicing again tomorrow and that we would learn new ways to use the weapon to help us during our fight. Richard and Tider waited for me while I walked over to Mr. Burwel to ask him a question

"What will happen if I can't create a weapon for the fight?" I asked.

Mr. Burwel hesitated. "I will speak with Mr. Mitchel, but he said you will all participate each week to improve your abilities, or you will be dropped from the class."

The longer I spent around Mr. Burwel, the more I realized he probably wasn't part of the Pulhu. Even though he followed Mr. Mitchel's teaching strategy, he didn't seem confident that it was a good idea. If he was Pulhu, it wouldn't bother him. It looked like Mr. Mitchel really did have the council fooled. I thanked Mr. Burwel, and we headed to the common room to meet Abby and Adam.

I let Richard and Tider explain what happened while I rested my head in my hands. I decided I would ask Mauevene if she knew a way to help me when I went to the south wing to practice with her later that night.

The name Chet interrupted my thoughts, and I tuned in to the conversation my friends were having.

"When did it happen?" Richard asked.

"Last night. My grandfather called me about an hour ago. He was busy taking stock of everything missing all day."

"He thinks it was the Pulhu?" Tider asked.

"Yes. He said everything on elementals was taken."

"Wait a second, I missed the beginning of this conversation. Chet was robbed?" I asked.

"Yes, his store was robbed last night," Adam said. "He thinks they are after the locations of all the true elementals."

"Did they get anything that would point them in the right direction?" I asked, my stomach sinking.

"They got enough that they may be able to piece together where the water and air elementals are. My grandfather didn't have anything in the store on the other elemental locations. They did get a lot of information about the true elementals though. There was even a book on possible weaknesses each elemental type would have."

"That's not good. Is Chet ok?" I asked, dreading the answer. I remembered the one time my dad had run into the Pulhu. I shuddered. He was lucky to still be here. They would have hurt him more if Dr. Griffith hadn't sent trained elementals to keep an eye on him.

"He's fine. He wasn't in the store when it happened. He wanted us all to know that he still has a few things for us. He was keeping them at his house until we needed them. He has moved them into hiding now. He doesn't want to send anything to us with the school being taken over by the council and Mr. Mitchel. He's worried they will search the package and find out information they don't need to know."

"I'm glad he is ok," I replied. "Tell him we will find a way to come see him as soon as we can."

"I will," Adam replied.

"By the way, Sally, my father will be coming to the school in a few weeks. I'm sure he is coming to check and see if I have taught you anything yet. We will have to pretend you are learning a lot of bad magic from me," Tider said.

"Like what?" I asked.

"We will work on some of the traps that can be deadly, but I will make sure we modify them so they don't hurt anyone. I can tell my father that it is modified so other students don't get hurt, or we would get in trouble. Having Mr. Mitchel here will help a little actually. We can blame his new rules about not practicing magic on why you haven't learned more."

"Great idea," I said. I wasn't looking forward to facing Tider's dad again. It was hard enough to pretend to be a stuck up snob the first time. "How are we going to practice any magic?" I asked Tider.

"I will tell you how to do the spell, and you will have to practice it at night when you go in the south wing with Mauevene. It's the only chance you have."

I sighed. I had too many things that needed to be done.

"Don't worry, Sally," Adam said. "We will get through this, and I'm sure Mrs. Sullivan will find a way to get reinstated."

"How? Mr. Mitchel has turned almost all of the council against her."

No one had an answer, so we let the subject drop. There wasn't anything we could do for Mrs. Sullivan right now, and she couldn't help us either, but I had an idea that might work. I would have to wait until I could talk to Mauevene though. I listened as my friends continued talking about the day. Adam and Abby spent the evening in the library trying to look up stuff on fire elementals, but a teacher was posted in the library at all times now.

All books had to be logged out if you wanted to read them, and you weren't allowed to have open discussions in there anymore. Everyone had to be quiet. Mr. Mitchel was making sure he knew everything at the school. We would need to find another way to learn about the true elementals.

CHAPTER SEVEN

The south wing was silent as I walked into the room I was practicing in. Mauevene let her magic swirl around the room, enclosing us. As soon as she finished, I started asking my questions.

"Can you take a message to Mrs. Sullivan or Jordan for me. I really need to get in touch with one of them. Mrs. Sullivan would be better since she can tell Jordan to come and get us. He will listen to her. I don't know if he will listen to me."

"Of course I will take them a message and let them know what is going on. While I'm gone, you won't be able to practice in here. Mr. Mitchel may be able to detect the magic used in here without my protective barrier. True elemental magic like you are working on is very powerful."

"I won't, but I can still come here to practice the traps Tider wants me to learn, right?"

"Yes. That will be ok as long as you are careful. Maybe you should take a few days off. You are exhausted."

"I can't. I need to learn all this stuff and quickly."

"Be careful, Sally. If you are tired, you will be more likely to slip up in front of Mr. Mitchel."

"I know, Mauevene. I will be."

The thought of relaxing was tempting. I was exhausted from staying up late every night and using so much energy to practice. I was getting much better at moving while staying invisible. All the practice walking down to the south wing was really helping.

"One more thing," I said to Mauevene before I forgot. "Can you help me with this air sword thing? I don't want to have to fight anyone without a weapon."

"It might be better if you fail at it and they drop you from master classes," Mauevene said.

I thought about it for a minute, but I didn't agree with her.

"I don't think so. The Pulhu aren't going to stop bothering me even if I get dropped from master classes. They have seen me fail before. Remember the obstacle course at the end of the term. They still think I'm too powerful. I would rather have a chance to learn more instead of hiding. I'm going to need every bit of help I can get, and I don't think Mr. Burwel is a bad teacher. Maybe I can get him to see that Mrs. Sullivan is a good headmistress. We need more of the council on our side."

Mauevene accepted my decision and changed the subject. She asked me to show her what I could do with the magic so far. I managed to make my air magic create the hilt of the sword, but as I was trying to make the rest of it, it started to fall apart. The magic lost its shape and blew away. I looked at Mauevene, hoping she could help.

"You are holding the magic too tightly. Magic is a living thing, you can't force your will on it. Well, you can, but it never works out that well, and it doesn't work for long. Instead, you need to ask it to help you. Have you tried using a little of the air queen's magic?"

"No. I don't want them knowing my magic is that powerful."

"You need to allow a small amount of it in. When the queen gave that to you, it became a part of you, just like the water elemental king's magic. You are blocking yourself off from those parts of yourself, and the magic knows it. If you truly want to learn how to create this sword, then you must stop closing parts of yourself off."

"So, it's not that I don't have enough imagination? That's what Mr. Burwel thinks."

"No. That will still give you trouble with certain things, but this isn't one of them. You've already seen that it can be done, so it's not your imagination holding you back. Now try it."

I tried pulling my air magic, and this time I let a little of the queen's magic flow through me, too. Immediately the air sword began to build itself, making a perfect replica of the short sword I held in class earlier.

I held it in front of me and gave it a few test swings. It stayed together flawlessly. I was shocked at how easy it was to create once I used all my air magic. Even though I didn't use a lot of power to create it, I could feel how balanced the air magic felt now that I wasn't separating the queen's magic from mine.

After a few more swings, I let the magic fade, and the sword disappeared. Instead of tucking the queen's magic back into the little box I liked to think of it being in, I let it flow through me. I felt a slight rush of energy as the magic released. I couldn't stop myself from smiling.

I looked over at Mauevene. She was smiling too. "You finally let it out. I wasn't sure if you ever would. You know you haven't let the water king's magic out fully yet either."

I realized she was right and did the same thing to the water elemental king's power, letting it flow through me.

"See, I knew you could do it," Mauevene said, laughing. "Now, you can truly start working on your magic."

"How will I keep Mr. Mitchel and the Pulhu from finding out about this power?"

"You can only try to be careful. They won't know that your magic is from the true elementals, but if you slip up, they will find out how powerful it is."

Mauevene asked me to work on using true elemental powers to make the water prison. This time, I was able to make a small cage around the ladybug. Now that the magic was balanced within me, it was easier to access the true elemental powers.

After working for a little bit longer, we called it a night. Mauevene let me know she would be leaving in the morning to find Mrs. Sullivan or Jordan. She wasn't sure how many days she would be gone, but I promised her I would be careful before I made my way out of the south wing and to my room.

Classes went by slowly, and I couldn't wait for them to be over. The only class that didn't go slowly was my masters class with Mr. Burwel. He had us continue working on our swords. I didn't create the sword right away, but I did make it appear fully for a second before it blew away. Mr. Burwel was pleased that I was able to do that and told me to keep practicing. By the end of class, I was letting the sword stay visible for a few minutes at a time.

"I'm glad to see each of you can sustain your elemental weapons. You have one more day before you fight each other. Sally, you and Sasha will be fighting each other, and Richard and Sean will be fighting each other. Tider, you will fight whoever wins between Richard and Sean, and then the last two winners will fight each other. Whoever wins at the end gets to go to town for the weekend," Mr. Burwel said before dismissing us.

I glanced at Sasha. She was smirking as she talked to Sean in hushed tones. I was sure they were up to something. I hurried to catch up with Tider and Richard as they left the dome.

"What are we going to do? We can't fight them."

"We have to," Richard replied. "But we shouldn't try to win."

"I will win," Tider said. "They expect me to use my full powers. If I don't, word will get back to my father, and I will be in trouble. Besides, if I go to town, maybe I can find out some more information since Mr. Mitchel won't be watching everything I do."

When we got to the common room, Adam was waiting for us, but I didn't see Abby.

"She is working on something in her room," Adam told me when I asked him. I started heading to the girl's wing, but Adam stopped me. "My grandfather called. He wants to meet us. He said it's important."

"We can't leave. Mr. Mitchel won't let us."

"I can meet him," Tider said. "If I win the fight, I will be in town this weekend. I could meet up with Chet and get the information."

"Good. I will let him know that you will be able to meet him," Adam said.

"Are you absolutely sure you can win?" I asked.

"Yes, Sean doesn't stand a chance."

"Unless he cheats like he did with the serpent during practicals."

"Even then, I should be able to beat him. He is already scared of me. He will make mistakes and get careless, trying to go for a quick win. He might be powerful, but he doesn't practice his magic as much as we do. He usually cheats his way through things, instead of learning how to do them correctly. That's not going to help him much during this fight."

"I'm still worried about these fights. Even if we don't try to win, we could get hurt," I said to Richard.

"The teachers won't let us get hurt badly. This is still a school, and Mr. Burwel works for the council. He won't want students hurt while he is teaching them. It will be fine. Let Sasha get in a few hits and then collapse. They will think it's too much for you. If you can't get up to fight, Sasha will be named the winner. I will do the same with Sean. Then Sasha and Sean can fight each other. I wonder if she will let him win?"

"Probably, she usually does whatever he says."

"You guys better be careful. Something about this fight doesn't feel right. I think Mr. Mitchel will try something," Adam said.

"We will be ok," Richard reassured him.

"We won't let Sally out of our sight either. She will be fine, and if Mr. Mitchel tries something, we will find a way to get out of there," Tider said.

"I doubt he will. There are too many other teachers around for him to do anything. I'm sure there will be other people besides Mr. Mitchel at the dome during the fight," Richard added.

Adam still looked uncertain, but he didn't argue about it. There was nothing we could do anyway. It's not like we had a choice. Mr. Mitchel was going to find a way to test me. It might as well be during class. At least then I might be protected by the other teachers if he went too far.

I left the guys to go check on Abby. It wasn't like her to not meet us when she said she would. Whatever she was working on had to be pretty important. When I got to her room, she opened the door and peeked out before ushering me in quickly.

"What are you up to, Abby? You didn't meet us like usual."

"I'm trying to make more potions."

"What? You can't. What if Mr. Mitchel finds out?"

"I don't think he will. It's doubtful he would search my room. To him, I have very little power. He doesn't know I can make potions."

"How will you get the ingredients?"

"Well," Abby started. "I snuck down to the potions room the day Mrs.

Sullivan left. I was worried something like this would happen with Mr. Mitchel. I took as many ingredients as I could that we might need. I've been working on the invisibility potion that we made last time and already have it started." She pointed to the corner of her room, and I could make out the pot we had used last time, hidden behind a stack of books.

"What else are you planning?" I asked.

"There is another potion that might come in handy. It's a heatproof potion. Since we are going into a volcano with fire elementals, I think we can use it."

"Is it easy to make?"

"Kind of. It uses a lot of ingredients, but they are all common, unlike the octatrug poison. I just need to mix them in the correct order. I already started it, but it takes some time. Different ingredients are added on different days."

"Will you have enough time? We need to go soon."

"I hope so. I will get as much done as I can. Did you figure out how to contact Jordan yet?"

"Yes. Mauevene is going to contact him or Mrs. Sullivan to set it up. I don't know what day it will be yet. Mauevene will let me know as soon as she talks to them. We will need to be ready."

"I will be," Abby said. "All I need to do is make these potions. When it's time to leave, we will take whatever is ready. It will have to be enough."

I stayed and talked to Abby a little longer. I told her how masters class was going and what Adam said. She looked worried but didn't try to persuade me to drop the class. She thought it was a good idea to learn as much as I could. She knew I was going to need it. Eventually, I went to my own room and thought about how I was going to battle Sasha and what I could do to make it believable when I lost.

I spent the next evening practicing with my elemental short sword, learning different ways to use it. Mr. Burwel taught us we could use our weapons as an extension of ourselves. I could use my elemental powers to shoot my element from the tip of the sword while swinging it around, creating a wave of air that shot out around me. It was pretty impressive.

Mr. Burwel called us all to the center of the room to tell us more about the fight. Everything sounded exactly as we expected the fight to go. While not fighting, we would be behind a protective shield to keep us from getting hurt. What he told us next caused me to worry.

If anyone was caught not giving it their all, they would have to face Mr. Mitchel himself in a fight. Mr. Burwel explained the reason for the rule was to keep someone from pretending to be weaker than they were. He said it was important for the teacher to know exactly how strong the students were so they could help them the best they could.

Richard kept glancing at me. I wouldn't be able to let Sasha win like we planned. Everyone knew I was stronger than her. If I let her win, Mr.

Mitchel would make me fight him.

I watched Sasha out of the corner of my eye. She was doing good with her weapon. Occasionally, she would lose focus, and her weapon would start to fade away. She also got tired faster than me. I started thinking of ways to beat her.

I switched my gaze to Richard. His weapon never wavered as he practiced with it. I knew he was still planning on letting Sean win. No one knew Richard was a lot more powerful than Sean, so it wouldn't seem like Richard was holding back, but I wished he would beat him. Sean was an even bigger jerk now that Mr. Mitchel was here. He seemed to think he could do no wrong. Letting him believe he was stronger than Richard was going to make him even harder to deal with.

By the end of class, I had an idea that might work and keep me from getting too hurt. My plan was to keep Sasha at arms distance with my sword and tire her out until she couldn't sustain her weapon any longer. I didn't want to actually hurt her, and I didn't want to get hurt, so I couldn't get close to her. Sasha would love to hurt me if she could, so I needed to be careful.

Mr. Burwel reminded us we would be fighting the next day and to get some rest so we would be prepared. I said bye to the guys and walked to my room by myself. I wasn't worried about Mr. Mitchel bothering me in the halls. He had control of the school and had found a way to test me with the council's permission. Until he knew how strong I was, he wouldn't try to hurt me. I was stuck here, after all.

I didn't go and see my friends after class. I preferred to be in my room. I spent the rest of the evening reading about elemental magic. Nothing I read would help me with the upcoming fight, but it might help me when I went to find the true fire elementals.

Abby knocked on my door as I was getting ready to lay down. She came in and sat on my bed, chewing on her bottom lip.

"What's wrong, Abby?"

"I don't think practicing your magic with Mr. Burwel is a good idea anymore. Mr. Mitchel is going to figure out how powerful you are during this fight or during one of your practices."

"I will try to keep him from finding out, Abby, but I can't hide forever. Besides, if I can't control my magic enough to fool the teachers, how can I expect to win against the darkness. The teachers think they have an idea of how powerful I am. As long as I don't do anything more powerful than that, I will be fine."

Abby didn't answer and fell silent. I sat next to her. "I'm scared too, Abby."

We sat there for a while, neither of us having any idea how to cheer the other up. Eventually, Abby gave me a hug, and we said good night.

After she left, I felt Sievroth curl up around my shoulders.

He never came with me anymore, and he stayed invisible all the time. I think he was worried about getting caught by Mr. Mitchel too. He was almost too big to curl around me. I felt his back legs slip down my back. I laughed and reached up to pet him.

"What do you think, Sievroth? Am I crazy to stay in a masters class?" I asked him, not expecting an answer.

"Stay in class, learn as much as you can," Sievroth's voice echoed in my head. I cocked my head at him.

"Why?" I asked, but this time he head-butted me and didn't respond.

CHAPTER EIGHT

I tossed and turned all night, thinking about the upcoming fight. It wasn't going to be fair. Sasha was going to try her hardest to hurt me after all the problems we had this term, but I didn't want to hurt her at all.

I dragged myself out of bed to get ready for the day. My teachers left me alone in all my regular classes. Somehow the whole school knew everyone in master classes would be fighting later.

Many of the students supported Richard. A large group also supported Sean. No one supported Tider, which didn't surprise me. He didn't have any other friends since they were too scared of him. A couple of students nodded to me as I walked through the halls, but I didn't pay attention. I wasn't excited about the upcoming class at all.

When we arrived at the dome, Mr. Mitchel was standing with Mr. Burwel. The dome had been cleared out. Only a few tables and chairs stood along one side of the room. Two of the chairs had council members in them, and the other two were empty. Probably for Mr. Mitchel and Mr. Burwel. They had us move to the center of the room.

"These five students are competing to see if they are strong enough to be in master classes." Mr. Mitchel addressed the two council members. "We will score them on their weapons, their abilities, and the length of time it takes for each test. At the end, one will win and be guaranteed a spot in masters classes for the rest of the term. The others may be allowed to continue masters classes if their scores are high enough."

The council members nodded, and Mr. Mitchel continued. "Mr. Burwel has trained them to create a weapon out of their element. Each of these students has been able to create and sustain their weapons for differing lengths of time. Now we will see if they have mastered how to use them."

Mr. Mitchel walked away to take his seat, and Mr. Burwel approached us. "Remember what I taught you, and you will all do fine. Good luck," he said before heading to the chair left for him. After he sat down, he called for Sean and Richard to step forward. The rest of us were told to stand on the opposite side of the room. Once we were there, Mr. Burwel raised a protective barrier up around us.

"Sean is going to win," Sasha said snidely.

"Probably," I agreed. Sasha stared at me. "What?" I asked.

"You aren't going to support your friend?"

"I would, but I doubt Richard will give it his all, he doesn't like taking part in stupid games like this." I knew I shouldn't goad her, but she really irritated me.

"You're only saying that because you know Sean is the better elemental."

"Ok," I responded, sounding bored.

She started to talk again, but Tider shushed her. I turned to watch as Richard dropped into a fighting stance. Mr. Mitchel counted down, and both guys made their weapons appear.

"Go," yelled Mr.Mitchel. Richard exploded into action, spinning away from Sean as their weapons crashed together. Richard grimaced as icicles flew toward his body. He used air to whisk them away and hit Sean with one in the calf.

Sean yelled and lost control of his weapon for a second. I glanced over at the judges. Their reactions worried me. They were enjoying the fight a little too much. The only one who looked bothered was Mr. Burwel. He saw me watching them and turned away.

I looked back to see Richard fall to one knee, acting like he was getting tired. He held his sword out and pushed air at Sean. A gust of wind knocked Sean back, but he got right back up and tried to wrap water around Richard. Richard easily cut through it with his sword.

While he was cutting the ropes of water, Sean took the opportunity and threw his ax at Richard. Richard could have avoided it. I saw him start to push it away with a burst of wind, but then he turned and let the wind miss the ax. The ax continued along its path and bit into Richard's shoulder.

Richard dropped to his knees as Mr. Burwel stood up and announced the end of the battle. Richard pulled the ax out of his shoulder and turned his face away from the council. When our eyes met, he winked. I relaxed. He was ok.

Mr. Burwel hurried to Richard and gave him a potion to drink. Within minutes his shoulder stopped bleeding, and he was escorted over to us as the council members, and Mr. Mitchel whispered. Sean walked over with his chest puffed up.

When he tried to brag, Mr. Burwel gave him a look and sent a small amount of magic at him. I saw Sean's body grow rigid, and his eyes widen in fear. It took only seconds for the rigidity to wear off, but Sean didn't say another word. I was really starting to like Mr. Burwel. Maybe we really could get him on our side, I thought.

"Sally, Sasha, it's your turn. Come out to the center of the room," Mr. Mitchel said.

I walked slowly behind Sasha. She was confident she would win this fight. I wasn't going to let her. She would be insufferable if she won, and Mr. Mitchel would know I hadn't used my full powers. He wasn't stupid enough to believe Sasha could beat me.

As he spoke, he looked at me and smirked. He thought he had me trapped and would find out how powerful I was. Once I beat Sasha, I would be going up against Sean, who I could let beat me easily, claiming exhaustion. It would stop our fight from getting out of control and wouldn't let Mr. Mitchel know any more about my powers.

Mr. Mitchel started the countdown, and I created my short sword. I watched Sasha create her dagger. She was moving before Mr. Mitchel said go. I watched as she rolled to her left, expecting me to attack her head-on. Instead, I stayed a few feet from her, backing up a few steps and moving sideways.

When she realized I wasn't going to attack, she came after me. She held her dagger up, and a stream of fire poured out of the tip, surrounding me. I used air to create a small bubble around me, keeping the fire from touching my skin.

Sasha continued the fire longer than she should have. When it finally died down, her dagger was shimmering. She was getting too tired to keep her focus on it. I slammed my weapon forward, letting a blast of air hit Sasha in the chest, knocking her to the ground. She jumped up and tried to send a fireball at me from her dagger. It was weak, and I had plenty of time to dodge it.

I sent another blast of air at Sasha, knocking her off her feet. This time she was slower getting up. She tried to run at me, using her dagger to cut through the wall of air in her way. I didn't make it very strong. I wanted the council to think I was only a little stronger than Sasha.

When she got close, she reached out and swiped her dagger at me. I swung my short sword at her wrist. I blunted the edge of the sword with air so it wouldn't cut Sasha and slammed it into her hand. Her fingers opened up around her dagger, and she dropped it as she screamed. Her dagger disappeared, and she fell to her knees, cradling her hand. The hit was hard enough to bruise her hand but not break it.

Mr. Burwel called an end to our fight and walked over to Sasha. He checked her hand but didn't give her a healing potion as he announced it wasn't broken.

"Why don't I get a healing potion?" she asked.

"We only use those for extreme cases. Your hand will be fine in a day or two."

Sasha grumbled the whole way back to the protective area. I stayed out in the center of the dome to fight Sean, but Mr. Mitchel stood up.

"I want to see Sean fight Johnathon," he said, using Tider's real name.

"But the plan was for Sean to fight Sally next. We know Johnathon will probably beat Sean. We need to see who is more powerful, Sean or Sally," Mr. Burwel said.

"I am changing it. Sean has proven that he should be given a chance to try to take on Johnathon. It wouldn't be fair to make him take on Sally first."

"Fine." Mr. Burwel gestured for me to go back into the protective area, and Sean and Tider stepped out. Tider looked pissed. We all knew something was up with Mr. Mitchel changing the fight. We didn't know what he had planned though. Leaving me to the last fight wouldn't be good. Something bad was going to happen. Mr. Mitchel wanted to know about my powers too much.

I reached out for Tider's mind and was swept away in the anger simmering inside him. "Tider," I yelled in his head. It took multiple tries, but I finally got his attention.

"Sally, you shouldn't be in my head. I need to focus."

"You could beat Sean in your sleep if you really wanted to," I scoffed. "What is wrong? Why are you so angry?"

"Sean knew this was going to happen. He was bragging about getting a chance to fight me while you were fighting Sasha. He overheard Mr. Mitchel saying he had special plans for you. He created something specifically for you to fight. He is going to do something awful to try to reveal your powers."

I wasn't surprised to hear that. I knew something was wrong. "Don't worry about it, Tider. I will be fine. Don't let them see you lose control. I'm sure they would love that."

"I won't, but I am going to give Sean what he deserves. I am going to use all my power on him. He won't know what's coming."

"Don't do anything you will regret," I said as Mr. Mitchel said go. I left Tider's head and watched the fight. Tider didn't even try to move away from Sean. Instead, he pulled all of his power to him and slammed it into his weapon. He threw the chakram away from himself and used a burst of air to push Sean backward.

Sean forgot about the chakram and tried to get closer to Tider so he could hit him with the ax. As he reached up to swing, the chakram came back at Tider. Tider turned, and Sean turned with him. The chakram silently flew toward the side of Sean's neck. He didn't even realize it was coming. I watched in horror as the chakram came closer. It stopped as it touched Sean's neck.

Mr. Burwel stood up and raced over along with the rest of the men. When they got closer, they were all stopped by a barrier Tider put up.

"I could have easily killed him," he said, slowly allowing the chakram to disappear. Only a thin line of blood was visible on Sean's neck. "Instead, I stopped my weapon so it wouldn't take his head off. This game you are playing is dangerous. You shouldn't be allowing children to fight." He released the barrier, and the men fell forward.

"I knew Johnathon was the strongest," one of the council said after they made sure Sean was ok, "but I didn't realize he was that powerful. He will be stronger than his father one day."

"He is obviously the winner here," the other council member said.

"Not really," Mr. Mitchel said. "As you all saw, Johnathon is too powerful to be considered on the same level as his classmates. He would do the same to Sally if we allowed him to fight her. It's not a fair test of her skills. She could be hurt, but we need to finish the test. We still don't know if she is ready to be in a masters class. She only fought Sasha, who was too weak for her. I'm sure we can all agree Sasha is not ready for these classes."

They all nodded. "Richard has already fought and would be a good match for her, but they are very good friends and won't fight each other. Sean is not in any condition to fight again after that." They turned toward Sean. He was still pale and shaky.

"What do you propose?" the first councilman asked.

"I have a spell that I have used with other students to see if they were really ready for masters classes. I propose using that to test Sally."

"That spell is not to be used without the council's permission any longer," Mr. Burwel interjected.

"We have four members of the council here. That is all we need to take a vote when the rest of the council isn't here."

"But," Mr. Burwel tried to say.

"There are no buts. We must finish the test," Mr. Mitchel said.

"Everyone in favor of testing Sally with my spell, raise your hand." Both councilmen and Mr. Mitchel raised their hands. "Those against?" Mr. Burwel raised his hand. "Then it is agreed. We will test Sally with my spell and see how she does." I looked at Richard in shock.

"What just happened?" I asked in his mind.

"We fell right into his trap. This is what he had planned the whole time. Somehow he knew Tider would act that way with Sean and push himself out of the competition. This was all arranged."

"What am I supposed to do?"

"I don't know."

"He will try to hurt me to get me to use my powers." Richard didn't have an answer for me, and I could see the same desperate look on his face that had to be on mine.

"Sally, come out here," Mr. Mitchel said.

"I decided I don't want to take master-level classes."

"Why? Are you scared of fighting a spell?"

"No, I just don't want to be in classes where someone could get hurt."

"Too bad, Sally. You show enough potential that you need to be trained.

We can't let an untrained elemental walk around. It could cause trouble for everyone. Remember what happened with the last person who wasn't trained?" Mr. Mitchel asked the councilmen. They both nodded.

"He is right," one of the councilmen said. "We need to know your powers, or you could be a danger to everyone. You will have to fight." I looked at Mr. Burwel, but he had his head down. He knew what was happening was wrong. I looked toward the door.

"Don't even think about it," Mr. Mitchel said quietly so only I could hear him. "I know where your parents are, and I will have one of my men take them if you don't complete this test."

I shook inside, knowing he could hurt my mom and dad if he wanted to. "Fine," I said. I relayed the information to Richard and Tider. Tider immediately took his phone out to text our security friend Gary at the Ireland haven where my parents were staying and get them to safety.

I looked at Mr. Mitchel. "Let's get this over with," I said and stalked to the center of the room. "Mr. Burwel," I called. He looked up at me. "Please make sure they don't hurt me too badly during this test and make sure the council knows I am doing this against my will."

Mr. Burwel nodded.

"Sally, be careful," Richard said in my head.

"I can't. Tell Abby to be ready to go. I won't be able to keep my powers hidden. If they try to take me, I'm going to have to fight my way out of here."

"I don't think it will be that bad. The council doesn't want anyone getting hurt even if Mr. Mitchel does. We will fight with you as soon as you give the word. We are ready."

I looked at Richard and Tider. They were both pissed and waiting to use their magic. I hid my smile. They would help me if I needed it. I pulled away from Richard as Mr. Mitchel raised his arms and chanted a spell in ancient. He said it low enough that I couldn't catch most of the words. The ones I did hear startled me. It sounded like he was creating a spell that would fight me in every element. I couldn't be sure that's what it was though.

The air in front of me coalesced into a dark figure. A hood covered its face, and I could only see darkness underneath it. The sleeves of its cloak rose, but no hands were visible. One of the arms pointed toward me, and I ducked, almost being seared by a thin line of fire. I created the weapon that I was supposed to be fighting with. I didn't want to give Mr. Mitchel any reason to say he needed to test me again if I made it through this.

The figure moved quickly and sent a stream of water at me next. It froze on its way to me, making a thin blade that would pierce through my skin easily. I slashed at it with my short word shattering it. I felt cold magic seeping into my hands through my sword and looked down in shock. Without focusing, I could see a little magic clinging to my hands. I jumped as the figure came after me again. I sent a wall of air at it and focused my attention back on my hands while it was busy trying to break through my wall.

The magic from the figure wasn't dissipating. Instead, it was trying to work its way up my hands, and it was pulling at my air magic. I pulled my magic back and watched the dark figure's magic try to grasp it. I used a sharp burst of air to push the dark magic off of me. As soon as I got it off, it disappeared.

Mr. Mitchel was using a spell to capture my magic so he could use it later. That's what this figure did. He made it look like a fight, but really it was sucking magic out of elementals. This is what we were worried about Mr. Damon having.

I told Richard about it quickly while trying to stay away from the thing. We needed to find out how both Mr. Mitchel and Mr. Damon had this power. I didn't know how to fight it. If I touched it, it would get stuck to me again and steal my magic. I kept throwing magic at it from a distance, only using air.

The more attacks I dodged, the faster the figure got. As I tried to slip past it again, it reached out and caught me on the arm with a spear of ice. Immediately I felt that cold sinking feeling and tried to push it off. It was harder to get off this time, and I felt my energy level drop. It kept coming after me while I was distracted and stabbed me in the side with a dagger made of air. The magic started sucking at my air magic, and I struggled with the dark magic.

I felt the figure moving closer again and tried to dodge, but it hit me on the other side with a flaming sword. I cried out as the flame cut into my side. The flames cauterized the wound, which kept me from bleeding, but the dark magic clung to me, causing me to fall to my knees. My head felt light, and I became dizzy. I could hear Mr. Burwel yelling at Mr. Mitchel to stop, but Mr. Mitchel wouldn't stop until the figure was done testing me.

I heard Richard in my head, begging me to get up. I saw the figure getting ready to hit me again, this time with a sword made of earth. If I didn't get this magic off of me, Mr. Mitchel would find out I had true elemental magic. I felt connections open to the water elemental king and the air elemental queen. They poured more power into me and told me to fight back.

With the extra magic, I was able to wipe the dark magic off of me and stand. As the figure came at me, I threw my hands up. I let the air stream out of one hand while water flowed from the other. They met each other in front of the figure and merged, becoming completely different.

A purple mist settled over the figure, and I could hear Sievroth in my head telling me to add fire to the mist to destroy the figure. I closed my eyes and followed Sievroth's directions, sending a giant fireball toward the mist. As soon as it hit, the mist exploded, destroying the figure and all the dark magic in the room. Mr. Mitchel screamed out in pain, and the other councilmen stared at me. I collapsed as the connections inside me closed, and I was able to feel my wounds.

Mr. Burwel and my friends ran to me. Mr. Burwel tried to give me a healing potion, but I passed out before I could take it. I lost too much blood, and the dark magic depleted all of my energy. The last thing I saw was Mr. Mitchel lying on the floor by the councilmen. I smiled as I slipped into darkness.

CHAPTER NINE

I opened my eyes slowly. I was getting tired of waking up after falling unconscious. I looked around and realized I was in Mrs. Newton's room. She was standing over me looking down, a small frown on her face.

"You are lucky, Sally, someone is watching over you. These wounds should have killed you. Even with my magic, they aren't going to heal easily. They will leave scars too. Whatever Mr. Mitchel hit you with wasn't ordinary magic."

"It was dark magic," I told her. I heard a gasp behind her and tried to see who else was in the room, but a sharp pain in my side caused me to fall back against the cot I was laying on.

I heard someone move closer. "Are you sure it was dark magic?" Mrs. Newton asked.

"Positive. It was trying to suck the magic out of me. Every time I was hit by the figure Mr. Mitchel created, dark magic would stick to me and start pulling on my own magic."

"Will she be ok?" A lady's voice asked as she moved into my line of sight. I had seen her before, but I wasn't sure where.

"Yes, I will help her," Mrs. Newton said.

"I must tell the rest of the council about this. If what she says is true, and I believe she is being honest, then Mr. Mitchel is not who we thought he was. We don't believe in dark magic." She looked down at me. "I'm sorry, Sally. This never should have happened to you. I don't know how we didn't realize what Mr. Mitchel was doing. He has been taken back to the council already. He is in a coma. Whatever you did caused his magic to backfire on him. You will be safe here now." The lady left the room before I had time to say anything.

"Who was that?" I asked Mrs. Newton.

"That was one of the council members. She has been with the council for over twenty years. Mrs. Sullivan trusts her. It looks like she hasn't been corrupted yet, but I wouldn't guarantee that the council is going to see things her way, especially if Mr. Mitchel wakes up. He has managed to fool them for so long that I doubt the word of a student will stop most of them from believing his lies. You need to prepare yourself to leave this school. It is no longer safe if he wakes up."

"What should I do?"

"For now rest. We will find out immediately if he wakes up. The healer for the council is a good friend of mine, and she has already promised to let me know the second he awakens. That will give you the time you need to do whatever you have planned. Talk to your friends, and I will contact Mrs. Sullivan. I'm sure you will all come up with something."

"What was that thing Mr. Mitchel attacked me with?"

"I'm pretty sure it was a magicus. A creature created by dark magic to steal another's magic. The stolen magic would be returned to the creator, and they could use it whenever they wanted. I've never dealt with this type of magic before, but what you are describing makes me think that's what Mr. Mitchel created."

Before I could ask more questions, Abby burst into the room. "Sally, are you ok?" she asked, running over to me.

"Relax, Abby," Mrs. Newton said. "Sally should be fine with a little rest. She has a lot to tell you, so I will leave you alone. I will be back in an hour to check on you, Sally. Make sure you stay in the cot until then so your wounds can heal more. After I check on you, you will be allowed to get up and go to your room."

Mrs. Newton walked out of the room, leaving me alone with Abby.

"Are you sure you're ok?" she asked. "Richard, Tider, and Adam are freaking out right now."

"I'm fine. Really sore, but fine. Where are they at?"

"They are busy trying to get in contact with Chet and Mrs. Sullivan. Your parents have already been moved. Gary wouldn't say where they are. He only said that they are safe, and no one will find them until this is all cleared up." I felt a weight lift off my shoulders. I knew Gary would find a way to protect them.

"Why are they trying to get in contact with Chet?"

"We need to find somewhere to go. The school isn't safe anymore. Richard doesn't think the council will believe a group of kids over Mr. Mitchel. He's probably right, and now Mr. Mitchel knows you have way more power than he thought. They are going to come after you with everything they have. We can't be here when that happens."

"If that happens," I said. "Maybe he won't wake up from his coma until after we defeat the darkness and the Pulhu."

"I hope he doesn't wake up, but we better be prepared for the worst-case scenario. Adam said Chet has somewhere safe for us, but we need to know where it is. Chet will tell us when he gets here. No one trusts the phones anymore."

"So, what happened after I passed out?"

"I'm not sure. Richard told me Mr. Burwel grabbed you and came running to the school, shouting for Mrs. Newton to heal you. He couldn't get you to drink the healing potion. You almost died." Abby started to cry, and I reached up to give her a hug.

"I'm ok now, Abby. Mrs. Newton healed me."

"I could have healed you if I was there."

"I know, but at least Mr. Mitchel doesn't know about your healing abilities."

"You aren't allowed to go anywhere without me anymore," Abby said.

"Ok, Abby." I smiled at her. "Now, tell me what else happened."

"Mr. Mitchel passed out, and the councilmen tried to revive him but couldn't. I guess one of them tried to grab him but burned their hands. Some kind of magic was covering Mr. Mitchel, so he couldn't be touched. It took a while for the magic to disappear. Once it did, they transported him back to the council. No one has said anything else about him."

"What about Sean and Sasha?"

"They are still here. They aren't saying much though. Everyone knows you beat Sasha, and Tider beat Sean. Sean tried to say he beat Richard, but Tider laughed about it and said Richard let him win. Half of the school believes Tider and half believe Sean. The school has really started to split."

"I think Mrs. Newton is right. We need to make a plan to get out of here. This school isn't going to be safe for us much longer, even if Mr. Mitchel doesn't wake up."

"Yeah, about that. The kids all know that you beat Mr. Mitchel. They think you are super powerful now. Some have even mentioned the prophecy. We weren't able to stop people from talking about it."

"It's ok," I sighed. "We knew it would eventually get out. It just happened sooner than I would have liked."

"So far, it is only rumors. No one actually knows about all your power or that you have more elements," Abby said quietly.

"Good. We don't need them knowing," I said.

Abby sat with me for the rest of the hour. She wanted to know all about the fight with Mr. Mitchel since she wasn't there. By the time Mrs. Newton got back, I was starting to fall asleep. She checked the wounds and said I could go get something to eat and go to my room to sleep.

I would have to meet her in the morning to recheck the wounds to make sure they were still healing. They were so bad that it would take multiple healings. She didn't let me see them when she took the bandages off, and I didn't try to. I saw Abby's face pale and decided I didn't need to see how bad they looked.

As I walked through the school, kids stopped to whisper. Some came up and said good job, but some glared at me as I walked past. Sean and Sasha were in the common room as I walked through and glared before turning to their friends. They whispered something that caused them all to laugh. I shook my head and turned into the cafeteria. I didn't need to get involved with anything they were doing.

A young kid walked up to me as I left the cafeteria to go to my room. I waited for him to talk.

"You did a good job, and I hope you defeat the Pulhu," he said quietly. I had seen this kid before. He waved to me on the school trip to the mountains, but his brother pulled him away. His brother was part of Sean's crew. This kid was too sweet to be involved with them.

I leaned down and whispered, "Thank you. I'm going to do my best to win." His eyes went wide as he realized I was confirming that I was going to fight the darkness. He smiled and closed his lips, acting like he wouldn't tell anyone.

I knew his brother would ask him about our conversation later, and I didn't want him to get in trouble for trying to keep secrets, so I shook my head. "It's ok if they know. Don't get in trouble for me. Keep your head down until this fight is over and don't use dark magic," I whispered. He smiled again as I walked toward my room to get some rest.

The next morning, Abby met me as I was getting ready to go down for breakfast.

"We need to go see Mr. Burwel when you finish eating. He will be in Mrs. Sullivan's office. He's taking over until the council decides what to do."

We ate quickly. Too many of the students were watching me and sharing whispered words. It made me uncomfortable. Richard and Tider were both absent from breakfast. When I connected with them, they told me they were working on plans to get me out of the school and somewhere safe.

Adam let me know his grandfather would be in town over the weekend for someone to meet. I didn't say anything, but I was planning on going to meet him. Now that Mr. Mitchel wasn't here, I could sneak out and see what Chet had to say for myself. I would let everyone know later when we had more privacy. They wouldn't be happy about it, and I didn't want anyone overhearing them when they tried to yell at me.

We headed down to see Mr. Burwel, Adam tagging along to make sure I was ok. I walked slowly. My side was starting to hurt. Each breath felt like a knife was digging into my ribs.

Mr. Burwel was waiting and ushered us into the room. As soon as I sat down, Abby stood in front of me.

"Let me see," she said, trying to put her hands over my wound.

I pushed her hands away, not wanting Mr. Burwel to see Abby healing me.

"Sally, knock it off. You need more healing, or you are going to undo all the progress Mrs. Newton made."

"What's going on?" Mr. Burwel asked. "Sally, aren't you fully healed yet?"

"I can heal her, but she doesn't want me doing it in front of you," Abby said. "She is in a lot of pain, and it's getting worse the more she moves around." She looked over at me. "You forget I can tell you are in pain. I'm a healer, Sally. I know it's bad."

"If she needs to be healed, we can call Mrs. Newton," Mr. Burwel said.

"She already healed her yesterday, and she is going to look at her again today, but she used a lot of energy, saving Sally's life. It is going to take her a few days to be able to do another big healing."

"If you can help her," Mr. Burwel said, "please do. I know you don't trust me after how things started when I came to the school, but I really only want what is best for the students."

"Fine, Abby, you can heal me." I closed my eyes and watched as her magic moved to my side. I loved the color of Abby's magic. It was a shimmery yellow color, and as soon as it touched me, I felt it begin to work, taking the pain away that was giving me difficulty breathing. Her magic worked further inside me, trying to heal the wound, but it hit a block.

Abby's eyes opened. "Do you feel that, Sally?"

"Yes. I can see it too." There was a smudge of dark magic still clinging to the deepest part of the wound in my side. It wouldn't allow Abby to fully heal me. "This is why I'm feeling worse. We can't heal this until the dark magic is gone."

Abby explained what was going on to Adam and Mr. Burwel while I focused on the magic, trying to dispel it from my body. I couldn't move it. It was firmly attached to me. Every time I tried, it ripped the wound apart farther. I wasn't strong enough to destroy the dark magic without possibly killing myself. It would tear the wound open worse than before, and I might bleed out before I could destroy it and let Abby heal me.

"How are we going to heal you?" Abby asked after I told them how bad it was.

"You can do it if we all join together," Adam said. "With the extra power, we might be able to destroy it." This time I explained to Mr. Burwel that I could connect with certain people and boost our powers.

"What is the downside of doing this?" he asked.

"When we stop touching, we no longer have the boost. If we use too much energy, it could cause us to pass out or possibly worse."

"We won't use that much power," Abby said. "Only enough to save you."

Mr. Burwel looked unsure until Adam spoke.

"We will need a strong healer here to help heal Sally in case Abby can't do it. Mrs. Newton should be able to handle healing the rest of us if we use too much energy. We need to talk to Mrs. Sullivan. She will know a healer we can trust to help Sally."

"I know a few healers we can call," Mr. Burwel said.

"Are they part of the council?" I asked. When he nodded, I shook my head. "No, we can't use them. We don't know who we can trust on the council." I interrupted him when he started to talk. "You trusted Mr. Mitchel and those two councilmen that allowed this. As you can see, the council has been compromised. We don't know who can be trusted anymore. We are taking a big enough risk trusting you."

Mr. Burwel nodded and took his phone out to call Mrs. Sullivan. When he got off the phone, he was grimacing. We all heard Mrs. Sullivan yelling at him when she found out what happened.

"She will be here soon with a healer. I need to go meet her at the gates so she can get in. Stay here."

Mr. Burwel left, and we waited for everyone to arrive. Adam let Richard and Tider know I needed them. It didn't take long for them to get to Mrs. Sullivan's office. When they heard everything going on, their powers started swirling around them.

"Calm down," I said. "We will need that power soon." I was gasping for breath by the time I finished the sentence. They both calmed immediately, coming to stand by me. I felt Richard slip into my mind and check how I was really feeling. I tried to block him, but it was no use. Our connection had grown to the point that we couldn't keep each other out anymore.

"We are going to need to hurry. She isn't going to be able to hold on much longer. She's in a lot more pain than she's letting on."

I glared at him but didn't say anything. He was right. The pain was becoming unbearable again. By the time Mr. Burwel got back with Mrs. Sullivan and another woman, I was barely hanging onto consciousness. Mrs. Sullivan rushed over. I smiled weakly at her.

"Do it now, Sally. We will protect you and your friends. Use all the power you need. You can trust everyone here." I felt her throw a protection spell around all of us. As soon as she did, Mauevene appeared to the surprise of everyone in the room.

"Sally, you need to use true elemental power to get rid of this. We will help you. Call to the true elementals after you connect to your friends."

She flew over to Mrs. Sullivan, landing on her shoulder. I looked at my friends and watched as they all grabbed hands. As soon as we were linked, I felt strength pouring into me from them. They were giving me everything they had. I opened my magic up, and let the true elemental powers flow through me. I could feel the water elemental king and the air elemental queen connect to my mind and send more power to me.

I sent all the magic in one concentrated burst toward the dark magic. I screamed as it hit and would have fallen if not for my friend's support. The dark magic was still there. My burst of magic wasn't enough, and the pain intensified.

"You can do it," I heard coming from my friends and the true elementals. Suddenly I felt a new presence in my mind. I heard a loud roar and yelling coming from the adults before fire magic poured into me.

I recognized Sievroth's voice as he told me to try again and use his magic to burn the dark magic. I pulled all the magic together and sent a burst of light at the dark magic. This time the pain caused me and my friends to fall, but we never let go of each other. When the stream of magic disappeared, the dark magic was gone. I looked closely, searching for any tiny speck of dark magic, but there was nothing.

"You are safe now," Sievroth said.

"Be safe," the water elemental king said.

"We will see you soon," the air elemental queen said, and then their presence was gone. I told my friends to let go slowly. I could feel as each person let go. I got weaker and weaker.

Only Richard kept ahold of my hand. Someone was healing me, and Richard knew the second he let go, both of us would be dangerously low on energy. He shifted next to me, and I let my head fall on his shoulder. The wound finally closed up all the way, and the healer moved away from me. I opened my eyes to see everyone staring.

I realized they weren't staring at me but behind me, and I turned my head to see what they were looking at. I hadn't seen Sievroth since Mr. Mitchel came to the school. He stayed invisible, but now he was showing himself off proudly. He stood behind me with his wings out. His wingspan was easily six feet already, and his body had grown to a few feet long. No wonder he couldn't stay on my shoulders anymore. He had grown so much.

He leaned forward and head-butted me gently. "I've missed seeing you," I told him.

He made the grumbling noise that reminded me of laughter before giving me one last head butt and turning his head toward everyone else. He growled once before disappearing again. I knew he was still behind me, curling up to keep an eye on me, but everyone else thought he was gone except Richard. He was still connected to me, so he knew Sievroth was hanging around.

Mauevene flew up to me, and I put my hand out for her to land on. "You need to stop getting into these close calls," she scolded me in ancient.

"It's not my fault. I told everyone I'm a magnet for trouble," I responded in the ancient language. She laughed and disappeared, saying she would see me later.

"What just happened?" Mr. Burwel asked. "That was a dragon and a water sprite. Why were they here? And they were helping. How do you know a dragon and a water sprite and the ancient language?" he sputtered.

I felt bad for him. It was a lot to take in. I looked at the healer, but she just winked at me. She looked a lot like Mrs. Sullivan, and I wondered if they were sisters. It would explain why she wasn't more surprised by everything. Mrs. Sullivan probably told her a lot about the situation.

Everyone ignored Mr. Burwel and peppered me with questions. When they finally calmed down, I explained that I was ok, and the dark magic was gone. Mrs. Sullivan told me to go get some food and relax for the rest of the day. There wouldn't be any classes for us. We were all grateful as we slowly left her office. They could sort things out with Mr. Burwel. I was sure Mrs. Sullivan would let me know if I needed to worry about anything. While she was here, I could relax.

CHAPTER TEN

Mrs. Sullivan was waiting for us later that day in her office. Mr. Burwel was there too. He looked better than a few hours ago and didn't seem nearly as confused.

"Sally, we need to discuss what your next step is," she said.

"What about him?" I asked, nodding at Mr. Burwel.

"It's ok, Sally, we can trust him. He even had me put a block on his mind to keep him from being able to tell the council about you."

"What do you think our next step should be?" I asked her.

"You need to get to the fire elementals before the Pulhu do. They are still on Mount Etna, and I think they are getting close. There has been more activity there lately."

"Can you get Jordan to take us?"

"Yes, but not yet. We already talked about it and think it would be best if you went next week. There is a council meeting scheduled to decide what to do about Mr. Mitchel, whether he is out of the coma or not. All of the council members that support him will want to be there, so they will have to leave Mount Etna. I'm sure there will still be Pulhu on the mountain but not as many. It might make it easier for you to get in undetected."

Mrs. Sullivan went over the plans with us for a few more minutes. When we left, Abby asked me to come to her room. I said goodbye to the guys and went with Abby. In her room, she showed me the different potions she made. We separated them between the two of us. If one of us got caught or lost our bags, we would still have some of the potions. I looked around her room. She still had two pots going with potions in them. When I asked her about them, she didn't answer right away.

"Come on, Abby. What are you making now?"

"Nothing important. One is the potion to withstand heat, and the other is more of an experiment."

"What kind of experiment?" The last thing we needed was to drink a potion and turn into mice for a day.

"I am trying to make a potion that will stop time."

"I'm sorry, what?"

"Well, I read something that said there used to be an elemental who always knew what was going to happen. Some people believed he could travel through time. Another book said it seemed like this man could only see what happened a few minutes into the future. There are ingredients that when mixed together, might give you that ability. Not to see into the future or travel through time, but stop time. Everyone around you would be stuck in time, and you could change how something was going to happen. Probably not much, but it might be enough to help you when you fight the darkness."

"Abby, how dangerous is this?"

"Pretty dangerous," she said slowly. "But it is a last resort. After everything that has been happening, I think we need a last resort item. Hopefully, we will never have to use it."

"How did you figure this out? Nobody else knows this is possible?" I asked.

"I don't know if anyone else knows, but I found a similar spell in the book you found in the south wing. When I cross-referenced it with a book Adam's grandfather sent me about old potions, I came up with this. I don't think anyone else would have access to the book Chet gave me. It's really, really old, and he found it at one of his archaeological sites. I have the only copy of it. He has the original locked up. The Pulhu didn't get it when they ransacked his shop."

"Ok, Abby, but we don't use it unless it's an emergency, like a life or death emergency, not any emergency. This is an untested potion. It could have awful side effects, and tampering with time is probably dangerous."

"Ok, Sally." Abby agreed. I left her to finish working on her potions and stepped across the hall to my own room. I was changing when I remembered something. I walked over to my desk and put my hand over the floor directly under it.

"Lakir."

I said the ancient word the air elemental queen had used. A book appeared under my hand, and I lifted it up. I walked over to the bed and made myself comfortable against the pillows before opening it. I completely forgot about the book with all the problems lately. This book contained all the information the true air elementals knew about void and its users.

"Void is not an element," I read out loud so Sievroth and Mauevene could hear me if they were in the room. "It is magic unlike any we have encountered. It is more powerful than all of the elements combined. We are not sure where it came from, but many think it originated on Earth, long before the elementals came. The users of void were specially selected, and very few were able to actually harness it." I paused, waiting to see if Mauevene or Sievroth would say anything. When they didn't, I went back to reading out loud.

"They studied it themselves, trying to unlock its mysteries. The only thing we know for sure from a void user is that only the most powerful could use void without being corrupted. They had many protections in place to combat a void user who lost control. A rumor was told to us that void magic came directly from the shadow king, but we haven't been able to substantiate that."

I stopped reading. If void magic was really the shadow king's magic than why would he kill the void users when he killed the elementals and destroyed their cities. It was said he didn't want any magic to be used by humans, which is why he sent the elementals into their own realms after all the fighting they did on the human realm. Something was missing. I didn't believe the shadow king would kill those that had his magic.

An idea came to me. I wondered if a shadow king could be corrupted. In the story about the elementals, one of the shadow kings was a real jerk and thought he was the best at everything. Maybe he destroyed the void users because he didn't want his brother sharing his powers with humans. It was a stretch, but it could make sense. I didn't know enough about the shadow kings to know if my idea was possible.

There was a knock on my door, and I jumped up to put the book back under the desk. I said, "Lakir," and the book disappeared as the person knocked again. I opened the door to Mrs. Sullivan.

"Come on, Sally. It's time for you to go."

"Where?"

"Chet is in town. Tider and Adam are waiting for you out front. They are going too. You will all stop by Dr. Griffith's office. He wants to check and make sure your wound is really better before you go into town. He also wants to make sure the dark magic didn't leave an invisible tracker on you."

"It can do that?"

"Possibly. I don't think you have anything, but it's best to be sure."

We walked down to the front doors together and met Adam and Tider. In the driveway was a sleek black car. I could see someone sitting in the driver's seat.

"Natasha will take you to Dr. Griffith's office. From there you can walk around the town. If you need anything, call me. We have already checked the town and haven't seen any sign of the Pulhu, but be careful. Watch out for each other. You have three hours to talk to Chet and get back here."

"Thanks, Mrs. Sullivan."

I slipped into the car, Tider and Adam right behind me. Natasha, our driver, took us to see Dr. Griffith before we headed into town on our own. I hadn't seen him since I first came to this school. He was the one who tested me and told me I had elemental powers. He also healed my dad after the Pulhu hurt him.

When we walked in, Nana, one of the nurses, came over and gave me a big hug.

"Sally, we have heard so much about everything going on around you. I'm sorry you have to deal with it. We couldn't come to the school to help you. The Pulhu don't know what side Dr. Griffith is on. Technically, he works for the council, taking care of children who uncover their powers and their parents don't know what is happening to them. He couldn't be seen siding with you, or the Pulhu on the council could cause problems for Dr. Griffith and the kids he tries to help. Plus, he helps regular kids with rare diseases when he can. He hates to turn any child away, even if they aren't elementals."

"Its ok, Nana. I don't want to cause anyone else trouble. Dr. Griffith needs to stay here in the town and take care of the other kids."

She gave me another hug as Dr. Griffith walked in.

"Sally, how have you been?" he asked.

"I'm ok, Dr. Griffith."

He gestured for me to follow him while my friends stayed in the waiting room.

"How are you really doing, Sally?" he asked when we were alone.

"It's tough, but I am doing fine. I miss my parents, and I worry about them every day still."

"I know you do. They are safe. I know Gary at the Ireland haven has taken care of them." He laughed at my shocked look. "I have been keeping tabs on you since you first came through these doors. I knew you were someone special. I'm not surprised you are the one who is going to defeat the darkness and stop the Pulhu."

"I don't know if we will win, but I'm going to try. I have something I need to ask you." I continued when he nodded. "Have you heard anything about an imposter? I found a reference to an imposter and the prophecy. How do I know that I'm the one in the prophecy and not the imposter?"

"I have heard of this. There is no way for you to know. You will have to decide for yourself. Maybe you will meet this other person, and then you will know the truth. For now, I would continue on as if you are the one the prophecy speaks of. No one else has been able to find the true elementals and get them to agree to fight with us. You have the water sprites, the sylphs, and the dragons backing you. I would trust in them."

He was right. Everyone believed I was the one meant to do this. I needed to start believing it too. Dr. Griffith did the routine doctor check-up and then called Nana into the room. "Ok, Sally, let's do a quick magical scan. Nana will be able to tell us if you have any other magical signatures on you besides your own. That way, no one can follow you."

Nana put her hands an inch from my body and ran her hands through the air over me. She stopped at each wound and spent extra time, making sure there was no magical tracker. When she finished, she smiled at me tiredly. "You are all set, Sally. Nothing is on you that can be tracked."

"Thanks, Nana."

Dr. Griffith cleared me to leave, and we hurried through the town to the little cafe. Chet was already there, and Adam walked to the booth to give his grandfather a big hug before sitting down. Chet gave me a hug next, and I squeezed into the seat next to Adam.

Tider sat next to Chet, and we all ordered something small when the waitress came over. Her eyes got wide when I ordered, but she didn't say anything, and no one else seemed to notice, so I dismissed it.

It was a cute cafe, and I spent a lot of time looking at it before Adam nudged me with his foot.

"Pay attention."

"Sorry. I've never been here before. It's a cute town." I glanced out the window again. "It's always been too dangerous to let me leave school. I guess now the school is just as dangerous."

"Sally, I have some information that might help you with the fire elementals. It's not much, but that's not why I'm really here."

That got my attention, and I leaned forward to listen.

"The school is no longer safe. After you leave to go to the fire realm, I don't think you should go back. Too many council members are siding with the Pulhu. I'm not sure what is happening, but even regular people are starting to be affected by something. There have been reports of killings all over the world. Something is causing people to act in ways they normally wouldn't. They are selfish and uncaring toward others."

"Why haven't we heard about this?" Adam asked.

"The council is insisting it's just another human war, and it will blow over, but most of us know something isn't right."

"How bad is it?" I asked.

"It has been getting worse the past few months, but this week has been really bad. Half of the states and most of Europe are now under curfew to keep people from hurting each other. Nighttime seems to be the worst. Not everyone is being affected, only a small portion, but it is causing a lot of trouble. If many more start to be affected, it will get worse quickly."

"How can we stop it?"

"I think the only way to stop it is to defeat the darkness. The Pulhu aren't strong enough to be the cause of this by themselves. It has to be the darkness the prophecy speaks of."

"Then there is nothing we can do until I find all the true elementals. I need to find the earth elementals and void before I can stop the darkness." We got quiet as the waitress brought our food to us.

"Don't worry, Sally. We are all rooting for you. When you finish with the fire elementals, I want you to tell Jordan to transport you to my shop in

Ireland. I have a way to keep you safe, but I don't want to reveal how right now. You never know who is listening," he whispered. I looked around the cafe. A few of the customers kept looking at our table, but they turned away as soon as I made eye contact with them. Something was definitely off here.

"Ok," I whispered back. Chet started talking about how things were going in Ireland, and Adam asked him about the break-in at his shop. Chet told us the details. He still couldn't locate his stuff. Whoever stole it put a blocking spell on everything so it couldn't be tracked.

Chet was pretty mad about his shop being broken into and kept telling us all the things that were taken. I listened to him, but I kept my eye on everyone around us. I felt very exposed in the cafe. I was glad when Chet started to grab his things.

"I have to leave now. Adam, keep an eye on her, and all of you keep an eye on each other."

"I will, Grandpa," Adam said. We told Chet we would be careful, and then he left.

"We have more time before we have to go back. Is there anything you want to do?" Tider asked.

"We should head right back. It's not safe here," Adam said.

"It's not safe anywhere," Tider replied. "Sally has never gotten a chance to look around the town. This may be her only chance. She has us with her if anything happens."

"I would like to go to the beach," I said. I remembered the first time I saw the beach after my powers had awoken. The water felt like it was calling to me, and I would have stayed and watched it for hours if I didn't need to go see Dr. Griffith back then.

"Come on," Tider said and took off down the street.

I followed him slowly, Adam trailing behind me. Occasionally we would pass one of the townspeople, but none of them looked up or said hi as we passed. It seemed like they were all afraid of something, I looked around, or someone. I didn't see anyone watching me, but I felt it. So far, no one had done anything but look oddly at me. I really wanted to go down to the beach, so I continued following Tider.

He waited for me to reach him. We took our shoes off and stepped into the sand. I let it squish between my toes and cherished the feel of it as I walked to the edge of the water. I had been in the ocean in Ireland, but this little piece of the beach still called to me. I sat in the sand and pushed my feet forward the extra few inches so they would get wet from the surf.

Tider and Adam were running up and down the beach. One of them found a frisbee, and they threw it back and forth to each other. I laughed as Adam lost his footing after a particularly large leap and fell into the water, soaking half his body. He looked around and quickly dried his clothes using his fire element.

I listened to them goofing around as I lost myself in the sight of the waves coming in. A creeping feeling crawled along my neck, and I turned around. Someone was watching us again. Eventually, I noticed a figure crouched on the edge of the beach, as far down as I could see. I wouldn't have noticed him except for a glint of light. He must have binoculars, and the sunlight caught them when I was looking.

I stood up slowly and dusted myself off.

"Hey, guys," I called. "It's time to go."

"But, Sally. We still have more time."

"We need to go now, guys," I said. I connected to each of them and told them someone was following us, and I wanted to leave.

Tider threw his arm around my shoulders and laughed, pretending everything was fine. We slipped our shoes back on and headed down the street, back toward the cafe. Another man was standing in front of the cafe. He was leaning against the side of the store, trying to act like he belonged, but his shiny dress shoes gave him away. This was a sleepy little town on the coast. No one was wearing shoes like that.

He had sunglasses on, but I could feel his eyes watching us as we walked past. Tider and Adam kept up a conversation about boats as we continued down the street, acting like everything was perfect. We made it back to the doctor's office without any incidents.

We explained what happened to Dr. Griffith. He told us they were probably watching us and reporting back to someone else about what we did while we were in town. He didn't think they were going to attack us, but to be safe, he sent us to the school right away. Natasha was already waiting, and we piled into her car.

CHAPTER ELEVEN

When we got back into the school, we told Mrs. Sullivan about our trip to town and the man we saw. "I'm not surprised they have people watching the town. We have been checking it but haven't seen them. They must have a hideout we don't know about."

"Most of the townspeople kept looking at me weird," I told her.

"Maybe they bribed or scared them into telling the Pulhu when they see you or any of the students from the school. That would explain why we haven't seen them. None of the students have been in the town lately. I will send someone to see if they can find and track them down."

We left Mrs. Sullivan's and agreed to meet up later that night in the south wing. The day went quickly without anything to do, and it was time to sneak out faster than I expected.

I didn't see anyone on my way to the south wing with Abby. We slipped inside and hurried to the meeting spot. Abby needed to grab a couple of books to bring with us, so we were a few minutes late. The guys were there and discussing how we would go about getting into the fire realm.

"It shouldn't be too hard," I said. "Mrs. Sullivan thinks most of the Pulhu from the council will be busy that day."

"Yeah, but what about their followers? We know they have a lot and are constantly getting more."

"I made more of the invisibility potions that we used in the air elemental realm. We can use those if we need too," Abby said.

"See," Tider told Richard. "I told you not to worry so much. It is going to be fine."

"I think the more important question is, what are we going to find once we go in? We have no idea what we are walking into. Adam said we haven't been able to find any information about what could be happening there."

"We should try to sneak in and look around before they know we are there," I replied.

"What if they are waiting for us? They have to know the Pulhu are trying to get in. They might think we are there to hurt them."

"We are not going to know what to do until we get there. There's no point in trying to figure it out without any more information. Let's just go and see what we find," I said.

"I agree," Abby said. "We are taking a lot of different potions, and we have all been in fights before. I think we can handle ourselves."

"What about Mr. Mitchel?" Richard asked.

"There is nothing we can do about that either. If he wakes up, we will need to hide from him. I'm sure he isn't going to want to talk next time we meet since I put him in a coma. He knows I'm very powerful now, so he will probably try to kill me. Chet said we can come to him to hide after we leave the fire realm. He doesn't have it ready yet, or we would go today. Mrs. Sullivan will protect us until then."

A whistle from down the hallway forced us to hide. I watched as the figure in the cloak walked past the door to the room we were in. She looked inside for a minute but continued on. I could see her through the crack between the two chairs I was hiding behind. I knew it was a female from the last time. She was wearing the same pointy black heels. I never saw any of the teachers wearing them though.

We heard the person moving down the hallway. A door opened and closed. The whistling was cut off, and I let the breath I was holding out. Everyone started whispering. I stood up and quietly moved toward the door.

"Where are you going?" Abby asked.

"I want to know who that person is."

"What if they catch you?"

"They won't. We need to know who keeps coming in here and what they are doing. We need more answers before we leave the school."

I snuck further down the hall, my friends following me. A light was coming from underneath the same door as the last time we had seen the cloaked figure. I tried to hear what they were saying, but whoever was in there was talking too quietly. We backed away and headed out of the south wing, waiting in the common room to see the person.

I put a shield of invisibility up around my friends and told them not to move. I was getting better at keeping us all invisible for longer periods of time, even with small movements, but I didn't want to take any chances.

The cloaked figure always seemed to sense our presence. The wait wasn't long, and soon she appeared in front of the south wing door. It still took me by surprise. When you walked out of the south wing, there was no door, but when you walked into the south wing, you had to open a door. It was part of the magic that had been placed on the south wing to keep everyone out.

The figure immediately turned toward us. She stared for a minute before walking out of sight. I followed her silently. My friends stayed with me and moved slowly so they wouldn't break my invisibility shield. I focused on the magic surrounding us.

We needed to move faster. I could see golden strands of magic trying to work their way into my shield, but I pushed them away. They were strands of void magic, and I refused to use them unless it was an emergency.

I didn't want to take that risk. Using void magic could kill me or twist me into a dark magic user. We were able to move faster as long as I kept my concentration on keeping the gold strands out. I saw the figure turn the corner up ahead and dropped the invisibility shield. We were all the way down the hallway and wouldn't be able to catch up to her moving so slowly.

"Wait here," I said. "I will see where she went."

I quietly ran down the hallway, slowing down as I reached the corner. I made myself invisible before peeking out into the next hall. The cloaked figure was walking faster and had already made it to the next corner. Before turning down it, she looked straight at me. I focused on the magic this time and watched as it turned a bright green color before the figure moved out of sight. I dropped the invisibility and gestured for my friends to come. They ran to me, trying to be quiet.

I ran down the next hallway and again made myself invisible before turning the corner. This time there was no one there. The figure had disappeared. I walked back to my friends.

"What happened?" whispered Richard.

"She's gone."

"Where did she go?"

"I have no idea. I would have seen her if she continued down the hallway. She must have gone into one of the rooms, but I don't know which one. We can wait and see who comes out."

"These are the teacher's rooms," Richard said. "We won't know which one of the female teachers was in the cloak. All of them are in this hallway."

I groaned. "I need to get near each of the teachers when they are doing magic. I know what the magic looks like and might be able to tell which one it was. The only one I can rule out is Mrs. Shaw. I've seen her use magic before, and it isn't the right color."

"Is everyone's magic always the same color?"

"So far. Tider always has the same blue color even when he is using different elements. So does Richard. I'm guessing it is the same for everyone. Since no one else can see the colors of magic, I am not certain. There is no book with the information."

"So let's go check their colors," Abby said.

"How? I don't have any classes with Mrs. Chanley, and Mrs. Newton only teaches regular classes, so she doesn't use magic."

"Are those the only two you need to check?" Adam asked.

"Have you seen Mrs. Sullivan's colors?" Abby asked.

"I doubt it's Mrs. Sullivan."

"It could be. You need to check everyone. Don't forget, there are a lot of staff members here too. I'm sure a good amount of them are females. They would have access to the south wing and probably have rooms down here too. If they thought they were being followed, they might have slipped into one of these rooms to hide. It could still be anyone," Tider said.

"That's a lot of people to check. Who do we start with?"

"We can start with the kitchen staff. They always use magic when they are preparing meals. If we get down there early enough, we can sneak in the back and watch as they work. You should be able to check them out without anyone knowing," Tider said.

I planned to meet Tider after a few hours of sleep. No one else needed to come. It wasn't dangerous, and it would be easier for the two of us to hide instead of all five of us.

My alarm went off, and I rolled out of bed, wishing I told Tider to wait until the next day. Staying up late and getting up early in the morning wasn't something I wanted to make a habit of doing. I stretched my arms over my head and almost hit Sievroth as he stretched out his wings. I spread my arms out, and he curled his neck around me.

He only stayed that way for a minute before settling on the bed. He really was growing fast. "I have to go," I told him. "I'm trying to figure out who keeps going into the south wing." Sievroth only stared at me. I gave him one last pat on the head before getting ready. I was used to him only answering me when he thought it was necessary. I headed down to the kitchen to meet Tider.

"Why are we hiding behind bags of potatoes?" I asked.

"This is a new shipment. They won't be touching these bags until later in the day or tomorrow."

"How do you know all this?"

"Before you came to the school, I had extra time on my hands and nothing to do, so I spent a lot of it learning exactly how the school operated."

I felt a pang of sadness, remembering that Tider had been an outcast until this year. Everyone was scared of his power and his family name. Plus, Sean had lied and made everyone believe Tider would use dark magic on them if they tried to be nice to him. Tider had a crappy few years of school because of it, but it was still better than him being at home.

I swung my arm around his shoulder and ruffled his hair. "Now, you have a great family."

He ducked out of my grasp and smiled. "I sure do, and I think your mom and dad call me more than they call you."

He stuck his tongue out at me. I told my parents about Tider when I first came here, and when they met him, they decided they would treat him like a son. It worked out great for both of us. My parents had someone else to worry about, Tider and I were best friends, and Tider had people that actually loved him and didn't care about his powers.

A group of people came walking into the kitchen, and we settled down to watch. I threw up my invisibility shield to be safe and started scanning the ladies. They weren't using magic, so I wasn't able to see if their magic matched.

"I thought they used magic," I hissed.

"They will. Be patient."

They went straight to work, washing their hands and getting out bowls and pots. Ovens were turned on, and flour was measured and poured into different mixers. I watched, mesmerized by how efficiently they all worked together. They knew exactly what they were doing and got right to it.

As we watched, I saw lumps of dough being lifted out of the mixers by small streams of air. The dough was placed along the counter, where it began to knead itself. I followed the trail of magic back to one lady who was handling the dough. Her magic was a light pink color, and I dismissed her and started looking for someone else.

The next lady was using air to break eggs and pour them into a hot pan. The whisk was moving on its own, and the smell of cooking eggs started to take over the kitchen. My mouth was watering by the time I looked at the magic she was using and saw it wasn't the green color I was looking for. This went on for another twenty minutes.

Eventually, I went through all the ladies in the kitchen. I ignored the men cooking since I was sure it was a female. No one had the color magic I was looking for. The only odd thing that I noticed was each person only used one element. When I mentioned it to Tider, he reminded me that it was rare for an elemental to have two elements. Having multiple students at one time with two elements was probably one of the reasons the council became so involved with the school in the first place.

We snuck back out of the kitchen but didn't go far. I was starving after watching all of the food being made, so we waited in the cafeteria for breakfast to be ready. Everyone else arrived as we were loading our plates with food. Richard had an idea to check the teachers out, and Abby had a way to check the staff that cleaned the school and took care of all the small things a school needed.

I would go with Richard first. He wanted me to ask Mrs. Chanley and Mrs. Newton for help learning how to do a spell that each of them should know. That way, I could see their magic without telling them why, and it wouldn't look like I was sneaking around. I liked the idea and decided we should do it at lunchtime. We didn't have time to wait. I wanted to know who the cloaked figure was before going to the fire realm. Especially since we probably wouldn't be coming back to the school.

If it wasn't either of them, I would have to go with Abby to talk to all the other staff. That would be the hardest because we would have to track down each one of them. Abby knew where to get their schedules, but it would still take a lot of work. We would start tomorrow if it wasn't one of the teachers.

I enjoyed my classes and was surprised when Mr. Connor asked me to meet him in the dome after classes. He wanted to teach me a few more things while the council wasn't watching. Mr. Burwel told Mr. Connor to teach me everything he could while we had a chance. I was glad Mr. Burwel switched to our side. He was a valued member of the council and could help us out if we needed it.

We waited until lunch to go see Mrs. Newton. She was in her classroom, getting ready for her next class. When we knocked on her door, she invited us in.

"Hi, Mrs. Newton. We hate to bother you during lunch, but Sally is having trouble with this one spell, and I remember my mom telling me you were really good with spells. Can you help her out, or show her how to do it?"

"Of course, I can help her. Show me what's going on, Sally." I did the spell but let the magic slip through my fingers at the last minute.

"Hmm, I think you need to concentrate less. You are creating the spell correctly. Here watch at the end where you lost it. Keep your magic calm and relaxed as you create the spell." I watched Mrs. Newton's magic as she created the spell. Her magic was a light orange color, nothing like the color I was looking for. She used a very delicate touch with her magic, and I followed along, relaxing my grip on my magic.

I didn't actually need help with the spell, but I wanted to see how my magic reacted to doing it differently. My magic flowed smoothly down my arms into the spell. It was easier to create the spell, but I could see that I didn't have as much power in it as usual. I wondered if I could use a soft touch like Mrs. Newton but still put a lot of power behind it.

"That's it, Sally. You did it."

I looked down and saw the coil of water had warped into the shape of a dog. When I instructed the magic to move, the dog walked across the floor.

"See, you didn't need much help. You are very advanced in magic."

"Thanks, Mrs. Newton. I guess learning from all males hasn't taught me anything about being gentle with magic."

She laughed. "Yes, men have a tendency to use their magic more forcefully. Now don't go practicing that magic anywhere. We don't want anyone knowing you can do such advanced magic. The Pulhu will find out. Though after what Mr. Mitchel did, they probably already know."

"Yeah, they know," I said.

"Be careful, Sally. I would hate to see anything happen to you."

"Thanks, Mrs. Newton. I will be as careful as I can."

Mrs. Newton sent us on our way, and I followed Richard to Mrs. Chanley's room. On the way, he asked me about Mrs. Newton. I told him her colors weren't right, but I learned something from the lesson, and I wanted to try it out with other spells. It didn't take long to make it to Mrs. Chanley's room. We knocked on the door, and she opened after a minute.

She looked surprised to see us and stepped back to allow us into her room. I looked around. I had never been in this room before. The walls were bare, but the tables pushed against the walls were covered in different types of rocks. Small transparent display cases with things inside I had never seen were spaced evenly between the rocks. It reminded me of a chemistry lab in my old school.

Richard gave Mrs. Chanley the same explanation that he gave to Mrs. Newton, but Mrs. Chanley didn't seem like she wanted to help.

"I would really appreciate your help," I told her. "I know you are busy, but it won't take long. I'm hoping that getting another perspective on the spell will help me understand it better."

Mrs. Chanley hesitated before speaking. "I'm very busy today. Maybe we can set up a time to do it later."

"She really needs to learn this, Mrs. Chanley. It won't take long for you to show her how you do the spell and give her some tips," Richard said.

"I really can't."

I was focusing on her magic and saw a small sliver of magic surround her hand. It didn't look like she was pulling the magic to her on purpose. She was upset or worried about showing us her magic, and the magic was reacting to her feelings.

"That's fine, Mrs. Chanley. You can show me the spell another time," I said.

I could see the surprise on Richard's face, but I didn't need to see any more magic from Mrs. Chanley.

"I only have one more question. Why have you been sneaking into the south wing to meet someone?"

"What?" Mrs. Chanley acted surprised.

"I know it's you. I want to know why. Are you helping the Pulhu?" I began pulling my own magic to me. Not a lot, only enough to subdue her if she gave any indication she would try to attack us.

"I don't know what you are talking about."

"Every person's magic is slightly different. Your magic has a very distinct green color. I can see that color around your hand right now. You are pulling a small amount of magic to yourself. It gave you away. Now, why are you meeting someone in the south wing?"

Mrs. Chanley sighed and moved to her chair. "I knew you would eventually figure it out. You saw me too many times. I'm surprised you figured it out so soon though. I didn't realize you could see magic too."

"Not many people know. The only reason I told you is to give you a chance to tell us the rest of the story before I tell Mrs. Sullivan."

"Don't tell anyone," Mrs. Chanley said. "What I am doing is for your protection, as long as you don't turn to the darkness. You weren't supposed to know about me yet. I am trying to help you overcome the Pulhu, but it must be done in secret. I will help you when I can."

"How? So far, I have barely spoken to you."

"I don't know yet, I only know that you will receive help if you are the one the prophecy speaks of."

"What about the imposter? We found it written down on the paper in the room you have been using in the south wing."

"The imposter is another elemental who thinks they are the chosen one. If they go up against the darkness, they will fail and destroy us all."

"Who is the imposter?" I asked.

"We don't know."

"So, it could be me."

"Yes. No one knows who the imposter is. You will have to figure it out on your own when you meet this other elemental."

"I'm going to meet them?"

"Yes. At some point, you will meet and have to figure out who is who. Until then, no one knows."

"Who is helping you in the south wing?" Richard asked.

"I can't tell you," Mrs. Chanley said. "That is something you don't need to know."

"How can we trust you if you won't tell us everything?"

"You will have to take my word. I won't reveal everything to you, or it could cause you to change your path. You are doing good staying away from dark magic and trying to protect those you love. Keep doing what you are doing. Eventually, you will find out everything."

I heard students moving through the halls. We needed to hurry up and get to class.

"That is all I can tell you for now. When it is time, I will tell you more," Mrs. Chanley said.

Kids started to walk into the class, and I walked out with Richard. I followed the connection Richard and I had and spoke into his mind as we walked. I told him I didn't trust anything Mrs. Chanley was saying.

Since she wouldn't tell us everything, I couldn't believe anything she said. He thought we should give her a chance. She never tried to hurt us, even the few times she sensed us in the south wing. I still wasn't sure, but I agreed not to go to Mrs. Sullivan yet.

CHAPTER TWELVE

Walking down to the dome with Abby made me uncomfortable. I hadn't been in the dome since Mr. Mitchel almost killed me. When we got closer, we saw Mr. Merrem waiting on the path. He stopped us before we walked into the dome.

"Are you ok, Sally? I know the last time you were here didn't turn out so well. None of us realized what Mr. Mitchell was going to do."

"I know, Mr. Merrem. I am doing fine," I assured him. He walked into the dome ahead of us. Mr. Connor was waiting inside and walked over to me.

"Sally, I'm glad you were able to come down here. We are going to teach you a few more offensive and defensive spells. Mrs. Sullivan told us some of your plans. We want you to be completely prepared."

They had me come to the center of the dome, and Mr. Connor asked me to try and use water and air at the same time and merge them. This time when I tried, I did exactly as Mauevene had shown me and was able to make them combine. Fog drifted from around me, getting thicker as I increased the power of the spell.

"Now, Sally, that is great for defense, but you may need some offensive spells too. We've taught you a few, but this one is going to be the hardest and has the potential to really hurt someone. I know you don't like this type of spell, but we think you need to learn it."

"I will learn it, but I won't use it unless I have to," I said.

"You need to add fire to the fog droplets, like when you made the bigger fireballs and covered them with air and buried them in the ground. Except here, you have millions of tiny air and water droplets that you need to add fire to. They won't realize it's a fire fog until it's too late. As soon as they step into the fog, the droplets will shatter, letting the fire out. Each tiny flame will only last a second, but hundreds of them will be bursting at the same time on a person's skin. It will feel like they have fire ants all over them."

"It doesn't sound like it can really hurt anyone," I said.

"If someone with fire magic throws their fire into the fog, it will ignite the flames and make them grow stronger," Mr. Connor said.

"Remember when you used your fire against mine, Sally. It's the same thing," Mr. Merrem said.

"I don't know about this," I said. Now I understood how someone could get hurt or even killed with this spell.

"Sally, you need to learn this. It might save our lives," Richard said directly into my mind.

I watched the fog swirling around me and slowly fed fire magic into it. I felt the fire collecting in the droplets, but before I could add fire to even half of the fog, I had to stop. I was exhausted. It used too much power. Sievroth appeared next to me, and Mr. Merrem and Mr. Connor backed up.

"Mrs. Sullivan told us you had a dragon with you, but I didn't realize he was always around."

"He usually stays invisible," I said worriedly. "What's wrong, Sievroth?"

He hung in the air, his wings flapping slowly as he reached his head out to me. He put his snout against my head, and a rush of magic flooded my body. Sievroth slowly disappeared again.

"What just happened?" asked Mr. Connor.

"He gave me more power. I'm at full strength. We can try again."

"That's ok, Sally. We have other things to teach you, but you need to practice it every day until you leave so it won't drain your energy. We know you can do it."

"I will practice it. What else do you want me to learn?" I asked.

"I want you to be able to stop a large group with earth. It's your least used element, so it's not as strong as the others. You need to work on it more. Earth is a great element, and it's always around you. You need to learn to use earth quickly. You can already raise the earth and create ditches, but you need more. We need to leave the dome for this lesson."

"But..."

"I know it's a risk, but it's worth it. Only masters can use earth powers the way I'm going to show you. I want you to control the trees. They are living things, so it's hard to control them. Flowers and weeds are easier because they are small and have very little will, but trees are rooted. They don't listen to anyone if they don't want to."

We headed out to the woods, the teachers checking to see if anyone was around. I didn't see anyone, and neither did they. We were no longer under the protection of the school. It didn't extend this far into the trees.

"Sally, all plants are living things. They have the same emotions that we do but on a much smaller scale. Trees are very slow-growing, so their emotions are also slow. You can talk to the trees and get them to listen if you know how. Trees will only listen to certain people. I think they will listen to you."

"Why?"

"Many reasons, but the main one is compassion. Trees don't like causing pain."

Mr. Merrem taught me how to push my earth magic into the trees and find their centers, which is where I would be able to connect with them. As soon as I did, I could feel the tree's emotions. It was slow like Mr. Merrem said, and the tree was full of contentment. It was nice to enjoy such a feeling.

When I heard Mr. Merrem ask me to talk to the tree and see if it would move, I balked at the idea. I didn't want to force the tree to do anything.

"Ask the tree, Sally, don't force it. You only need to force them if it is an emergency."

I asked the tree to move but also decided I would never force the trees to do something they didn't want to do. If they didn't want to help me in an emergency, I would have to find another way. I wouldn't want anyone forcing me to do something.

The tree responded slowly. I felt his answer before I heard it. A massive crack sounded, and the tree rose, giant roots breaking the surface of the ground. My tree took a single step, and I ran to catch up with him. He sank his roots back into the ground and stopped moving. I thanked him and turned back to Mr. Merrem.

"Good job, Sally. Now that you know how to do that, we should head back to the school. Don't practice this unless you are positive no one else is around. Not only do we want to keep that power hidden from the Pulhu, but normal people would be terrified if trees started moving around by themselves."

Back at the school, Abby was waiting and said Mrs. Sullivan wanted to see us. We headed right to her office. The only reason Mrs. Sullivan would be calling us down was if something was wrong. I had a feeling I knew what it was, but I hoped I was wrong. We knocked on her door and went in. Everyone else was already there.

"What is it?" I asked. "I know something's wrong."

"Mr. Mitchel is awake," Mrs. Sullivan told me. "He woke up a few hours ago. So far, he hasn't been able to tell the healers anything. He doesn't remember much, but they are expecting him to make a full recovery in the next couple of days. Once he remembers, he will be looking for you, Sally."

"What about the council? Will they protect Sally?"

"We don't know. As of right now, we know many of the council will side with Mr. Mitchel."

"Even after what he did? Mr. Burwel can tell them exactly what happened."

"He will," Mrs. Sullivan replied. "But the other two council members will also be testifying, and I doubt they will tell the truth. After all, they gave permission to Mr. Mitchel to use that on you, and they will get in trouble if the council finds out. I'm sure they have crafted a good lie explaining away what really happened. We will remain hopeful that the council won't believe them, but I think it's best if we are ready."

"We are ready, Mrs. Sullivan. Tell us what we need to do."

"When Mr. Mitchel regains his memories, we will be sending you away. There is another town not far from here that Natasha will take you to. We've already rented a hotel room for you to stay in. It has three bedrooms so you can all stay together. I will let Jordan know where you are so he can transport you to Mount Etna. Until he gets there, you will need to stay hidden. I will be sending a few people I trust to keep an eye on you, so you should be fine, but once you get to the mountain, we don't know what you will encounter."

"When should we be ready to go?" I asked.

"Get everything you need ready tonight, but I think you have another day or two. I want all your bags packed and in my office this evening, and keep a small bag with you in case something happens."

We left Mrs. Sullivan's office, each of us heading to our rooms to pack what we needed. Most of my stuff was already ready to go.

Abby knocked on the door a little while later. "What do we do now?" she asked.

"Nothing. We have to go about our day as if nothing changed. We don't want Sean or Sasha reporting to the Pulhu that we are preparing for something."

"It's going to be awfully hard," Abby said.

"I know."

We ate dinner and tried to act like nothing was wrong, but I kept a close eye on everything around us. By evening I was exhausted. It was hard worrying about everything all the time. Classes the next morning went by like always. Nothing unusual happened. I kept waiting to hear from Mrs. Sullivan, but she never called me.

I checked in on Richard and the others periodically throughout the day, but they hadn't heard anything either. I was heading to the dome for one more lesson when Richard spoke into my mind telling me to be careful. He had gone to look for Mrs. Sullivan but couldn't find her. Frowning, I continued toward the dome, hoping Mr. Merrem or Mr. Connor would be able to tell me where Mrs. Sullivan was. I reached out with my mind for her, but I couldn't find the connection. Something was wrong.

The door to the dome was standing open when I arrived. I moved back to the path and put up my invisibility shield. I crept forward, keeping my steps as silent as I could. I searched for Tider's mind and opened our connection.

"Tider, where are you? The door to the dome is open."

"I'm on my way," he said. "I got waylaid by Sean. Don't go in the door. I think it's a trap. I saw a group of council members arriving at the school a few minutes ago while Sean was harassing me. I think someone gave Mrs. Sullivan incorrect information about Mr. Mitchel. I think he has his memory and is already coming for you. Get back to the school, I will meet you on the path."

I reached out to the others and told them where to meet us and to be careful.

I couldn't stop myself from moving closer to the open door. I wanted to see what was going on inside. I felt my connection with Richard open up.

"Where are you, Sally? You better not be doing what I think you are."

"What do you think I'm doing?" I asked as I moved even closer to the door. Only a few more steps and I could peek in.

"Trying to see what is going on in the dome. Tider told you to get back to the school. Something isn't right."

"I know. That's why I want to see what's going on in the building. Mr. Merrem or Mr. Connor could be hurt."

I could feel Richard's frustration and worry. I felt him sigh. He knew I was right. If one of our teachers was hurt, I had to help them. I took the last few steps to the door. I peeked in but didn't see anyone. Mr. Merrem and Mr. Connor weren't here, but neither were the Pulhu. I started to step into the dome, but Richard's warning stopped me. I didn't see any traps, but I didn't want to take chances.

I moved back up the path, keeping my invisibility shield up. When I saw Tider, I stopped and pulled him inside as he walked past.

"Sally, don't do that. I could've hurt you," he said, lowering his hands. He had raised them, thinking I was attacking him when I pulled him into my shield.

"Sorry, I wasn't thinking," I apologized. We slowly made our way to the school. It wasn't too hard to keep the shield up around only two of us. Richard was waiting, and I dropped the shield as we got closer to him.

"Alright, guys. I think we need to go," Richard said. "Mrs. Sullivan is missing. So are Mr. Merrem and Mr. Connor. It looks like someone is taking out the teachers that have been helping Sally. I'm sure they will be after us next."

"Where are Abby and Adam?" I asked.

"They are trying to sneak into the office down the hall from Mrs. Sullivan's. It's where she put all of the stuff that we brought to her for safekeeping. She gave Abby the code in case of an emergency. They are meeting us around the side of the school closest to the woods."

I reached out to check on Abby. When we connected, I could feel her frustration. She was trying to get into the room to grab our stuff. As soon as I knew she was safe, I left her alone. She needed to concentrate on what she was doing. The council was close, and she didn't want to get caught.

"How will we get out of here?" I asked.

"We are going to sneak through the woods and bypass the town. We will need to keep walking until we get to the next town, which is where Jordan was planning on meeting us to transport us to Mount Etna. Hopefully, Mrs. Sullivan told him yesterday, and he will meet us there in a couple of days. Until then, we will lay low at the hotel. Mrs. Sullivan already booked it, so we should be able to give the name of the reservation and stay there."

"Do you know the name on the reservation?" I asked.

"No, but I'm hoping Abby does. Mrs. Sullivan entrusted her with a lot of information in case something happened."

We stopped talking as a group of kids walked by. They glanced at us a few times but didn't stop to say anything.

I grabbed Richard and Tider's hands and pulled them around the school. We walked quickly to the spot where we would be meeting Adam and Abby. We waited quietly, Tider occasionally whispering to Richard.

Abby and Adam rounded the front corner at a run, arms full of bags. "We grabbed as much as we could carry. I think I got everything, but I may have missed a few things," she said.

We grabbed the bags as she passed them out.

"We need to go," Adam said, looking over his shoulder. "One of the council members was trying to follow us. We gave him the slip, but if we stay here, they will find us."

We ran to the woods and into the trees. The branches blocked out most of the sunlight, and we slowed down, walking carefully over the uneven ground. I could feel the trees around us as I reached out with my magic.

I sent my magic flowing from tree to tree. I didn't ask them to move. I wouldn't have been able to control them all anyway, but I did send a silent plea to hide us from the Pulhu or let us know if they were coming. I didn't know if it would work, but I had to try.

We were almost through the woods when a shiver went through the trees. I could hear the rustling of the leaves far behind us moving closer until the trees nearest to us shivered, and their leaves twirled from the movement.

I reached out to the trees and heard them speaking in one voice. "They come," the voice said in my head. "Run." I sent a wave of thanks out to the trees and turned to my friends, telling them to run, the Pulhu or the council were coming.

We ran out of the woods and into the street. I looked both ways. "Which way?"

"This way," Richard said, pointing to the left. "We need to follow the road until we get closer to town and then go around it. It is going to take a few hours, at least."

"Good thing we have the time. We are a few days early," Adam said.

"We need to find somewhere to hide so the council and the Pulhu don't find us. They will be coming out of the woods in a few minutes," I told everyone.

I looked around, spotting a ditch on the far side of the road. Abby spotted it at the same time and said we should stay in there and use an invisibility spell.

"No," I said. "They will look for us there, and we have to assume they know I can use invisibility. They may fire magic or throw those sleeping potions down, hoping to hit us. I think we should go that way." I pointed to the right. "There isn't anything that way, right?"

"Not for a long time. It's only fields and farmland that way."

"Then they won't think we went that way. If we walk up that way half a mile or so, we could hide and wait for them to come out of the trees. They will assume we headed to town and turn that way."

Everyone agreed, and we quickly ran up the road. When I thought we were far enough away, we stopped and sat down near the trees. I put the invisibility shield up, and we stayed there for a few minutes without seeing anything. Finally, the first person came out of the woods. He looked disheveled. There were leaves and small twigs stuck in his hair, and his clothes looked ripped in multiple places. The trees must have decided to help me on their own and slowed the men down.

I smiled. I always loved trees. I would have to remember to come back here and send them a big thank you. It didn't take long for more people to start coming out of the woods. They stood around, talking for a few minutes until a man came striding out of the woods, shouting something. The men moved to the sides of the road, shooting magic down each ditch.

The man turned toward us, and I grimaced. It was Mr. Mitchel, and he looked livid. He continued shouting at the men. He pulled a phone from his pocket and made a call before going back to yelling. They continued walking away from us. None of them even looked back this way. A car showed up and picked Mr. Mitchel and two of the guys up. They headed toward the town while the rest of the men walked along the sides of the road. We were going to be stuck here for a while while they walked down the road.

"We could go through the woods on this side, so we don't have to stay here," Richard whispered, knowing I couldn't hold the shield forever.

"Good idea," I said. "Let's go." We walked to the other side of the road and slipped into the woods. I kept the invisibility shield up around us until we were deep in the woods. I sent a thank you to the trees and felt an answering warmth coming from them.

"Stop talking to the trees," Tider hissed quietly. "We don't want them to know you are in the woods, and they will figure it out if the trees keep responding to you." I looked down, embarrassed. I wasn't great at hiding from people.

I pulled my magic back from the trees, and they stilled.

CHAPTER THIRTEEN

We made our way through the woods heading in a diagonal line toward the town. "By the time we get there, we should be on the edge of town and be able to skirt around it with no problem," Richard said, using GPS on his phone to help guide us. We walked for a few hours before stopping.

"I think we need to make camp here," Richard said. "We still have a few hours hike tomorrow to get to the other town."

"How far have we walked?" I asked.

"We are past the town at this point but only barely. We can't make a fire, or people might see it."

"We are that close?"

"Yes, and I'm sure Mr. Mitchel has the town under surveillance. He might have the next town under surveillance too, but I think I have a way past that."

"How?"

"I will show you tomorrow. Right now, let's get some shelter set up."

"Why don't we do the same thing we did in the water elemental realm. I can raise the ground and make a little underground room for us. It worked well there."

Richard nodded, and I looked around the tiny clearing we were in.

"It's going to be pretty small," I said as I put my hands down to the ground and called the earth to rise up, leaving a space for us to sleep. It reminded me of a hobbit house, except not as pretty. I used the roots of the plants to create a barrier once we all squeezed in. It would keep the cool air out, but it was easy to move if we needed to get outside.

We went through our packs, divvying out food and drinks. It wasn't much since we left so quickly, but we each had a granola bar and an apple. We even had enough water bottles for everyone. We would need to refill the bottles in the morning, but that was easy. I could pull water from the air around us and let it fill the bottles. So could Tider.

I took the first watch, waking Adam after a few hours. In the morning, we had a quick breakfast of granola bars again, and I pushed the earth back down. We continued heading for the next town. We walked for half of the day before Richard told us to stop.

"We are close. We need to turn south here, and we will come to the main road in about thirty minutes. I will go in first and find the hotel. Once I check us in, I will let Sally know, and you can all come to the hotel one at a time. They are looking for a group of us. We should be able to get through the town unnoticed if we aren't together. Keep your heads down and act naturally on your way to the hotel. Sally, you will need to use your invisibility shield. They will be keeping an eye out specifically for you."

No one argued with him. What he said made sense. We continued through the woods until we came close to the town. Richard said a quick goodbye, and we sat down to wait. I opened our connection and stayed with him as he maneuvered his way through town. It was surprisingly busy as he got closer to the center.

It wasn't as small as the town near the school. He told me about it as he walked through the streets. He stayed on the main road most of the trip, only turning right at one point to get to the hotel. He didn't have any trouble checking in and getting a pair of keys to use. Mrs. Sullivan gave Abby the reservation name before she went missing.

The front desk clerk told Richard he could use the entrance on the side of the building and take the elevator up to the third floor. Richard told me it was six floors when I asked. He thanked the clerk and made his way to the room, checking it over to make sure it wasn't tampered with. It looked ok, and he told me to have Abby come next.

I gave her directions, and she left. I told Richard to let me know when she arrived. I sat back against a tree and relaxed. Abby didn't have any trouble, and neither did Adam when he left. Tider looked at me and asked if I was ready. He wouldn't let me go by myself, so I would stay invisible, and he would walk slowly so I could keep up. If I needed him to stop, I would reach out with our connection and let him know.

No one bothered Tider as he walked through the town, but I did catch a few people look his way more than once. When I caught a mean-looking man glance at Tider a few different times, I reached out, letting him know to pick up his pace and lose the guy.

I would keep heading to the hotel, and we could meet back up. He didn't want to leave me, but he couldn't lead the guy right to the hotel we were staying in. He left and took off down an alley as I continued along. A few people almost ran into me without Tider to walk behind, but I made it to the hotel safely.

Tider arrived a few minutes later, and I followed him to the door. Abby was waiting for us and showed us where the room was.

It was a big enough space for all of us, and I took my invisibility down and sank onto one of the couches. Holding the shield for so long was draining.

"Our room is through here, Sally," Abby called, pointing our door out to me. I thanked her and closed my eyes, listening to Tider tell everyone about the guy that followed him. Once Richard was sure he wasn't followed to the hotel, they all relaxed too.

There wasn't much to do in the hotel room except watch TV, which got boring pretty fast. I slipped away with Abby to go down to the pool for a quick swim. We wore shorts and tank tops since we didn't have bathing suits. It was indoors, so I didn't think it would be a problem until I heard Richard's voice in my head.

"Where are you?" he yelled.

I flinched. Hearing screaming in my own head was incredibly irritating. "I'm swimming with Abby. We are still inside."

"What if someone sees you?"

"We checked to make sure no one was in here first, Richard."

"You need to stay in the room," he said. "It's only for a few days."

"We are almost finished anyway," I told him. I was irritated that he yelled at me. "We will head up there as soon as we dry off. I think you are overreacting. I doubt Mr. Mitchel or the councilmen will stay here. This hotel isn't fancy enough for them."

"Yeah, but they might look to see if we are staying here."

He had a point, so I didn't answer. I felt his satisfaction at winning our argument and gave him a light mental slap. His amusement at my irritation seeped through, and I frowned, which caught Abby's attention.

"What's wrong?" she asked.

"Richard says we need to go back to the room. It isn't safe enough here."

Abby fell silent, but I could tell she wasn't happy either. We trudged back to our room sullenly. The guys took one look at our faces and turned back to the TV. After we changed, we ordered room service and relaxed for the rest of the day.

I was going stir crazy by lunch the next day, but Richard didn't want me leaving. He went out that morning to see if people were watching the town still. Within a few blocks of the hotel, he ran across three different guys who all looked like they could be Pulhu. We stayed inside again that evening. We only had one more day until Jordan was supposed to meet us.

It was incredibly boring, but I got through another night. I played cards with Abby while Tider and Richard watched TV. Adam sat on the couch, reading a book from his grandfather.

Mauevene appeared in front of us the next morning while we were eating breakfast.

"You need to leave now," she said hurriedly.

"What's wrong, Mauevene?"

"They've released some sort of poison in the hotel. It's making its way up from the first floor. We need to get to the roof."

Everyone jumped to their feet, grabbing their packs and shoving their feet into shoes. We didn't even take time to tie them. We ran out of the room.

"Wait, what about the other people here?" I asked. There wasn't an alarm going off to let everyone know something was wrong.

"I don't know," Mauevene said. "I don't know what kind of poison this is. I haven't seen it before. I was in the lobby, keeping an eye on the front doors when a man walked in and set a vial down. He left quickly while the hotel clerk tried to ask him what he was doing. As soon as he stepped outside, the vial exploded, and a mist started to spread through the lobby. When it touched the clerk, he fell over and didn't move. I flew up here as fast as I could to warn you."

"We need to save everyone else too. What if it kills them?"

I looked around, finally spotting what I wanted. I ran to the fire alarm and pulled it. I used my magic to create small fires in the lobby. I made the smoke rise quickly. I couldn't see what my magic was actually doing down there, but I felt it and hoped it was doing what I wanted. The smoke seeping up the stairs moved quickly. I was hoping anyone trying to get out would think there was a massive fire down below and head for the roof.

People came running from their rooms, and we yelled for them to move toward the roof, that there was smoke below us. They all listened and ran up the stairs. We were all using our magic subtly to keep people from getting hurt. If not for a burst of wind here or a spark of fire there people would have run each other over in their panic.

We got to the roof and watched as more people came pouring out from another roof entrance. A few stragglers came up the stairs after us, and I held the door for them. When it looked like everyone was out, I walked back into the stairwell.

"What are you doing?" Tider asked.

"I need to stop the poison. It could hurt all these people," I said, looking around.

Children were crying in their parent's arms. I wasn't going to let them get hurt. I could hear sirens in the distance, but they wouldn't make it in time. I could feel the poison magic moving closer. I tried stopping it with a barrier, but the hotel was too big and spread out. The mist just moved around it. It couldn't be blown away either. My magic didn't want to work on the mist. Whatever spell they had used was powerful.

"What do we do?" Abby asked when she realized I couldn't stop it.

"There must be a way down," Adam said. He started walking around the edge of the building. We could all get down using air magic, but the ordinary people on the roof would still be stuck.

"Here," Adam said to us. We followed him along the edge of the roof. "We can get over to the next building." There was a gap about eight feet wide to the other building.

"These people can't get over that."

"We can help them. Look, there's a piece of wood and a ladder on that roof. If we keep everyone's attention focused on the other side of the roof, Sally or Richard can float the wood and ladder across the roof to this side. Then they can say they found the piece of wood, and we can all move it, so it lays across the gap.

"It won't be long enough," I said.

"That's what the ladder is for. It can go across first. It's one of those ladders that get bigger."

"An extension ladder," Richard said, thinking through the plan. "It could work. It's our only choice right now."

"Whatever we are going to do, we need to do it now. The poison is almost to the level below us."

"Let's go," Adam said to Abby and Tider. They ran to the other side of the roof and started pointing and yelling, saying they may have found a way down. There was already a crowd of people around the hotel, so I tried making the ladder and wood invisible before moving it.

"Sally, I can't see it now," Richard said.

"I know, but those people will see it moving. It needs to be invisible. I will move it."

I started to raise both objects, moving them toward our roof. It didn't take long before I dropped them on our side and let the invisibility shield drop.

"Hey, everyone, over here. We can use this." Smoke was now coming out of the roof door, and the people were panicking even more. Richard tried to move the ladder himself, and a bunch of guys came running up to help him. They managed to position it between the two roofs and get the wood on top of it. I used air to keep it steady without anyone knowing.

Some of the guys got across easily and held the other side. We tried to get the mothers and children over next. It wasn't easy. The kids didn't want to let go of their parents, but they couldn't carry them all. I scooped up a little boy and soothed him, slowly walking across the wood. I turned back and stood in the middle of the wood.

The kids would be able to reach me without their parents, and I could help them to the other side this way. I coaxed the next child to me, Richard holding them by the arm as they scooted out onto the piece of wood. It worked, and the other kids moved faster.

Once the kids were over, the parents came. The rest of the people started screaming, and I looked over. The mist was creeping toward them.

"What is that?" one of them screamed.

"Hurry up," Richard yelled. "Get across."

I put a barrier up between the mist and the people, but within seconds it was seeping around the edges to get to us. The last of the people crossed, and Abby and Adam ran across, not worrying for a second that I would let anything happen to them.

Tider came next and then Richard. As I stood up to move to the other side, the mist picked up speed. I jumped to the other side and let a blast of air dislodge the ladder and wood from the rooftop. The mist stopped at the edge of the roof. Whoever had done the spell had confined it to one building. They didn't think we would find a way out.

People were already running down the stairs, and we joined them. As we came through the door and onto the street, I noticed two men watching us. I stayed close to the other people, watching the men to make sure they didn't try anything. I didn't think they would in a crowd this size. I let my friends know about the two men.

We walked away from the buildings with the rest of the group as the firefighters tried to check us over. The paramedics hadn't arrived yet, but I could hear them getting closer. A low whistle caused me to turn my head, looking for the sound. I saw Jordan hiding in an alleyway only a few feet from us.

I looked back. The men were still watching and trying to get closer. I grabbed Abby and Tider and told them to grab the others. "On three," I said, looking at Jordan. He nodded.

"One, two, three." We all ran forward, holding hands. Jordan stepped back behind a dumpster, and we ran to him, grabbing his hands as we all ducked down to hide. I looked back before we bent down. The men were running toward us. I closed my eyes and felt the world spin away from me. When I felt steady again, I opened my eyes. We were standing in a wooded area, but I could see a mountain far ahead of us through the trees.

I looked at Jordan questioningly.

"I thought this would be better for now. We need to talk before you go up on the mountain. It's crawling with Pulhu. Activity has increased in the past two days, but I'm not sure why. I haven't been able to get in contact with Mrs. Sullivan."

"We think she has been kidnapped along with Mr. Merrem and Mr. Connor. They are all missing, and Mr. Mitchel is awake. He probably has been for a few days. We think he remembers everything and is trying to get rid of anyone who is helping Sally. Someone fed Mrs. Sullivan false information. He almost got us too," Tider explained.

"I'm glad you are all safe. I don't know if you should go to the mountain. It is too dangerous."

"We have no choice, Jordan," I said.

"I know. Mrs. Sullivan filled me in on everything. I'm here to support you, whatever you decide to do, but I don't like you putting yourselves in danger like this."

"Can we take a few hours to rest and then decide how we are going to get in?" Abby asked.

"Is there anywhere nearby we can rest and get something to eat?" I asked Jordan.

"Yes, come with me. I'm staying at a house through these woods. It belongs to a friend of Mrs. Sullivan's and is safe. I have been watching the Pulhu, so I can help you with their movements."

We followed Jordan to the house and started to prepare.

CHAPTER FOURTEEN

The house was more of a small cabin with two bedrooms. The kitchen was stocked with food, and we sat around the table, eating while Jordan told us what he found out about the Pulhu on the mountain. Their numbers were increasing again. At least another twenty people had arrived and were scanning the mountain, looking for something.

"They keep bringing more people in," Jordan said. "They are going to find what they want soon. Almost all of their people must be here."

He pulled a map of Mount Etna out. I found the area we had been at last time Jordan brought me. I traced it up to the spot where the fire elemental realm entrance was. There were black dots all around that area. More black dots were scattered throughout the rest of the mountain. A few spots had larger concentrations of dots but none as large as where we needed to go.

"What are these dots for?" I asked, dreading the answer

"The number of Pulhu in that area," Jordan replied.

"I thought so. It is going to be hard to get past that many and get into the fire realm without them seeing us." I looked back at the dots. Around fifteen dots were in the area where we would be going.

"Maybe there is another entrance into the fire realm," Jordan said. "I doubt they only have one. They would be trapped easily."

"They probably have another portal, but I don't have a clue where it is. This is the only one I know about, and we don't have time to waste trying to find a different one. The Pulhu could break in any time now. Then they would be able to control the fire elementals. We need the true elementals on our side. We will have to find a way through this portal."

Jordan's lips thinned, but he didn't say anything else. He knew I was right, even if he didn't like it. I understood why he was upset. To him, we were only a bunch of kids. We hadn't even finished high school yet, and everyone was counting on us to save the world. It sounded crazy when I thought about it that way.

I didn't think I was ready to save the world either, but I didn't have a choice. "I know you don't like it, Jordan, but it needs to be done, and we need to get in through this portal," I said, pointing at the spot on the map where the portal and a large number of Pulhu were.

"We better figure out a good plan to get you through all of them," he finally said. I smiled. He was still going to help us.

"What's the plan?" Adam asked.

"We are going to need a distraction," I said. "Something far enough away that the Pulhu will be drawn to it, and we can sneak in."

"We could create an explosion farther down the trail. That might send them running to it."

"What about last time? Sievroth blew fire, and they all came running. They thought he was a fire elemental. Remember?" Abby asked.

"That could work, but I don't know if Sievroth will be able to get back to us in time, and I don't want him getting hurt. I'm sure they put up more traps to catch anything trying to leave or enter the fire realm."

"Is he here? We could ask him if he wants to do it. You said he sometimes answers you back, right?"

I knew Sievroth was close. I could always feel his presence when he was nearby. I asked him if he thought our plan would work, but I didn't get a response. I tried one more time but still got nothing.

"I don't think he is ok with it. He isn't responding to me," I told everyone.

"That's ok. We will figure something else out. I think the explosion is the best idea. We can use the invisibility potions to keep them from seeing us as we sneak in. Do we have any bomb potions left? That would be great for distracting them."

"I have one," Tider said. "Mr. Connor gave me his last one when we went on our last trip. He was worried and wanted us to have something to help if we needed it."

"Great. I can transport to whichever spot you choose and throw the potion before transporting right back out. I will make sure you get into the fire realm before I transport back to the cabin," Jordan said.

"No. You need to go right back to the cabin. If we end up having to fight, I don't want to be worried about hitting you if you are hiding in the trees somewhere. If you are at the cabin, I won't have to worry. We will be fine. As long as the Pulhu are distracted, we will be able to slip in."

Jordan agreed after another minute of arguing. I didn't want to fight the Pulhu to get in, but we would probably have too. They weren't going to leave the area entirely unprotected when they thought that was the entrance. I didn't want Jordan getting hurt again. He wasn't a fighter. We spent a few more hours going over our plans before taking a break.

I slipped outside to enjoy the rest of the evening. We would rest here for the night before Jordan transported us. We didn't want to go while it was dark. The fire I would need to heat up the rock that opened the portal would be too visible. It was better to sneak in during the day.

Abby came out to join me, and we sat quietly together.

"Do you think we will be able to get in?" she finally asked.

"Yes. We will be invisible. They won't have any idea that we are nearby until it is too late."

Abby didn't look convinced. "Nothing seems to go the way we plan it," she said.

"I know," I sighed. "I'm hoping this one will be better. We have a good plan, and Jordan is going to help us."

Tider sat down next to us. "It's going to go fine," he said, overhearing our conversation. "We need to believe that or it really will go bad. All we can do is keep trying."

"I'm worried about our families. If things are getting as bad as Chet says, what will happen to them? I just got my dad back, I don't want to lose him again."

I didn't know what to say to Abby. I didn't want her to lose her dad again either. The curse on him had almost ruined their relationship. It was getting better now that he was himself. Abby spent as much time talking to him as possible. Since we left the school, she hadn't been able to contact him. I hadn't talked to my parents either. I knew they were safe for now, but it could change.

"They are going to be ok," Tider said, wrapping his arm around Abby's shoulders. "I know it doesn't seem like it sometimes, but look at everything we've accomplished. We saved the water elementals and the air elementals. No one even knew they were in trouble. If we keep working together, everything will be fine. Your parents are both in a safe place, and Chet will let us know if anything changes. So will Gary. We haven't heard anything so I doubt there are any problems. If there was trouble with them, Jordan would know, and he hasn't lied to us about anything."

Sometimes I forgot that Tider could tell if someone was lying by the color of the aura. He didn't talk about it much, so it was easy to forget.

"I'm worried about what will happen as the darkness gets closer," Abby said. "Chet told us regular people were acting more aggressive. Will it eventually cause elementals to act that way too? Will our parents act that way? How do we help if it starts to affect them?"

"I don't have the answers, Abby," Tider said. "I am going to stay positive. We will figure it out as we go. We are doing a good job so far. We will get the fire elementals on our side, and then we can go see your dad and Sally's parents. I'm sure you will be sitting down with your dad within the week. We usually don't take that long in the elemental realms."

Abby looked a little happier after that. She sat outside for a few more minutes before saying goodnight and heading to bed. Tider took off too. I waited for Richard to come out from around the house. He had been watching, keeping an eye on all of us while we talked to Abby.

"Hi," I said when he sat next to me.

"Hi."

"Why didn't you come over?" I asked. The only reason I knew he was watching was the connection we had to each other. I always knew where he was.

"You and Tider had it under control. I'm not good at that kind of thing and didn't want to upset her more. This has been pretty hard on her so far."

"It's been hard on all of us, you too."

"I'm fine," Richard said.

"I know you are, but you are worried about your family. I know you are concerned about your sister. Remember, I'm in your mind as much as you are in mine." I laughed when he elbowed me. "We will find a way to stop the darkness," I told him.

"And if we don't?" Richard asked.

"Then you don't have to worry about the Pulhu trying to force your sister to their side. We will all be corrupted by the darkness."

He laughed. "Thanks, Sally. Not exactly what I wanted to hear."

"Yeah, but it made you laugh." I became serious. "We have a lot to do, Richard, and I feel like we are running out of time."

"I do too. I don't know what else we can do though. We are going as fast as we can. We will be able to go faster after this since we aren't going back to the school. We won't have to do everything in secret or worry about one of the other students spying on us. I'm sure wherever Chet has in mind for all of us to hide will be good. I bet he even has a practice area for you."

"Maybe," I said. "I want this part over. I want to go check on my parents and make sure they are ok."

"Me too." I stayed outside with Richard for a long time, gazing at the stars. We didn't talk anymore. There wasn't anything to say. We would be going into the fire elemental realm in the morning and hopefully convincing them to side with us.

Jordan eventually called us in, telling us to get some rest. I walked inside slowly. I didn't feel like sleeping even though I knew I needed some rest. I laid down and quietly went over everything in my head. It took a long time to fall asleep.

In the morning, I was awake before everyone else. I started to get all my stuff together before breakfast. Jordan made food. He had eggs, bacon, toast, and even some fruit on the table for us.

"Where did you get all this?" I asked him. I hadn't seen any of this in the fridge last night.

"I popped over to town to grab some supplies. You need a good breakfast before you go into the unknown."

"What town did you go to? There weren't any Pulhu were there? They might know who you are," Richard said.

"Don't worry. I went to a town much farther away. I wasn't anywhere close to Mount Etna. I don't want to run into the Pulhu either."

We sat around the table, eating our breakfast and talking about last-minute ideas. When we finished, and it was time to go, Jordan stood up. "Please make sure you are careful. You all have my number if you need me. Let me know as soon as you are finished in the fire realm, and I will come and get you."

"Thanks, Jordan," I said. I stood up, and we cleared the table while my friends got our stuff together.

We went through our packs, making sure everything was set up before meeting Jordan by the door. We took our invisibility potions and grabbed hands. Jordan took a potion too, so he wouldn't get caught and then transported us back to the woods as close to the entrance as we could get.

Since it was surrounded by trees, we were almost on top of it. I peeked around a tree looking for the rock with the indent on it. The Pulhu hadn't moved it, but they were standing around the entrance, pointing some sort of equipment at it.

They were closer to opening the portal than I thought. We needed them to move now. I nodded at Jordan, and he disappeared. A few minutes later, I felt the ground shake and heard the explosion. Many of the Pulhu turned and raced through the trees toward the sound, but a few stayed behind.

"Let's go," I whispered. We crept forward, trying to come up behind each of the Pulhu. Before we got to them, one turned around and pointed at us. Somehow they could see us. The invisibility potion didn't work.

"Watch out," he yelled, his companions turning toward us and throwing up shields. "It's her, call the others," they shouted. One of them pulled out a phone, and I sent a stream of air at him intending to knock the phone from his hand, but my magic hit a wall of resistance. I heard him tell someone to come quickly. He put his phone away, as we all tried to get past their barriers.

This wasn't going the way I expected. They could see us, and we couldn't even touch them. I tried to scoot around them and get to the entrance, but they blocked the way. I tried fire next, shooting small streams at their barriers. It worked, and the barriers started to come down. Adam noticed and used his power over fire to help me.

As the barriers fell, the Pulhu started throwing their own magic at us. Two of them used air, and one used fire. I left my friends to deal with them, knowing they would be ok. I ran to the stone and placed my hand on it. I sent fire magic around it, but nothing happened. I tried again, using the ancient word for open. Still, nothing happened.

"Sievroth," I yelled. "I need you." I felt heat sear my cheek as flames came from behind me and engulfed my hand and the stone. Before I could pull my hand back, shimmers around the edge of the pile of stones appeared. The flames continued hitting the rock, but my hand didn't burn. I felt Sievroth talk to me.

"It's almost open. Be prepared. The Pulhu are coming, we can't let them in."

"Sally," Abby yelled, and I turned my head. Pulhu were pouring from the trees. They had gotten the message that we were here, and they planned on stopping us. I threw a barrier up around my friends and myself as the entrance glowed. Sievroth stopped blowing fire, and the portal started to open.

I didn't get to watch it open the rest of the way before the Pulhu started flinging power everywhere. I sagged as my shield took multiple hits. I needed my friends to get closer together, so I would only have to control one shield instead of multiple. They tried to get to me, but the Pulhu cut us off from each other, surrounding each shield with multiple people.

"Sally," Abby screamed, and I watched in horror as Mr. Mitchel emerged from the trees. He headed toward Abby. I refused to let him hurt her. I threw a stream of air at him to knock him back. He recovered quickly and laughed.

"You know I will take her, Sally. Unless you do as I say, she will be mine. So will the rest of your friends. You can't protect them all. I will destroy them."

"I won't let you touch her," I said, as he held his hand up.

I staggered as he placed his hand on the shield causing it to start turning grey. The shield started to fail everywhere the grey color touched. Mr. Damon had done this to my shield too. I didn't know what magic they were using, but I couldn't fight against it. Abby screamed and moved a few steps back, but she couldn't go anywhere. The Pulhu were surrounding her too.

I pulled all my power together and shot a burst of wind at the Pulhu around Abby, causing them to be blown back a few feet. Abby ran toward me before they could stop her. I sent wind at the Pulhu around me too, opening a path for Abby to take. She ran to me, grabbing my hand and shaking. She was terrified of Mr. Mitchel after what he did to me.

I was scared of him too, and I wanted to put more distance between us. I felt Richard in my head. "We need to attack, Sally. Otherwise, he will destroy all the shields, and we will be captured."

"Ok," I sent back to him. "On three." I let the others know the plan and then counted down. On three, I dropped the shields, and we all threw our hands up, allowing our powers to hit the Pulhu closest to us. Tider created a wall of water that swallowed a few of the Pulhu. Adam used small flames to light some of the Pulhu's clothes on fire. It wasn't deadly, but it would keep them distracted.

Abby stayed with me, her greatest power was in being able to heal us if we needed it. I used small tornadoes to pick up the Pulhu nearest to me and fling them into the woods. Mr. Mitchel watched the whole thing without a word. He held his hands out, moving toward me. I tried to stop him, but my magic was flung aside. He continued walking toward us.

I looked around trying to find a safe place for Abby. More Pulhu were still coming into the clearing, and the guys were busy trying to keep the Pulhu off of themselves. Air began to swirl around us, picking up speed. I focused and saw Richard's magic surrounding the entire clearing. I used earth to make roots burst from the ground and entwine themselves around our legs as Richard's power increased.

The wind was howling as Richard let his full powers out. The Pulhu were lifted into the sky and slammed back down. I grimaced as one close to me hit the ground, and I heard a crack as his arm landed under him. I turned my head away from the sight.

Mr. Mitchel wasn't moving any closer to us. He was trying to keep himself from being sucked up into the whirlwind Richard was creating. He threw his hands out, and a stream of fire hurtled toward Richard. I pulled water from the air to smother the fire, and Mr. Mitchell looked back at me.

The air was losing its ferocity as Richard used up more of his power. Tider was keeping as many Pulhu down as possible by smothering them in a blanket of water, and Adam was still trying to light a few of them on fire.

It looked like we might win, but then Mr. Mitchel sent his magic around the clearing. A dark cloud swirled around Richard's whirlwind, and each time it touched one of the Pulhu, they regained their strength and were able to stand up against Richard's attack.

As his wind died down completely, Mr. Mitchel smiled cruelly. "Now, you are all mine. You will do as I say, and the Pulhu will rule beside the darkness."

"Never," I said, shooting a blast of fire at him. He easily swiped it to the side and moved toward me.

"You are overpowered," he said. I looked behind him to see my friends barely holding the Pulhu off. They were almost out of energy. There were too many Pulhu and not enough of us.

I put my hands out and said the spell for the fog. I told my friends what I was doing and cautioned them to put up their own shields if they could. I let the fog slowly drift toward the Pulhu. I moved it around Mr. Mitchel, not wanting him to dispel it.

He laughed. "Do you think a little fog will stop us. There is nowhere for you to run. I have people stationed all over this mountain to catch you if you escape here."

"I'm not trying to escape," I said. The fog wrapped itself around almost all of the Pulhu, and I raised my hands, eyeing Mr. Mitchel warily. I needed him distracted for a minute so I could add fire to the fog.

"Why are you doing this?" Richard yelled, causing Mr. Mitchel to turn toward him.

I sent a quick thanks to Richard and let the fire magic connect with the fog. The Pulhu immediately started to yell and run. The fog was burning them, allowing my friends a break. I threw a shield between them and Mr. Mitchel so they could get to me.

When we were together, Richard put his arm around my shoulders to help support me. Immediately my power started to return. If we stayed touching, we would eventually both succumb to energy exhaustion, but it would give us a fighting chance. I leaned into Richard pretending to still be depleted. Abby grabbed my hand, giving me even more energy.

I could see power coalescing around Mr. Mitchel. Whatever he was going to do would be huge. When he raised his hands and sent the magic at us, it was the same black form of the magicus that had come at me in the dome back at school. I tried to make our shield stronger, but his power ate right through it. I kept throwing shields up to keep the dark monster away from us.

We couldn't fight it. It would absorb our magic. "Sievroth," I yelled. "Help me."

I felt Sievroth next to us, and I dropped the shield as his fire slammed into the magicus, blasting it backward. It didn't explode like the one in the dome though. Mr. Mitchel must have made it stronger. Sievroth blasted it again, but it still stood before us. I felt the portal behind me shift as a group of people in armor came rushing out.

"Fire, Sievroth," they yelled. When he let another stream of fire out, they added their own fire magic to it. Their magic twisted around Sievroth's before blending together right before it hit the magicus. The explosion threw us all back. As I opened my eyes and looked around, I saw Mr. Mitchel staggering to his feet. The rest of the Pulhu were still scattered across the ground. Mr. Mitchel took one last look at us and disappeared.

Someone reached a hand down to me, and I looked up. A man stood in front of me, covered in heavy red armor. Only his arms were bare. I let him help me up. As I lost contact with Richard, my knees buckled, and the man scooped me up before I could hit the ground.

"Thank you," I said.

"Rest. We will talk more soon." He carried me toward the portal. I tried to see my friends, but his shoulders were blocking my view. "Don't worry, we will take care of your friends. You are safe for now." I let my head rest against him as we walked through the portal.

I didn't sleep though. I watched as the fire realm came into view, and I tried to look everywhere at once. It was nothing like what I expected. I thought their realm would be similar to a desert, but it wasn't. I could see a lush jungle valley in front of us, and a mountain rose in the distance.

The sky was a gorgeous orange color, and as we walked, I waited for the colors to change, thinking it was the sunset that made the sky so orange, but it never changed. The man holding me must have realized I was waiting for the sky to change because he started talking to me.

"That is the color of our sky. Occasionally a few purples or reds can be seen, but it's almost always orange just like yours is blue. We aren't sure why but you get used to it."

"Who are you?" I asked. I noticed that they didn't have the same magical signatures of true elementals. They looked like ordinary elementals, like everyone at my school.

"I am Gavin. I am a member of the fireguard. We protect the true elementals and the dragons from any trespassers."

"Then why are you helping us? We don't belong here, but you came out of the portal and saved us. You could have closed the portal and stayed hidden."

"Eventually, that man would have found a way in. Plus, Sievroth told me you were needed here. We have been waiting for you for a long time." I looked at him again. He couldn't be more than twenty-five years old. He laughed. "When we are in the fire realm, time stops for us. I have been alive since before the shadow king forced us to live in these realms. Only children age normally until they reach adulthood."

"How? The true fire elementals were not supposed to take any followers with them."

"They didn't listen. The fire elemental king allowed every follower who survived the shadow king's wrath to come with them. We've been here since them. We can only go out into the human realm for short periods. Our aging starts again when we leave here. I've aged maybe three years since I came here because I've needed to go into the human realm for the true fire elementals at times."

"That's amazing," I said.

"It can be, it can also be pretty boring."

I fell silent. I wouldn't want to live forever if given a chance. I wondered if these elementals felt that way too.

"Where are the true elementals?" I asked.

"We will take you to them soon. First, we need to make it to the town and then refresh ourselves before heading to the palace."

"Where is the town?"

"Through there," he said, pointing at the forest. "It will take many hours to get to the town, but we have a small outpost inside the tree line where we will stop until you can all walk."

My friends must be in bad shape too. I reached out and connected to each of them, making sure they were ok. Abby was being carried, but the guys were walking. We were all feeling exhausted from our fight with Mr. Mitchel. Everyone's mood picked up when we made it to the outpost. The man carrying me put me down on a bed, and I immediately tried to sit up.

"Wait," he said, putting his hand on my shoulder to prevent me from moving. He took a small bottle from a young woman who walked in right after us. "This is our healer. She will give each of you an energy potion to help you feel more like yourselves."

He handed each of us a bottle. They all looked at me, waiting to see what I would do. I went to drink it, but Adam stopped me. "Let me drink it first. If it isn't what they say, we will know in a few minutes."

"I don't want you getting hurt," I said, frowning.

"It's my choice. We need the rest of you to fight if they aren't as friendly as they seem to be. Abby can heal me while you three get us out of here." He didn't give me a choice, he downed the whole potion before I could stop him. I waited impatiently, worried he would fall over sick from the drink. He didn't say anything for a minute, but then he smiled.

"It's an energy potion, and it's very potent. You guys are going to feel better than yourselves after you drink it."

I looked at the man who had carried me in. "We wouldn't poison you, but judging by how much energy your friend has, you won't be able to take another potion for at least a week. That amount only gives us a small jolt of energy." I looked at Adam. He was bouncing on his toes, ready to go. I made my decision and drank my potion. Everyone else did too.

Within a minute, energy started to fill me, and soon I was up and standing. "I feel great," I said. "Let's get going."

CHAPTER FIFTEEN

We headed deeper into the rainforest, following a path through the dense underbrush. I wanted to get to the true fire elementals as quickly as possible. I was sure the Pulhu would still be trying to get into the fire realm. Now that they knew where the portal door was and how to open it, they would focus all of their efforts on it. It wouldn't take long to find a way through.

After a few hours, we stopped for lunch. Gavin gave us a variety of fruits and bread. They also gave us water and fruit juice. When I asked Gavin how much longer we would be in the jungle, he told me we should be to their town by nightfall. He didn't say how long it would take to get to the true elementals, but I was sure it would be at least another full day.

I was starting to get antsy. I felt like Gavin and his men were keeping something from us. Every time we tried to talk about the true fire elementals with them, they would clam up and change the subject, saying that we would see them when we got to the palace. It also felt like we were taking a very roundabout path. When I asked Richard, he said he felt the same.

There was definitely something going on, but until I figured out what, we would have to play along and follow Gavin and his men. If we left them, we could be lost in this jungle for days and who knew what kind of creatures were in here. We hadn't seen anything yet, but the men and women all carried weapons on them, and if they weren't fighting each other, they must need the weapons for some reason.

I talked to Richard through our connection as we walked. I didn't want them knowing what our plans were in case they decided to turn on us. Gavin walked back to me and started pointing out different things in the jungle. There were different trees than we were used to, and even the birds were oddly colored. I saw a particular bird watching us. It was purple with a bright blue beak, and it stared at us as we passed by.

When I stopped to watch it, it turned and met my eyes. I would swear the bird knew exactly what we were doing and who we were. It made a loud screech and took off into the treetops. I heard answering calls throughout the jungle, and Gavin looked spooked.

"What's wrong?" I asked.

"That was a tarandul. They are not native to the fire realm. We don't know where they came from. Something about them makes me cautious," he said. "They seem to be able to understand us and communicate with others far away. They always know what we're doing. Sometimes I wonder if they aren't reporting back to someone on our activities."

"Maybe the true fire elementals use them to keep an eye on you," I said.

"No, it's definitely not them," Gavin replied.

The way he said it made me think something was wrong with the true elementals. It didn't sound as if he thought they wouldn't ever do that to them, but more that they couldn't do it.

I tried asking about them again but got the same result. Gavin switched the topic to something else. I let it drop. We would find out soon enough what was going on.

When we walked into the town, I was surprised by the flurry of activity. Everywhere we looked, people were working. Some were working in gardens and fields while others cleaned the roads. We moved through the town toward the center, people stopping to stare at us. I'm sure they were surprised to see people from the human realm since they had been here so long without anyone being allowed to come through.

No one stopped us, and they cleared a path for Gavin and his men. Gavin must have a lot of power over them. I wondered what his position was exactly. The people weren't scared of him. They showed him a lot of respect. The people looked excited as we moved farther into the town. As we reached the town center, a man with long white hair came running up to us. Gavin and his men bowed slightly to him.

"This is Tristan," Gavin said. "He would like to speak with you."

"Is he the leader in this town?"

"Yes, he is the leader of all the towns in the fire realm. He is here to greet you. He has traveled a long distance to get here." My suspicions amped up. I thought Gavin was taking us a roundabout route, and now I was pretty sure he did it to allow this man, Tristan, to meet us here.

"Why does he want to speak with us," I asked, eyeing the new man.

"I will tell you all you need to know about this realm," the man said. "Come with me."

He led us to a house nearby. We went inside and sat on pillows on the floor. A woman brought heated water on a tray with cups. She set it on the floor in the center of us. The man added tea leaves to the water and let them steep. Abby went to say something, but I shushed her. I wanted to see what this man had to say. After he poured a glass of tea for everyone, he sat back on his own pillow.

"Drink up, it's not poison. It's a tea made from the leaves of the buhbul tree in the rainforest. It doesn't do anything to you. I enjoy the taste." He raised his own glass and took a sip. I reached down and grabbed my cup, taking a small sip. My friends did the same. It felt like this was a test of sorts but for what I didn't know.

Tristan finished his tea and put his cup back on the tray. "I know you have questions, and I will answer them, but first I need to ask for your help."

"What do you need?" Tider asked.

"What about the true fire elementals?" Adam asked at the same time. "Can't they help you?"

"The true fire elementals haven't been able to help us for a long time. We were running out of hope until Sievroth's egg started to hatch. It was said a dragon egg would hatch when the chosen accepted their gift. Only then would we be able to awaken the true elementals."

"What do you mean, awaken? Are they asleep?"

"They are in some sort of stupor. It happened slowly. We all thought they were just getting tired, even lazy from being stuck in this realm for so long with nothing to fight for. They stopped coming to the towns. Then they stopped inviting people to the palace to train. By the time the first true elemental fell into a stupor, it was too late to do anything. We tried to protect the rest of them, taking them from the castle, but nothing worked. Eventually, even the king and queen fell."

"Where are they now?" I asked.

"We brought them back to the castle. All the true elementals are there now. We think you can wake them."

Tristan and Gavin were watching me, waiting for my reaction. It took me a minute to answer. "Of course, we will help, but if you haven't found the cause of the stupor, what are we supposed to do?"

"We know it has something to do with the dragons. They have also fallen into a stupor. We think they fell first. We stopped seeing them in the skies around the mountain years before the true elementals fell. When we asked about the dragons, the true elementals told us they were fine. They were spending more time in their caves because they were getting ready for an important event. No one thought it was a lie until the stupor started to hit the true elementals."

"If it started with the dragons, then we need to figure out what caused it with them first. Can we go see them?" I asked.

"Yes, but we will stop at the palace first. We will need to get the talismans."

"What are the talismans?"

"Only a few elementals had talismans that allowed them to walk into the dragon's den without getting hurt. You will each need one to pass through the mountain unharmed. Usually, only one person goes into the mountain at a time to check on the dragons. The rest of the talismans are in safekeeping at the palace under guard."

"Will they allow us to take them?"

"Yes, once Gavin explains who you are," Tristan said.

"We will rest here tonight, and tomorrow start our journey to the palace. It is too dangerous to leave now. We would be stuck in the forest when predators wake up and hunt. Even though our sky always remains the same, we still have nighttime and daytime. Many of the predators in the forest prowl around at night. Even for us, it can be dangerous. Especially with those birds around."

"Why haven't you tried to get rid of the birds?" I asked.

"We have, but they come back in greater numbers. It's better to let them be. All they do is watch us. They never try hurting us."

Tristan stood up and gestured for Gavin to take us. We followed him through the town center and to another house. Gavin directed us to our rooms and left, saying he would be back shortly to take us to dinner. Abby and I went to our room and cleaned ourselves up.

When we finished, we headed back out into the main room. The guys were already cleaned up and waiting for us. Tider tried to say something, but I shook my head. I created the silence bubble around us before speaking. "Let's be careful here, guys. We don't actually know what they want or what's wrong with the fire elementals. We could be walking into a trap."

"That's what I was going to say," Tider said. "I just forgot to create a silence bubble first."

"So far, they don't seem like they want to hurt us," Richard said. "I know that doesn't mean they won't," he continued when I gave him a look. "But I think we need to look at them as friends rather than enemies, after all, they did help us with the Pulhu."

"We won't look at them as enemies, but I'm not ready to look at them as friends yet. They could have gotten us to this town much faster but instead chose a roundabout route in order to give Tristan time to arrive here. They could've told us in the beginning what was going on."

"Would you have waited here, or would you have tried to get to the palace tonight?" Adam asked. They all knew me so well. I would have wanted to get to the palace today. When I didn't answer right away, they laughed.

We didn't have long to wait. Gavin knocked on the door before entering. After making sure we had everything we needed for the night, he escorted us out of the house and down a few streets. We approached a large building with a few scattered tables around the side of it. I could hear music and laughter coming from inside.

When we walked through the doors, the laughter stopped. Heads turned our way, everyone looking us over until their eyes landed on Gavin. Suddenly, they threw their heads back and laughed more, some coming over to slap us on our backs and shout good luck. I looked at Gavin.

Once we were seated, he tried to explain. "They all know you are here to help save the true elementals. They are celebrating and wishing you luck on the journey. No one has been able to help them. We are all hoping that you will be able to do it."

I looked at the people again. They all appeared to be in good health and happy. "Why are they so excited to wake the true elementals?"

"The true elementals are our friends and our teachers. They saved us when the shadow king was destroying all elemental humans. It's our turn to save them."

A woman came over to our table, asking what we would like to eat. Since we weren't given menus, we looked at Gavin. He ordered pizza for everyone.

"What?" he said when he saw our faces. "I told you we occasionally go out in the human realm. Last time Beeble went out, he came back with a recipe for pizza. We have been making it ever since. Everyone loves pizza. It's the same in the human realm, right?"

We laughed. "Yes. Many people love pizza."

Our pizza came, and we enjoyed ourselves, watching everyone joke around and celebrate. When we were almost finished, a man came over and sat at our table in Gavin's seat. Gavin had gone to talk to one of his friends and wouldn't be back for a few minutes.

The man didn't say a word. I looked him over and tried not to shrink away from him. He had a scar across his eyebrow that obviously hadn't healed properly, and his hands were gnarled and scarred too. His beard was matted, and when he grinned, I could see his yellowing teeth. This man hadn't been taking good care of himself.

"What can we do for you?" Richard asked politely.

"You can leave," he replied. "You will destroy everything. You need to leave now before you make things worse."

"What do you mean before we make things worse?" I asked.

"You don't belong here. The true elementals need to remain asleep."

"Why?" Richard asked.

"Because they refused to listen to the shadow king. This is their punishment. They were not supposed to bring human followers with them. I'm sure the shadow king is punishing them, and that is why they won't wake up."

"How do you know it's the shadow king?"

"What else could it be? It's the only thing that makes sense," he said. "If you continue trying to wake them, we will stop you."

"Who will stop us?" Tider asked.

"The brotherhood of the flame. We are everywhere. We will be watching you," he said, standing and moving quickly to the door. When Gavin returned, he could tell something was wrong and asked what happened. After we explained it to him, he slammed his fist on the table.

"Damn the brotherhood," he said. "They have been a nuisance to us for so long. We have tried getting rid of them, but they keep growing."

"How many of them are there?" I asked.

"We don't know. We think there are close to a hundred, but most of them are older, or they are weak in their elemental power. They are not a big threat."

"Are you sure? He seemed pretty certain they would stop us."

"Unless something has changed, they are not powerful enough or numerous enough to cause any problems. I will look into it to make sure, but I don't see there being any issues. We will continue on in the morning like we were planning."

We went back to our temporary house a few minutes later. After our warning, none of us were in the mood to stay. I laid my hand over my pack, saying the word lakir. The book on void appeared, and I pulled it out of the pack and sat on the bed to read before going to sleep. I was still wound up from the odd man we met.

I opened the book to the page I was reading. I was about a quarter of the way through the book. I read a few more pages but didn't learn much. It talked about how void users were never seen. They stayed away from others in an effort to protect themselves from becoming corrupted.

A corrupted void user was more powerful than any other elemental, and only another void user could defeat them once they were corrupted. That is why there were so few void users. They couldn't take the chance of just anyone getting the power. It was too dangerous.

There was so much speculation in the book, but it was better than the other books I read on void. I slipped under my covers and tried to get some sleep after putting the book away. Abby was already asleep and snoring softly. I smiled. I was glad my friends were with me.

Something woke me, and I opened my eyes. A soft click came from the front door. I climbed slowly out of bed and padded across the room. I peeked into the main room. The front door was still closed, but I could hear noise coming from the other side.

"Wake up," I yelled into all my friend's heads. I heard covers being thrown back and Tider cursing softly under his breath as he fell out of bed. We all ran to the center of the room with our packs as I heard another click. The doorknob slowly started to turn. Someone had managed to pick the lock.

I let an invisibility shield drop on top of us as Richard put up a silence bubble. Two men snuck into the room, not making a sound. I recognized one of the men from dinner. It was the old man who told us we would be stopped from helping the fire elementals. They separated and started looking through the room. There wasn't much to see. We hadn't brought a lot with us, and the few important things were spelled so no one could see them.

When the first man got to the guy's room, he peeked in and then stepped back quickly. He poked his head in again and took a few steps into the room. He came out, striding quietly over to the other man who was looking into my room.

"They aren't here," he said. "They must have gotten past us."

"How? Brotherhood members are stationed everywhere. Someone would have seen them."

"Well, they aren't here. Maybe they left to get to the palace before we could stop them."

"It won't matter. They will never get past the traps we have laid out for them. We need to hurry and catch up to them so we can kidnap them after they are disabled by the traps. I'm glad we put the traps up when we did. "

"They don't have a guide with them. They will be moving slowly. We will catch up to them in no time," the old man laughed. "This will be easier than I thought. I was worried we would have to deal with Gavin, but they left him behind."

"Are you sure Gavin didn't sneak out too?"

"Yes. I checked on him before coming over here."

"Let's get going then. I want to finish this quickly before we get caught. I don't want to be imprisoned for kidnapping the one who can wake the true elementals."

"Another hundred years and we will have the majority on our side. The longer we go without the true elementals, the more bitter the people become toward them. They don't remember how much they loved them, and our words keep them doubting the true elementals ever cared for them in the first place. We will win this fight. We only need to be patient."

"We have been patient," grumbled the one man. He stopped complaining when the other man looked at him sharply.

"Stop whining, and let's go. We have a lot to do before Gavin wakes up and realizes he has been left behind."

CHAPTER SIXTEEN

We waited for a few minutes after they left before taking down our shields.

"We need to warn Gavin about the traps and get out of here," Adam said.

"We don't know where Gavin lives. How will we warn him?" Abby asked.

"I think we should wait here until morning. It's only a few more hours, and then Gavin will come here looking for us. We can tell him what happened and make a plan. Maybe there is a different way to get to the palace. Plus, the brotherhood will think we have already passed their traps without getting caught in them. They will be trying to catch up to us, but we will be behind them the whole time. It will make it easier to get to the palace without them following our steps."

"I think Sally's right," Richard said. "We can start making our own plan and see what Gavin says when he gets here. What is Sievroth saying?"

"Nothing. I haven't heard from him since we got here. He is staying invisible, so he must not feel comfortable. I will try to talk to him next time he comes back. He keeps taking off."

No one could fall back asleep, so Tider pulled out a pack of cards, and we played games until morning. When we heard a knock on the door, we stood together and put a shield of invisibility up. When Gavin walked in and shut the door, we let the invisibility fall.

"What are you guys doing," he sputtered. "You scared me. Why were you invisible? Is this your idea of a joke?"

"Calm down, Gavin, and keep your voice down." I looked at Richard, and he spoke the words to put the silence bubble around us. "We had visitors last night."

We told him everything that happened and what we thought we should do. He listened to everything we said and slowly shook his head after we stopped talking.

"There is no other way to the palace. Trying to go off the jungle path is too dangerous. We need to follow it. Once we are through the jungle, we will travel across a stretch of open land that leads to the palace. There is nowhere to hide during that stretch. We will have to be very careful. The brotherhood is becoming more than a nuisance. I still can't believe they are going to try and kidnap you all."

"That's what they were saying," Tider said.

He shook his head. "They must be going insane with nothing else to do in this realm. After the true fire elementals wake up, I'm sure they will stop all this nonsense."

I wasn't so sure. The brotherhood seemed pretty determined to live without the true fire elementals. I spent a lot of time thinking about it overnight. They didn't seem like evil people, but someone was putting bad thoughts about the true elementals into their heads.

I wanted to find out who. They might know what really happened to the dragons and true elementals. I doubted the shadow king would have done this. It didn't make sense. He was powerful enough to wipe them out if he wanted to. Putting them to sleep didn't punish them since they wouldn't remember being asleep. Something else was going on.

We decided to stay invisible and follow Gavin to the path that would take us to the palace. It wasn't far away, only a few roads over so I would be able to keep us all invisible. The brotherhood would expect Gavin to go down the path, thinking he was trying to catch up with us.

Once we were far enough that the townspeople wouldn't see us, I would drop the invisibility, and we would continue. We would watch out for traps, but we figured they would be disabled so the brotherhood could get by without tripping them since they thought we were farther ahead.

Gavin already had everything he needed, so we grabbed our bags and headed into town. Gavin strolled down the street, stopping to talk to people along the way. It was hard for me to keep the shield up while we were moving, so he went slowly. Every time I shielded my friends it got easier, and I was able to keep up with Gavin without trouble.

When we finally made it to the path, I sighed in relief.

I heard Gavin whisper, "Only a little longer, and you can drop the shield." I smiled. He was looking the wrong way.

We followed him deeper into the jungle. When he stopped again, I sat down, trying to recoup some of my energy. I let the shield drop so he could see us.

Richard handed me a chocolate bar, and I smiled gratefully.

"I brought a few of these, knowing you would need extra energy." The sugar rush always made me feel better faster than regular food. "Eat this too. You need some real food." He handed me a granola bar. I took it and ate it as soon as I finished the chocolate bar.

"You ok?" Tider asked.

"Yep. I'm ready to go."

Gavin led us forward. The walk was easy, and we didn't run into any trouble. We passed a few areas that had been disturbed, and I could see trace amounts of magic along the ground, but whatever had been there was gone. So far, the brotherhood was acting exactly as we hoped.

When we finally reached the edge of the jungle, we were tired and hungry. We sat down and had a small lunch looking out at the desert stretched in front of us.

"It seems bigger than it actually is," Gavin told us. "There are sinkholes and quicksand everywhere except the path. The desert was spelled long ago to keep anyone from trying to get to the fire elemental palace by taking a different route. It only takes a few hours to cross. We will be at the palace by nightfall."

"If the brotherhood doesn't stop us, or make us leave the path," Tider said.

"I'm sure they will try. By now, they will have reached the palace and realized you weren't ahead of them, and they will double back. I'm sure we will meet them on the way to the palace. They will be easy enough to overpower. I doubt they brought many of the brotherhood with them since they expected to catch you in a trap."

"I don't want to hurt them," I said.

"Neither do I. We will try not to, but if they fight us, we may not have a choice. Our healers will take care of them though. They are not bad, they are misinformed and bored. It makes it easy for their minds to be fearful of change. The true elementals have been asleep so long that waking them will be a huge change for many of the people living here."

We finished eating and set out across the desert. The farther we went from the jungle, the hotter the temperature got. Abby and Tider were sweating almost immediately and complained of the dry heat. I handed Abby my water bottle as she finished hers, and Adam gave Tider his.

Neither of them had a fire element, so they were struggling in the heat. It was definitely hotter than the desert in the human realm, and I worried they would have to take the heat potion. We would run out if we started using them already.

Gavin noticed the situation and opened his pack. "Here," he said, handing a small vial to both of them. "This will help you. It's made from a cactus in this desert. You will be able to feel the heat, but it won't bother you. We make it for those of us that have a very weak fire element. It helps them handle the desert. Especially once they get close to the volcano. I brought one for each of you. I didn't know if you all had fire or not."

I watched as Abby and Tider took the potion, and their faces became less red and strained. Abby handed my water bottle back. "I feel much better now," she said.

We continued on. I noticed figures in the distance a little while later. I pointed them out, and we kept an eye on them. After a few minutes, we realized they were heading toward us. It would take them an hour or longer to reach us. We stepped off the path, and I put an invisibility shield up. It was easier than trying to fight them if it was the brotherhood. Richard used a small burst of air to cover our tracks as far back as he could.

He couldn't cover all the way to the jungle, so if the brotherhood was paying attention, they would see our tracks in the sand and know we had come through. Then they would be after us again.

"We will need to watch for traps down the path. If they realized you didn't come through yet, they might be resetting the traps," Gavin cautioned.

We stilled as the figures came closer. It was the two guys who had snuck into our rooms. They were talking loudly as they walked closer.

"Maybe they snuck out last night to look around the town and then went back to their room to wait for Gavin. We would have seen them if they had come to the palace."

"What will we do now?" the whiny guy asked.

"We will meet them on the path. I'm sure they will be coming this way soon. We replaced these traps, and we will do the same to the ones in the jungle until we see them. We can let them pass us and follow behind." The men moved out of hearing range, and we all snickered. The brotherhood really wasn't that much of a threat. We would still need to be careful of the traps though. Those could be a problem.

We moved through the desert faster now that we knew where the brotherhood was. The first trap we came to was pretty simple. Once it was triggered, the sand would collapse, trapping us in quicksand. It would hold us until the brotherhood arrived. Richard was able to easily disarm the trap, and we continued on our way.

I could see the palace in the distance. It looked like a mirage. The heat coming off the sand distorted the view making it shimmer in the sky. Gavin informed us we would make it to the palace in less than an hour. Halfway there, I saw another trap, this one more complex. Instead of trapping us in quicksand, it would catch us in a swirling vortex of sand. Before Richard could disarm it, I stopped him.

"Let's leave this one," I said. "It will confuse them more if this trap hasn't been disabled. They will think we tried to go around, but there won't be any footprints. They might even think they somehow got past us again."

Richard helped me use air to fly everyone over the trap. It was bigger than I expected and would have added hours onto our travel time if we tried to go around it. It wasn't very tall though since they didn't know we had air magic.

Once we were safely on the other side, we continued our walk. The palace got bigger and bigger as we got closer, and the heat from the desert didn't warp its appearance anymore. It was massive, and all along its walls, I could see areas for them to shoot fire out but still stay protected.

"Why was the palace built with so much defense in mind?" I asked.

"The other elementals were always trying to start wars with us. They said we were too aggressive, but the truth was they were scared of our power and constantly tried to destroy as many of the true fire elemental followers as possible."

I wondered if this was true. It wasn't what the other elementals said, but since I wasn't around when they were fighting, I couldn't know for sure. I would give the true fire elementals a chance. Their followers had been very nice and welcoming, except the brotherhood, and I doubted they would be so nice if the true elementals were bad.

A guard stood on either side of the gigantic gate and greeted Gavin as we walked closer.

"My friends, we request entrance into the hall of elementals. We are here to try and save the true elementals with your permission." The guards sucked in their breath and looked us over.

"They have finally come?" One of them said to Gavin.

"We think so. They have traveled far to get here and have many enemies, including the brotherhood of flame. The brotherhood laid traps for them and even snuck into their room, hoping to kidnap them."

"We have seen them. They came here earlier today, asking for news of any travelers. We sent them away."

"Yes, they were after us, but we had a few tricks up our sleeves and easily got past them." The guards laughed.

"A child could get past those two. I never understood why the brotherhood would choose them to do anything."

"Please enter," the other guard said, opening the door for us. It took a bit of work with the gates being so large. "Good luck. We would love to see our true elementals awakened. If there is anything you need, ask."

"We will need talismans for each of them," Gavin said. "They think the dragons are the start of this and would like to examine them."

"I will send word ahead to Lily. She is guarding the talismans right now." He turned to another guard standing inside the gates and told him to find Lily and prepare the talismans. The guard took off into the palace. "Lily will have them ready for you, but you must wait until morning to go to the dragons. The path has become unstable recently. We think the brotherhood is messing with it, but we can't find any trace of their magic," the guard told us.

I shook my head but didn't say anything. The constant stopping was starting to get to me. I wanted to get to the dragons and figure this out before the Pulhu made it inside the fire realm. We thanked the guards and headed inside, the doors shutting loudly behind us.

Gavin took us straight to Lily, who already had a talisman for each of us.

After introductions, she laid them out. I reached down and picked one up. It was shaped like a diamond with a small flame inside of it. The diamond was intricately created, with twists and swirls along the front and back of it.

At the top of the diamond was a small symbol. I looked at the other talismans. Each one had a different symbol. Lily told me it was the symbol of a specific dragon. Every dragon was given a talisman, and they added the mark, claiming it. If they were awake, only the person they trusted most would hold their talisman and be able to get into the dragon's lair without having to go through the guard.

I looked down at the one I was holding. "Who's is this?"

"It belongs to Kavli. She is the leader of all dragons. The baby dragon that hatched is hers. It is only fitting for you to use it since Sievroth brought you here."

She went through the others, telling them the names of the dragon associated with their talisman. When we were all set, she bowed and wished us luck. Gavin took us through the halls until he came to a large door.

"The true elementals lay in here. We have it set up as a sick room, so it is easier to check on them all."

He opened the doors, and we stared inside. Cots were set up in rows throughout the whole room. Hundreds of elementals lay sleeping. Gavin led us to the king and queen. They were lying on a large bed together. I stepped closer, but Gavin put his hand on my arm to stop me.

"Don't hurt them," he said, looking unsure.

"I won't, Gavin, but I need to look at them." He let go, and I moved closer. I shut my eyes, concentrating on their magic. In seconds I was backing away. I looked at Tider. He could see auras, and I asked him what he saw.

"Nothing unusual. Their colors are all muted, but besides that, there is nothing to tell me what is wrong. Why? What do you see?"

"There magic is muted like their auras," I said to Tider. "They both have grey magic encircling their own magic."

"A curse like the water elemental king?"

"No. I don't think so. It's like their powers have been contained somehow."

"A spell?"

"Maybe. Could they have been spelled?" I asked Gavin.

"Doubtful. It happened too slow to be a spell."

"Maybe it was poison," Abby said. "In one of my potion books, there was a spell that could slowly fix a person's complexion as long as they kept taking it. It worked very slow, over the course of weeks, but it would keep their skin clear forever as long as it was consumed every few days."

"Gavin, could they have been slowly poisoned?" I asked when he didn't answer Abby.

"I suppose, but how could they all be poisoned at the same time. And wouldn't they have noticed?"

"Not if it was a tiny amount of poison that could gradually build up in their bloodstream. They would never even notice something was wrong."

"What would be causing it?"

"Since they are all still asleep, someone must be giving them the poison if that's what is keeping them sleeping."

"Only our most trusted guards are allowed in here. And everything we give them is checked to make sure it can't hurt them."

"We need to go to the dragons. There is nothing I can do for them. It isn't a curse that I can defeat. We need to find the source."

"We will go to the dragons first thing in the morning. For now, let's get something to eat, and you can all relax for a couple of hours. It's been a long day. I want to go speak with the guards about the Brotherhood of Flame too. We need to keep a better eye on them."

We went to the kitchens where the cook prepared us a meal. We were all starving and ate everything he made. I wasn't even sure what some of the things on my plate were. It was all delicious, and I started to feel better as soon as I finished. I thanked the cook and turned to Gavin.

"Is there a library in here?" I asked, not ready to lay down.

"Yes," Gavin said. "I will show you once your friends are in their rooms unless you all want to come."

I could see the decision in their eyes. They would come with me to keep me safe. "Go rest, guys. I will be fine. There are guards posted at the entrance. I will wake you if I need you." They agreed after some more convincing, and Gavin showed them to the guest rooms before leading me to the library.

"Is there something you are looking for in particular?"

"No, I am going to browse if you don't mind," I said. I didn't want him knowing I had void and was looking for a book on it. The air elemental queen's book was giving me some new information, but maybe the fire elementals knew something the air elementals didn't.

Gavin must have heard something in my voice. He told me he would wait across the hall in another room and to come get him when I finished. I thanked him, and he left. I started searching the shelves. The room was as large as the cafeteria back at the school and at least two stories tall. Every available shelf was filled with books. I kept searching but wasn't having any luck. Even Mauevene came out to help me search the higher areas but didn't find anything.

"Stop it," Mauevene yelled, and I tilted my head up, my hands coming out to defend her. Sievroth flew around the room, his tongue snaking out every time he got close to Mauevene.

"Sievroth," I yelled, "you get your butt down here right now. How many times do I need to tell you not to eat Mauevene? She is my friend, and it isn't nice to eat friends." Sievroth landed in front of me, his chest rumbling.

"It's not funny. Look at poor Mauevene. She's never going to come out with you around."

I heard Sievroth rumble again and gave him a light smack on the nose. "Bad, Sievroth." I put my arms around his neck. "Don't do that again, ok?"

He nodded his head and then took off into the air. He flew to one bookcase and hovered there, pushing his nose at one of the books. I ran to him and used air to lift myself up to reach the book he was pointing at. It was a plain brown leather book. There was no writing on the cover to tell me what it was. I opened it, curious to see what Sievroth wanted me to look at. Void was written across the first page. Sievroth had found the book I needed. I started reading before I was even seated at the table.

It started off talking about where void came from, but instead of ideas, this book was written by a void user. It said void users were created by the shadow king to help save the Earth from a disaster that would hit one day in the future. Until then, they were supposed to stay hidden from everyone. When they didn't, and the elementals came into contact with them, it changed the prophecy.

The void users were supposed to work in secret to keep everyone united, but they couldn't do that once the true elementals found out about them. Without them using the pure magic of void to create happiness, the elementals started to fight with each other. Eventually, it got so bad, the shadow king had to destroy most of the followers and send the true elementals away into their own realms.

This was a completely different story than what I had been taught, but it sounded more truthful than any other account I had read. I wanted to learn more, but I was falling asleep. I grabbed the book and headed for the door. I told him I was ready to go and asked to borrow the book. He was fine with that as long as I returned it before I left for the human realm. I promised him I would, and we headed to our rooms to get some rest.

CHAPTER SEVENTEEN

We left through a different set of doors to get to the mountain after a quick breakfast. There were two guards at these doors, and they wished us luck too. Everyone seemed to be counting on us, but I still didn't know how we were going to save the true fire elementals.

On this side of the palace, there was no desert. Only the base of the mountain. Gavin pointed to a plateau high above us. "That's where the entrance is."

I traced the path back to us. It was going to be dangerous. Parts of the trail were missing, and rock slides had taken down multiple areas of trees directly next to the path.

"This was safer last time I came," Gavin said. "The guards are right. This is getting very dangerous. We need to find out what is happening before we can't get to the dragons at all. They will die if we can't take care of them."

"Why?" Abby asked. "They are sleeping. They can't go anywhere."

"They are still alive. They are in a stupor. They need water and nutrients still. We feed them every few days. That is all they need. When they are healthy, they only need to eat once a month after they have reached full strength."

"How are you feeding them if they are in a stupor?"

"We have a nutrient-rich potion that we mix with water. It is easy enough to pour into their mouths. They swallow without any trouble."

"I wonder if that is what is poisoning them. Are you giving the same thing to the true elementals?"

"No. They have a different potion that they take. The dragon's potion would be too powerful for them. It can't be the potion making them sick.

"What about the water?" Abby asked.

"We drink the water too, and we are fine."

"Yes, but you aren't true elementals. The poison might be designed specifically for true elementals and the dragons."

"Let's check the dragons before we jump to any conclusion," Richard said. "Then we can talk about this more."

We hiked up the mountain, careful to watch for loose rocks along the way. Every time I heard a pebble tumbling down the mountain, I braced for a mudslide. I was so busy watching the side of the mountain waiting for boulders to come crashing down that I didn't realize Adam stopped. He stumbled as I walked into his back, pushing him forward and against Tider.

"Whoa, everyone, back up," Gavin said.

I peeked around Adam as we all took a few steps back. The path in front of us fell away into a giant hole. Gavin tossed a pebble into the hole, and we all listened, waiting for it to hit. Eventually, we heard a small ting.

"It's at least a one hundred foot drop."

"Is this normal?" I asked.

"No. This is really bad. We will have to go around. We can climb up the side of the mountain to get past this. We will need to be careful not to slip on the rocks. If anyone falls down into that hole, it's a death sentence. You can't survive it."

"Except Richard and I. We could use air to stop our descent."

"I could use water," Tider said.

Adam and Abby didn't say anything. Their powers wouldn't be able to save them.

"We could fly everyone over again," Richard said. "It will weaken us a little, but it's less risky than climbing the side of the mountain.

"I keep forgetting you guys can do that stuff. I'm used to only being around people with fire elements," Gavin said.

Working together, we managed to get everyone over to the other side of the hole in one trip. When we were on the other side, I let go of Richard's hand and felt my energy decrease. We wouldn't be able to work together like that again until I ate or got some sleep.

We continued forward, this time moving slower, watching for anything else that could potentially harm us. Only a few hundred yards up the path, another hole was forming. It was only two feet across, but as we watched, another inch of ground fell into the hole, making it wider.

We scooted past carefully, trying to stay as far from the edge as possible. We were almost to the entrance of the dragon's lair. I wanted to move faster, but Gavin kept us moving slowly.

We climbed over a recent mudslide. The ground was still soft underfoot and even wet in some areas. As we crossed, I made sure my magic was ready in case one of us fell, but we made it without anyone getting hurt or needing my magic.

I stood in front of the entrance, a little let down. This was supposed to be the dragon's lair. Their home. I was expecting grand doors with a guard that led into a beautifully decorated hall with fancy treasures everywhere. I thought dragons were treasure hoarders.

This was a cave entrance. I bent down, inspecting the rock. I could make out claw marks all along the walls. The dragons had created this by digging it out. I wondered how long it took them to do it. It was easily twenty feet tall and twice as wide.

Abby hesitated at the entrance, "Do you think this is a smart decision? The cave isn't going to come crashing down on us, right? What if there are giant holes inside too."

"It will be ok," Gavin replied. "The cave was built by the dragons. They would have made sure nothing could hurt it. Plus, we will be able to see if there is any damage to the cave."

"How?" I asked, peering into the inky blackness of the cave mouth.

"Watch." He spread his hands and shot a blast of fire at each side of the cave. Something in the walls lit on fire, and the flame raced away from us into the cave, illuminating everything. "The oil will stay lit until we leave."

I could see into the cave with the fire burning softly on both sides. The ground was smooth from years of people walking across it. We walked through the tunnel, occasionally pausing when we thought we heard a noise, but it was always silent when we stopped.

The farther we walked into the cave, the hotter it got. Gavin gave Abby and Tider another potion to help with the heat. The cavern we came to was filled with sleeping dragons. I shook my head in wonder. The fire glittered off their scales as their bodies moved up and down in time with their breathing. They were all different colors shooting a rainbow into the sky as their chests moved.

Some of the dragons were massive, while a few were only twice as big as Sievroth. I stared at the dragon closest to me. His scales were a deep green color, but the color changed to a light orange as it traveled up his neck. It was beautiful.

"They are amazing," Abby whispered.

Gavin laughed. "You don't have to whisper. You won't wake them."

A crack echoed across the chamber, making me jump. After a second, the echo died away, and the chamber was silent again.

"What was that?" Adam asked.

"It sounded like…" Gavin moved around the chamber quickly, crossing to the other side. I followed him, but I wasn't prepared for what I saw. A nest was built behind the sleeping dragons. Two dragons had their necks stretched around the nest, trying to protect it. They were both dark blue, but one of them had silver streaks outlining some of her scales. The other one was only blue.

One of the eggs had a crack across the top of it. As we watched, another crack appeared, and the same noise filled the cavern.

"It can't be. We haven't had a dragon birth since the stupor began, and now we've had two in one year. This definitely means you are the one. You can save them."

He moved forward, placing his hands on the egg. He gave it a light knock. Another crack reverberated across the room. I moved into the nest, placing my hands on the egg too. It wasn't large, about the size of a basketball, but it was hard. I tried to gently lift it, but I could barely move it. It felt like it was made of rock.

The egg warmed under my hand, and I looked down at it. It was starting to glow a light orange on one side.

"The baby is heating up the egg so it can be cracked. Their eggs are almost indestructible. Only high heat can soften them enough for the baby to break free. It won't be long now. He is almost there."

"It's a he?" Abby asked.

"Probably. Most of the dragons are male. Very few females are born. They are the rulers of the dragons."

I looked at the sleeping dragons protecting the nest.

"They are sisters. This one here," he said, pointing to the largest one, "is the queen and the other females are called little queens. The queens always protect the nests." The queen was the blue and silver dragon. Her sister was the blue dragon. I wondered if all the females were blue.

Another crack sounded through the cavern, but this time Sievroth bellowed as he came flying into the cave. He landed as close as he could to the queens. He stretched his neck over them to tap the egg with his snout. He blew a steady stream of fire at the egg, turning the whole thing orange.

"Stop Sievroth, you'll hurt it. It needs to get out on its own," Gavin said. Sievroth shook his head and snorted before continuing to blow more fire at the egg. When Gavin tried to stop him, Sievroth flicked his tail out and hit Gavin, causing him to fly halfway across the cavern and land in a crumpled heap. Richard ran to make sure he was ok.

"Sievroth, what are you doing? Why would you hurt our friend?" I asked. Sievroth shook his head at me again and stopped his flame. He touched his snout to me, and I saw a picture of a baby dragon, stuck in the egg, too weak to crack it open. "He's too weak?" I asked.

Sievroth nodded and went back to heating the egg.

"Abby, come up here. I'm going to need you. Something is wrong with the baby dragon. Sievroth says it's too sick and weak to get out on its own. That's why he is heating it. You will need to try to heal it when it finally gets out."

"I don't know how to heal a dragon, Sally."

"I know, but we have to try. We can't let it die or be drawn into the stupor."

More cracks came from the egg, and Sievroth stopped his flame. He reached for the egg with his claw, slowly tapping one sharp claw against it over and over. The noise echoed through the chamber, making it sound like a hundred eggs were cracking open at once.

Finally, Sievroth's claw pierced the egg. He removed it and started the same process a few inches down. When his claw went through this time, a crack appeared between the two holes. A few more and the baby should be able to push the egg out of the way and get out.

It only took a few more minutes for Sievroth to crack the egg. The shell started to slide away, and the baby's head emerged. It was a beautiful green color. It let out a small mewling noise, and I quickly encouraged it to keep pushing. It needed to get out of the shell. I didn't want to lift it in case I hurt it.

I kept my hands out to stop the egg from tipping over and hurting the baby dragon. Slowly, it maneuvered it's body so it was clinging to the edge of the egg with its claws. It sneezed and lost its grip, tumbling into my arms. It tried to get its wings out, but they were slick with moisture from the egg. Sievroth let out his grumble, and the little dragon trembled, turning its head quickly to look at Sievroth.

"Stop laughing at the baby and help it," I told him. He shook his head, and I heard his voice in my mind.

"She is a little queen. She barely made it out of that egg, She has a lot of will, but she is dying," he said, his voice becoming sad.

"How? What's wrong with her?"

"She shouldn't have hatched yet. She is too small. Something must have happened in the cavern that caused her to hatch. Queens will hatch early if there is a threat to the other queen's lives. We must try to protect the little queen and find out why she hatched." He turned away from us. I could feel his sadness that the little queen was so weak. There was nothing he could do to help her.

"Abby, try to heal her," I said, gently lifting the dragon who was still lying in my arms. She was too weak to move anymore.

Abby scooted closer and laid her hands on the dragon. I shifted the little queen in my lap and grabbed Abby's shoulder, transferring some of my power to her. I watched her shimmering yellow magic flow out of her hands and down into the baby dragon. The colors around the dragon were the same muted colors as the fire elementals. I looked back at the other dragons, concentrating on their colors. They were all muted.

"Is it the stupor doing this to her?" I asked Abby.

"I don't know. I don't know if I can heal her either. She is so weak."

I pushed more power into Abby. I wasn't going to let the little queen die or fall into the stupor. We would save her. I continued feeding Abby magic until I started to get tired.

"Guys, we need you. It's going to take all of our energy to help her." They made their way to me and grabbed each other's hands. Richard placed his hand on my shoulder, increasing my magic. I pushed everything at Abby. The muted color was starting to lift. We gave Abby everything we had as the last of the muted color faded away.

"I think you did it," I said to Abby. "Her colors look much better now."

"We need to let go, but when we do, we are going to be weak. Gavin, you need to get us something to eat."

"There is a smaller cavern up ahead stocked with supplies for the guards. I will go get something right away."

"Let's all lay down before we let go. That way, if we used too much energy and pass out, we won't hit our heads or break anything."

Once we were all settled, I counted to three and let go. I immediately felt woozy, and I heard Abby gasp. I turned my head to look at her. It was hard to move my head that little bit, and I worried about Abby. When I finally saw her, my heart sank, her eyes were closed, and she wasn't moving. I could see her chest rising, so I knew she was breathing, but it looked shallow.

"Everyone ok?" Richard asked quietly.

"Yes," Tider whispered.

"I am," Adam said faintly.

"I'm fine, but Abby passed out," I told them, barely able to get the words out.

Gavin came running back into the cavern and gave us something similar to a granola bar. He had to help me eat I was so weak. I could feel the baby dragon lying across my legs. She wasn't moving either, and I was worried all this had been for nothing. By the time I finished the food, I was already starting to feel better. Gavin helped me into a sitting position, and I looked at the little queen.

She hadn't moved from my lap at all. I reached down to pet her. Her eyes flicked open, and she purred as I pet her scales. The guys were getting up as Gavin handed me another bar. I ate this one on my own. When I finished I scooted back toward Abby and laid my hand on her shoulder.

I poured a small amount of my energy into her. Her breathing deepened, and my friends sighed in relief. Abby would be fine. I gave her a little more but stopped when I started to feel lightheaded again. She needed to sleep now. I did too, but I had to take care of the little queen first. I moved my arms under her, forcing her to stand up. She stumbled on unsteady legs, her wings fluttering around uselessly.

"Come on, little queen." I encouraged her when she tried to sit back down. "You need to move around. We need to get this stuff off the rest of your scales too."

Gavin handed me a towel he brought back when he got the food, and I went to work, rubbing the scales until they sparkled in the firelight. I left her wings alone, not sure if I should try to dry them. They were very thin and fragile looking.

"It's ok," Gavin said. "They are tougher than you think. They need to be cleaned off. Usually, her mother would clean her. She needs her wings to be dry so they can start to work properly."

After drying her wings, she spread them out and took a few steps forward, flapping them. She wasn't able to fly, but it made me laugh watching her try.

After a few more minutes, I laid back down and closed my eyes, telling Gavin I needed to sleep for a while. My friends had fallen asleep while I took care of the little queen.

When I awoke, my friends weren't with me, but I could hear their voices coming from across the cavern. I slowly stood up, noticing the little queen was missing from my lap. I walked toward my friends and found them standing near a large red dragon.

"We can try to heal him, but I don't know if it will work. You saw how much energy it took to heal the little queen," Abby was saying as I moved closer.

"We should at least try. He may be able to tell us what happened." Richard said.

"Why do you want to try to heal this one and not one of the queens?" I asked.

"He is the oldest dragon. If any of them know what is happening, it will be him," Gavin said.

"I say we try it. We need to know what happened to them," I said.

We agreed, and the little queen gave a soft yip. She was standing on the leg of the giant dragon, butting him with her head. She was so tiny compared to him. It amazed me, knowing she would one day grow into a creature so large. I stood next to the dragon and put my hands down for the little queen to climb into. I realized my hand was smaller than the big dragon's paw. If we healed him and he was angry, we could get seriously hurt.

I voiced my concerns to Gavin, but he laughed, saying as long as we had the talismans, the dragons would never hurt us. They could sense the talisman each person carried. I hoped he was right.

"Let's try this," I said.

"Now?" Abby asked.

"Yes. Let's get it over with quickly. I'm sure the brotherhood will be trying to find us, not to mention the Pulhu are still trying to get in. We need to get this figured out and wake the elementals."

Abby laid her hands on the dragon, and we all joined hands. Abby pushed her healing magic into the dragon, and he stirred almost immediately. A growl entered my head, "What are you doing, human?"

"We are trying to help you," I replied.

"Don't. It is too dangerous for you to heal me."

"What happened?"

"Our water has been poisoned. It is in the well."

"How can we help you?"

"We need to drink from the well to wake up, but without the poison in it."

"Do you know what kind of poison or how the poison works?"

"The poison slowly seeped into our bodies, causing us to lose the will to live. Eventually, we fell into this stupor. Do not let your friend give me any more of her healing magic. Use it to save us all. Find a way to stop the poison from getting into the well and bring us the water when you are finished. If you pour it over us, the magic might begin to seep away, bringing us back to our former selves, eventually."

"Where is the well?"

I got a picture in my head. The well was past the caverns and through the center of the mountain. In the picture, I could see a river of lava flowing past the path that we needed to take to get to the well.

"Save the well, and you will save us all," the big dragon said before I felt his presence fade from my mind.

I told Gavin and my friends what happened. Gavin knew where the well was located, but he had never been there before. Only the dragons and true fire elementals went that far into the mountain. It was too dangerous for the human elementals. The heat was too intense. We would need to use Abby's potions.

CHAPTER EIGHTEEN

Abby gave everyone a potion, and we stuffed them into our pockets before moving deeper into the cave. We stopped in the cavern next to the sleeping dragons to grab some food. The little queen started making noises when we left the other dragons, but she calmed down as soon as Sievroth flew ahead of us. She wasn't strong enough to fly, so I held her as we walked.

The cave grew hotter as we moved farther into it. It sloped slightly downward the whole time we walked. We were moving deeper into the ground. Abby and Tider finally called for us to stop so they could take their potions. They couldn't come any further without them.

Once they took them, they were fine. Everyone else was ok, so we continued. A few times, the tunnel split into different caverns, but Gavin didn't know what they were for. We rounded a turn and a wave of heat hit me. It was so hot I struggled to breathe. I stepped back around the corner, taking in deep breaths. Everyone else was gasping except Abby and Tider.

We needed to take our potions. Abby even gave one to Gavin so he could come with us to the well. The potion only took seconds to work. This time when I walked around the corner, I could breathe. It was still hot but not like before. Across the room, lava poured from a hole in the wall and into a pool of molten rock.

"Guys, there is lava over there," Abby said.

"It's not called lava, Abby. It's magma. Technically, it's still in the earth's crust," Tider smirked.

"They are the same thing, Tider. I'm more concerned with how we are supposed to get past it."

"We don't have to get past it," I said. "We need to walk alongside it." Ahead of us, a small trail shot off from the main path. It followed the pool of lava around until it butted into another path.

We walked along the path, single file. There wasn't enough room to walk side by side. We stayed as close to the wall as possible. We may be able to handle the heat, but if the lava hit us, we would get burned. When we switched to the next path, I was able to see the river of lava spread out in front of us. There was a path on either side of it that we could take. I looked at Gavin.

"I don't know which one to take," he said.

"Let's choose, and if it isn't the right side, we will take the other one," Richard said.

"Wait," I said before they could move forward. "Sievroth," I called. He didn't answer, so I called again. Even the little queen started making noises. Sievroth came back and stopped in front of me with his head down to the little queen. I waited until he lifted his head and asked where the well was.

"The little queen has commanded me to tell you. She is growing stronger," he said with pride. "Take the left side and hurry. I can feel the magic in the fire realm weakening. I think your Pulhu friends are doing something to open the portal."

We moved faster down the path until we reached an opening into a large room. I felt something pulling me into the room. I tried to turn away and continue toward the well, but the little queen hopped out of my arms. She managed to glide a decent distance into the room, and I yelled to my friends to wait. I stepped into the room, and the pull intensified.

The little queen was hopping and flapping her way across the room into another cavern. I rushed to catch up with her. She was faster than I expected. I finally grabbed her in the next room, but she flapped her wings so much I couldn't hold on.

"Where are you going, little queen?" I yelled as she moved farther into the room. There wasn't any fire along the walls, so I created a fireball to see what we had stumbled upon. I could see the little queen's scales shimmering in the firelight as she made her way across the room. She was heading for a giant object lying on the ground.

I could barely see it in the darkness. I moved closer, following the little queen's yips. When I was almost to the object, I saw the little queen sit down in front of the object. I moved my fireball closer, trying to see what it was, but the light from the fire was having trouble piercing the shadows around the object.

"What is that?" Abby called from behind me. I was only a foot away now, and I finally recognized it.

I gasped. "It's a dragon."

The others stumbled closer. "It is a dragon," Richard said.

"It's Garuld. No one has seen him in so long that we thought he had died," Gavin said. "He was ancient even when the dragons came to earth."

"What's wrong with him?" I asked.

The little queen flared her wings to get my attention and hopped back and forth, her head swiveling around to look at something on the other side of Garuld. I moved around to the far side as Richard crept around the other side of the old dragon.

Cowering on the ground was a man in a tattered robe. He had a giant needle and a vial in his hand. I lashed out with my power, causing the ground to become mud under his feet. It quickly covered his hands and feet before turning back into hard ground.

He started to whimper, but I told him to be quiet. I reached down and grabbed the vial and the needle that had fallen to the ground.

"What are these?" When he didn't answer, I pulled more power to me, shaping the small amount of moisture from the air into an ice spear. I pointed at the man, and he whimpered more.

"I'll tell you. Don't hurt me," he whined.

"What are you doing to Garuld?" Gavin asked angrily.

"I'm taking his blood, it doesn't hurt him. He is asleep. They all are." He laughed. Something wasn't quite right with this person. He was acting a little crazy. Richard hadn't shown himself yet, and I connected with him to tell him to stay hidden in case we needed a surprise attack on this guy.

"Why are you taking his blood?"

"Because I need it." He laughed again. I pushed my ice spear closer to him. I wouldn't actually hurt him with it, but he didn't know that, and we needed answers. "Ok, ok," he whimpered. "It's to keep them asleep. His ancient blood, combined with a powerful sleeping spell, has caused them all to fall asleep."

"Why would you do that?" I asked, horrified that this person had been doing this to all the dragons.

"They trap us here in the fire realm. They didn't tell us we would be stuck here forever. I left all my family. They all died while I was trapped here."

"I thought all the followers came willingly," I said to Gavin.

"They did. I don't remember this sniveling weasel coming through, and I watched every single person come in. I've never seen him before."

"No lying," I said to the man, thrusting my spear at him. It was only inches from his chest.

"I'm not. I swear. I snuck in with the others. I used an invisibility spell. I wasn't planning on staying here forever. I only wanted to hide out until the shadow king finished destroying all the cities, then I was going to go back."

"Why didn't you leave then?"

"I couldn't. The fire elementals didn't allow anyone to leave. They said it wasn't worth angering the shadow king again, and we would stay in our own realm for a few decades to make sure he was calm. Decades turned into centuries. I was trapped."

I felt bad for him but kept the spear pointed at his chest. Even if he did sneak in and get stuck, he shouldn't have tried to hurt the dragons. "Why didn't you go to them and explain what happened?"

"I didn't want them knowing I snuck in."

"Why not?"

He refused to answer me, and I wasn't willing to threaten him anymore.

"Fine, keep your secret. What's your name?"

"Zacharius."

"I know that name. You can't be. There hasn't been anyone named Zacharius in the realm because the last person named that…"

"Yes," the man said, laughing maniacally. "I am Zacharius."

"You started the fighting between the elementals. You started teaching black magic to followers. Everything that has happened is because of you. That's why we were punished so harshly compared to the other elementals. You were one of ours. Why did you betray us and use dark magic?"

"I wanted more power, of course." He threw his hands up into the air, streaks of fire flowing from them. Before he could use them on us, Richard hit him from behind with air trapping him in place.

"How do we fix the dragons?" I asked him. I couldn't believe I had felt sorry for him a few minutes ago.

"You don't. Only I can, and I never will." He laughed again and didn't stop. Richard finally used his magic to hit him over the head with a rock, and he crumpled to the ground. Richard kept him tied up with air ropes, and Abby made sure he would live. We didn't want to kill anyone. Even this crazy man.

"So this dragon's blood is poisoning the well. If his blood isn't getting into it, then they should all get better, right?"

"That could take years to filter all the dragon blood out. We don't have that kind of time. We need to save them now." I laid my hand on the dragon. He looked different than the others. The poison must affect him differently since his own blood helped create it.

The little queen started flapping and yipping for attention. I moved over to her and picked her up. She was trying to show me something, but I couldn't figure out what until Sievroth appeared in the room.

"She is a bossy little thing, Sally. She is going to make a great queen one day." I heard his voice in my head. "She wants you to take some of her blood and give it to Garuld. She thinks it will wake him since her blood is free of the poison. Fill the needle and inject it into Garuld."

"Little queen, this is not a good idea," I told her, but she yipped at me until I grabbed the needle. "Are you sure?" She nodded and turned so I could access her side. I inserted the needle, and it started to fill with blood. I called Abby over to make sure I didn't take too much. When Abby told me to stop, the needle was halfway full.

I took it over to Garuld with the little queen wrapped up in my other arm and inserted it into his neck. Nothing happened right away, so we sat down to wait. I murmured soothingly to the little queen. I was watching Garuld and saw his colors starting to come back. It was slow at first, but it got faster. Soon his scales gleamed in the firelight.

He moved his head around slowly, still not opening his eyes. "Who is here?" He spoke to all of us in our heads. My friends gasped, they weren't used to dragons speaking directly into their minds. I had gotten used to it with Sievroth, so it didn't surprise me. Gavin introduced us and told Garuld all that had been happening. He moved his neck to come close to the little queen, snuggled up in my arms.

"You did well, little queen. You will be a good ruler when you grow up," we heard him tell her. She yipped at him and nudged his head with her own. "You will need to save the other dragons now."

"We don't know how," I told him.

"It will be a lot of work, but I'm sure you can do it. You must first bring the water from the well to me, we will purify it here to make sure there is no more poison in it. Then you must take it back to the dragons and pour it over them and make them drink some. It will wash away the poison, and they will awaken. "You," he pointed with his head to Abby, "stay here. You can help me make the purifying rocks."

Abby shrugged, and the rest of us left to go get the water. We made it to the well without any trouble and filled the buckets we had taken from the room Garuld was in. I used air to carry them back so they wouldn't spill everywhere. By the time we got back, Abby and Garuld had crafted a large tub made of rock and filled it with pieces of stone and sand. Garuld had us pour the water over it, and it ran down through the stones.

Once we filled the tub, he breathed fire under it, heating the rock to a bright orange color. Before the rock melted, he stopped. The water was bubbling, and he had Abby throw some ingredients from a table along the back wall in.

"There. Now take that to the dragons," he told Richard and Gavin. "You two go get more water," he said to Tider and me.

We did as Garuld told us, and soon Richard and Gavin reported that some of the dragons were starting to wake up. We kept bringing more water, and they kept taking it to the dragons. It took a long time, but finally, Garuld told us to stop.

We grabbed the remaining water and all headed to the cavern to watch the last dragons wake up. When I entered the cavern, a loud rumble swept through, and the two queens stood up, moving toward me.

The little queen started yipping and jumped from my arms, gliding toward the queens. They bumped heads, and all made soothing noises to each other. It was sweet watching the older queens greet the little queen. It didn't take long before all of the dragons were awake. Garuld came out of the chamber behind me and landed in front of the queens, bowing his head.

I couldn't hear their exchange, but they seemed shocked to see him. I was sure he was explaining everything that happened recently. As one, the dragons turned toward us and bowed. I bowed back, unsure what was going on.

"Come humans. We must reach the palace quickly. The portal is almost open, and the fire elementals still sleep. We must wake them before the portal falls, or we are all in grave danger," Garuld said into our minds.

I started walking toward the entrance, but Gavin stopped me. "No. They want us to ride. It will take too long if we walk." I looked at the dragons. Six had moved to the center of the room and kneeled down for us to climb on their backs.

"Do not worry humans, we will not drop you," the queen said into our heads.

We all chose a dragon to ride and climbed on. Richard used magic to lift Zacharius onto the dragon he was riding and held him in place. There was nowhere to grab on their smooth scales, so I lay forward and tried to wrap my arms around the dragon's neck. The queens took off in front of us and flew through the tunnel.

My dragon slowly unfurled his wings and started to beat them, getting a little higher each time. When he was ready, he took off down the tunnel. I let out a yell and closed my eyes, hanging on as hard as I could. I felt the dragon rumble below me and knew he was laughing.

I opened my eyes and looked to my right. Sievroth was flying as close to me as he could, keeping an eye on our progress. As we flew toward the palace, I tried to look around, but we were moving so fast my eyes were tearing up. I used air magic to make a shield for my eyes and carefully wiped them off.

We were flying over the path we had walked to get up to the mountain. Another hole had opened up in the path, and as I was watching, it grew bigger, swallowing an entire tree. I was glad we didn't need to take the path back. Far in the distance, I could make out the jungle we had come through.

Past the jungle, everything started to look hazy. It was too far for me to see. The palace walls came closer and closer until my dragon landed in front of the palace gates. The guards dropped to their knees as the queens moved toward them.

When I slid down my dragon's side, the guards looked up, staring in astonishment. My friends landed next and came to stand with me. Gavin walked up to the guards. "We need to get in to see the elementals," he said.

"Of course, sorry. We just..."

"We haven't seen the dragons in so long," the other guard finished. "You woke them. Can you wake the true elementals?"

"We are going to try," I said.

"Take this guy and put him in the dungeons," Gavin said, handing over Zacharius. "Be careful. He is very powerful. He is the one who put the elementals and the dragons in a stupor."

The guard grabbed him and wove his own threads of fire ropes around Zacharius before taking him into the palace.

We walked to the room with all the true fire elementals, and Garuld came forward, sniffing and nudging them. He turned toward us. "They need to bathe in the hot springs. It will replenish their energy."

"What about the poison?"

"We need to purify the springs and stop any water from coming in until the poison is out of the well. Once we awaken them, they will be able to purify the springs themselves until we are sure the water is safe."

"Where are the hot springs, and how will they get there?"

"They will have to ride us. You can tie them to the rest of the dragons and get them all there in a few trips. You all work on that. I will take Abby with me to get the supplies we need to purify the hot springs," Garuld said into our heads. "We will meet you there."

Abby took off with Garuld, and the rest of us got to work. Gavin called Lily and the other guards that could be spared to help us. They started lifting the true elementals onto the dragon's backs, tying them in place with bands of fire magic. Most of the dragons could take at least three elementals at a time. I climbed onto the dragon I had ridden before, and Richard and Tider joined me. Their dragons were carrying true elementals.

We took off, flying low through the castle and out the gates of the palace. We didn't have to go far. The hot springs were less than an hour walk behind the castle walls. We slid off the dragon, and he took off into the air.

He would go back to the castle to get another group of true elementals. Richard and Tider started bringing the elementals closer to the hot springs. I walked over where Abby and Garuld were waiting. They were adding different ingredients into the hot springs.

"Sally, you will need to create a barrier between the hot springs and the water flowing into them," Garuld said.

"How? As soon as I run out of energy, it will fail. It will take weeks to clean all the water."

"You can attach the barrier to something nearby. It will pull all the energy from that object instead of you. Once the object has no energy left, the spell will end."

"What can I use around here?"

"Those trees over there would work nicely. They will have enough energy for what we need. It only needs to be a thin barrier that holds back all the poisoned water that will be coming from the well."

I nodded and went to work, concentrating on making the barrier. When I had it in place, I looked at Garuld.

"Excellent. Now pretend the magic powering that barrier is connected to you through a rope. Take the rope and move it to those three trees. Wrap it around them and let go."

As soon as the figurative rope was tied around the trees, I felt my energy stop decreasing. The trees looked the same as before. "Will it hurt them?" I asked.

"No, we will be finished with the barrier before the trees die, and one of the true elementals will be able to take it down. Since it is no longer connected to you, anyone with magic can now work with it."

"That is awesome." I thought about how much energy I could save.

"Be careful with this knowledge, Sally. If you decide to do this and your enemies get ahold of one of your spells, they could corrupt it with dark magic. They wouldn't need to be very powerful since you already did the hard work of making the magic. That is why not many humans were ever given this knowledge."

"Thank you for trusting me, Garuld. I will be cautious."

CHAPTER NINETEEN

Working together, we were able to start carrying the true fire elementals into the hot springs. Abby stayed in the water, trying to hold the true elementals up so they wouldn't drown. We started with the king and queen. It didn't take long for them to begin waking up. After a few more minutes in the hot springs, they began to move around.

Garuld brought his face close to them as they opened their eyes. They were startled to see him, and when they looked at Abby holding them up in the hot springs, their expressions turned blank. They both turned back to Garuld. Every few seconds, they nodded, and their bodies seemed to relax. He was telling them what occurred.

Adam and Tider brought more elementals into the hot springs, and I helped place them in positions they would be able to sit in and not fall over. It was a slow process. Even though the hot springs were huge and could hold a lot of elementals, we could only carry so many at once and hold them in the water. We were all exhausted, and there were still a lot to go. After the king and queen were able to get up and leave the hot springs, they started gathering the true elementals to the side as they woke.

Once they told the elementals everything that happened, they sent them over to us to help. It became easier and easier with everyone's help. Eventually, we stopped and sat down off to the side, watching the true elementals help each other. It was sad to see that they had no idea anything had even happened. Many of them kept peeking at us but didn't say anything. There was a small amount of talking as they woke up, but otherwise, it was quiet.

The little queen and Sievroth took a break with us. Sievroth was curled up behind me, and the little queen was on my lap again. I leaned against Sievroth as I pet the little queen. He spoke into my mind a few times, telling me the fire elementals were being quiet while they processed what happened. Many would have trouble believing it until they saw all the changes in their realm. It was a lot to take in.

I tried not to worry. The true fire elementals didn't seem mean or even rude. They all looked stunned. When they were all awake, the king and queen walked up to our group. I went to stand up, but the queen told me to stay seated.

"We know you are tired," she said. "We want to thank you for saving us and for trying to save our entire realm. We are still waking up from this awful nightmare, and we aren't sure how to react. I apologize if we have ignored you. We have been getting an account of everything that has transpired since we fell asleep from Sievroth and Gavin. A lot is going on right now from what I understand."

"Yes, your majesty," I said, unsure what title she wanted me to use.

"You can call me Fiara. We don't use titles between friends. It's so hard to remember what happened. I remember being worried about the dragons, and then I was so tired. It was hard to worry about anything. I got into bed one day and never got back out. Thank you again for saving us. Gavin said his men tried everything, but they couldn't figure out what was wrong, so they took care of us the best that they could."

"I'm sorry. I know this is a lot to take in, but we have bigger problems coming. I doubt we have long until the Pulhu are here. They have a weapon they can use against you to force you to do what they want. You will be caught in another war and blamed for it again if the Pulhu control you."

"Yes, Garuld and Gavin told me about them. I can feel them working at the portal. They will break in soon." She turned to everyone and raised her voice. "We all need to go protect our land from them," she said. The true fire elementals looked worried, and some still looked confused.

"Can you stop them from opening the portal?" I asked.

"We have to close the portal for good. It is the only way to ensure they can't get in."

"What about us?" Abby cried. "We need to get back home."

"Don't worry, the dragons will take you to another portal that you can use to get home. There are many different portals into our realm, but most are heavily guarded by the creatures that live here."

"Where will we show up in the human realm?"

"The dragon's portal is in the air above their home. It will take you out in the air above the Nebrodi mountains. The dragons will fly you as far down the mountain as they can. You will be far from the Pulhu. Sievroth says you can call someone to come and get you once you are in the human realm."

"Yes, we can. Thank you. How do we seal the portal?" I asked. I wanted to make sure it was sealed before we left the fire realm.

"Let's head to the castle. I have supplies there that will help. It is difficult to seal a portal and even harder to create one, but if my crystal is still charged with energy, we will be able to do it."

We started heading back to the castle with the true fire elementals. The little queen hopped out of my arms and glided over to the dragon queens. She would stay with them until they were ready to head to the portal. After an hour, we made it to the castle only to stop short. Around a hundred men were standing in front of the gates, magic swirling around their hands. I recognized the two men from the brotherhood.

The king and queen went to move forward, but I stopped them. "They have been without you for a long time. A man named Zacharius filled their heads with doubt and fear that the shadow king was punishing you, and if you awoke, they would all be killed. Let me talk to them."

I strode forward with my hands up, showing them I wasn't there to fight.

"You," sputtered the old man. "You did this to us. We will all die because of you."

"No one is going to die," I told him. "You have all been tricked and lied to. You think the shadow king caused all the true elementals to fall into a stupor along with the dragons, but that is not true. Instead, one of your own has been doing it, poisoning the true elementals and the dragons, and using you to keep anyone from helping them."

"You lie," someone shouted.

"Really? Guards, get the prisoner and blindfold him so he doesn't know who he is talking to," I shouted. The guards rushed inside the castle, and we waited for them to return. Whispers ran through the brotherhood. They weren't sure who to believe yet. Most of them were good people that had been fooled into thinking their friends were the enemy.

The guards brought Zacharius through the gates. "Unbind me you fools, I have things to do," he screeched.

"Zacharius, it's me, Sally."

"I already told you everything I'm going to say," he giggled. "You can't stop it. By the time the poison wears off, the Pulhu will be through the portal, and the true elementals will be theirs to control. I will finally be free to leave this cursed place. I'm sure the Pulhu would love to have me on their side."

"Why did you poison them all?" I asked. "Did the shadow king tell you to?"

He started laughing again. "The shadow king doesn't care what we do. He probably forgot about us long ago. I did this for revenge." His laughter became even higher-pitched, and I winced.

"Take him back to the dungeons," Fiara told the guards.

"Wait, who said that?" Zacharius asked. "That sounded like, no, you couldn't have. Was that the true elemental queen?" Fiara nodded to the guard, who took the blindfold off. He stared in horror at everyone watching him. "No, it can't be. You saved them. Why?" He screamed as the guard dragged him away. "They should all die," he yelled as he was dragged through the castle.

"Now, do you believe me?" I asked the brotherhood. "You were all tricked. That man's name is Zacharius, and I think you all knew him as the one who started the wars long ago between elementals." They gasped and looked to the two older men, their leaders.

"We didn't know. We thought we were protecting the realm," the older man said to Fiara.

"It's ok. You were doing what you thought was right to save your families. Next time come to us. We would never let anything happen to all of you. We have always protected you, and we always will. It must have been hard to have faith in us when we were in a stupor for so long. You are forgiven, but now we have a new enemy to defeat. These Pulhu are as bad as Zacharius. We must keep them out of the fire realm."

A roar filled the sky as the dragons flew above us. Their heads tipped back, and they let another ferocious cry out. They landed as close as they could to the elementals, shaking their heads and flapping their wings. Something had them all worked up.

"There is no more time," Fiara said. "We must seal the portal now. They are almost through. They will break through by the end of the day. Everyone, let's go. Three people per dragon. We need to hurry." I looked at the dragons. There weren't enough dragons to carry everyone. At least fifty people would be left behind.

"Those of you who don't have a dragon, start fortifying the castle. We may have wounded when we return, and if they break through, the townspeople will head to the castle and its protections," Fiara said. "Sally, come with me. We will need to talk about how to close the portal. I will need your help. Many of us are still too weak to attempt using the required magic necessary for closing a portal."

I followed Fiara into the castle. Garuld was standing at the gate, waiting for us. Abby, Tider, Richard, and Adam headed out to the portal and would wait for me there.

The queen ran through the castle, and I had a hard time keeping up. When she ran into the main room where all the cots were set up, she stopped. "This is where we all were?"

"Yes. They put you all together so they could take care of you easier."

She moved through the room slowly until she came to the largest bed. "My king was laid here with me. Even in sleep, we were still together." She stared at the bed for another minute before moving through the room and farther into the castle.

We came to a room I hadn't been in before. It looked like the ingredients room back at the school, but bigger. There were jars of ingredients everywhere. Some of the jars stood as tall as my knee. I moved closer to one of the jars as Fiara ran down the aisles. Bollywort was written on the label. I had never heard of it. I reached out to pick it off the shelf and see what it looked like, but Fiara came around the corner.

"Don't touch that. It would kill you in seconds if you opened it up."

I quickly stepped back and walked over to the door. I didn't want to accidentally knock something over and kill us both. Fiara rushed up and down the aisles, searching for different ingredients. When she passed me, she added vials to my hands, telling me to hold them.

"Let's go," she told me, running back into the hallway. Garuld was waiting for us, and we climbed onto his back. He jumped into the air using his wings to lift us off of the ground with one stroke. He turned, aiming for the portal and flew forward. He glided through the sky, his wings beating quickly to get us there as fast as possible. I could see the other dragons far in the distance. We were gaining on them, but they would make it to the portal before us.

I felt a shift in the air as we got closer. I couldn't see the other dragons anymore. They already landed. The shift in the air came again.

"What is that?" I yelled to Fiara.

"That is the portal opening." Garuld put on a burst of speed. I could see the true elementals standing in front of the portal and the dragons behind them. A swarm of the weird purple birds flew out of the jungle behind us. They were headed right for the portal too.

Garuld managed to move even faster, and we landed as the portal shimmered and opened, revealing the Pulhu. I could see through the portal to the clearing beyond it. Row after row of Pulhu were lined up, ready to storm into the fire realm.

The ones in the front had something in their hands, and I heard someone yell, "Now." They each threw the object in their hand through the portal.

"Shields," I yelled, throwing one up in front of as many of the fire elementals as possible. I saw the objects bounce off the shields and start spewing gray smoke.

"They are smoke bombs. Richard, help clear the air before they get in. We raised our arms and blew the smoke up and away from the portal. The Pulhu were starting to stream through. The dragons let out roars, and the Pulhu stopped, staring at the dragons before being pushed forward by those waiting in the back.

"Sally, come here," Fiara said, dragging me to the side of the portal and away from the battle.

"What are we doing? We need to stop them."

"We need to close the portal first, or they will keep coming in. Didn't you see how many there were? If they all get in and they have a weapon that can hurt us like you said, we won't be able to win."

"Ok, let's close this. How?"

Fiara grabbed all the ingredients we had thrown into the sack she carried and laid them out. I kept an eye on the battle, making sure my friends were ok. They were all in the front except Abby. I couldn't see her anywhere. I connected to her mind, and she told me she was near the back, healing people as they were hurt.

I turned my attention back to Richard. He was using air to keep the Pulhu from rushing through the portal, but he was weakening, and enough were getting through to cause havoc among the fire elementals. The Pulhu seemed to be immune to the fire elementals attacks, and I realized they must have created a potion that could stop the flames before they burned them.

Tider was using icicles to stop the Pulhu that got past Richard, and Adam was using fire with no success. He switched to hitting the Pulhu with his fists when they got too close. The other elementals were all engaging the Pulhu too.

The dragons reared up and started flying around the clearing as the purple birds tried to attack them. The birds flew around the dragons, ripping at their wings with their sharp little beaks. It wasn't likely that they would mortally wound the dragons, but they were keeping them occupied so they couldn't help with the ground attack.

I watched as Garuld breathed fire, and one of the birds fell to the ground. Others immediately took its place, and Garuld flew higher into the air, trying to get away from the little birds. They were fast and so small they could maneuver around Garuld easily. He managed to hit another one with his tail. The rest of the dragons were doing the same thing. I watched birds falling to the ground, but more were coming. They were still flying in from the jungle.

A shout from the portal caused me to look back at it. Tider created a weapon of ice to attack the Pulhu, but there were too many coming through. Without the true fire elementals being able to do any damage to the Pulhu, they were quickly being overrun.

"Sally, I'm ready," Fiara said. "I need you to use your fire magic to help me close the portal. I will say the spell and release the power, but you must channel your magic into me."

I looked at her, surprised. I hadn't told her I could share my magic.

"It's something only a few elementals can do. I know you can do it. I can sense it. Now hurry."

I grabbed her hand, and she started speaking in ancient. I felt her power moving toward the portal and channeled my magic into her. Her magic swirled around the portal and through it. I concentrated and watched as the orange magic took on a darker hue. She continued funneling magic into the portal, almost yelling the ancient words.

"Stop them," I heard someone yell. I saw the Pulhu turn toward us, and I started to put up a shield, but Fiara stopped me.

"We can't. We need all of your power and mine. Protect us," Fiara yelled, and the elementals moved to stop the Pulhu. They knew they wouldn't be effective against them, but they stood in the way for their queen anyway. They would try to buy us as much time as they could. Richard, Tider, and Adam shifted toward us too. Everyone was trying to protect us from the Pulhu. The Pulhu knew we were trying to seal the portal and fought even harder.

"Get Mr. Mitchel in here before it seals," one of the Pulhu yelled. My skin went cold. We couldn't let him get in. If he did, he would destroy us all. He could suck our magic out of us, and we wouldn't be able to seal the portal.

"Hurry," I yelled to Fiara, "We need to seal it now." She felt my terror and shoved more power at the portal. I gathered all the magic I had left and sent it into her making her knees buckle.

"Too much," she said.

Instead of pulling my power back, I traced the path her magic was taking and pushed mine along the same path, entwining our magic together as it reached the portal. As I forced the last of my magic into the portal, a large crack echoed across the area, and the portal slammed shut. We could still see out of it, but the Pulhu on the outside couldn't get in or see through it. We watched as they beat their fists against it.

With the portal closed, the birds stopped their attack on the dragons and flew back toward the jungle. Somehow they were being controlled when the portal was open. With the dragons no longer distracted, it didn't take long to stop the rest of the Pulhu.

While the last of the Pulhu were being tied up, I walked over to the portal. It was slowly fading.

"We will no longer be able to see out into the world from here once the portal is completely closed," Fiara said.

We watched as the Pulhu moved away from the portal. Mr. Mitchel walked up to it and placed his hand on the rock. Dark magic swirled around his hand, and I flinched when it touched the portal. Mr. Mitchel's face was a mask of rage as he slammed his fist into the portal over and over again.

When he looked up, I would have sworn he was able to see me. His eyes turned black for a minute before he regained control. He turned and strode away from the portal. We watched for a few more minutes as the Pulhu in the clearing started to gather their things and leave. As the portal disappeared completely, I breathed a sigh of relief. Now they wouldn't be able to get to the fire elementals.

CHAPTER TWENTY

I was helping the wounded when Fiara called me away. "Something is wrong at the town," she said. A woman was standing next to her, panting. "This is Alicia. She ran here, taking the shortcuts, to get to us in time. It was a perilous journey, and she could have died. Someone else is trying to poison us, except this time it is making the human fire elementals sick too. Everyone in the town is sick. We need to get there immediately and find out what happened."

I rode on Garuld again with Fiara. We grabbed Abby too. Adam, Tider, and Richard would stay and help with the wounded. They would meet us at the town later. We left the little queen and Sievroth behind, asking Gavin to keep an eye on the little queen. The dragon queens were keeping an eye on her too, but she still couldn't fly and needed to be carried around. She really was too small to have hatched. I was worried she would get hurt if someone wasn't with her.

I was going to need my friends if we had to do any more magic. I was tapped out after helping close the portal. I would love to sleep for an entire day, but we had to help the townspeople. They had been kind to us, and I didn't want to see any of them hurt.

I tried to think of what could be wrong while we flew to the town. Maybe some of the Pulhu had gotten through, but that didn't make sense. They wouldn't have made it to the town yet unless they had powerful air magic. They could have flown to the town then, but I hadn't seen anyone flying away from the battle. I would have to wait until we got there to find out what happened.

As we landed, Tristan came running out. "My queen, we need you. Something has struck the townspeople. It is a poison, I think. So many are sick already. We can't stop it."

"Tell me about the symptoms," Fiara said.

"The symptoms are slightly different for everyone. They all have a fever, but some have stomach pains, while others have headaches. Some even have full body aches. None can stand after the fever shows up. They are too weak to take care of themselves. We have set up a sick area so we can care for them easily."

"Could it be the same poison Zacharius used on you, but without the dragon blood? They are all too tired to get up, similar to how you all fell into a stupor," I asked Fiara.

"The poison could have been altered to make human elementals sick too, I suppose. I'm not sure that's it though. We never got ill, we only grew more tired each day, not even realizing something was happening. These people are very sick and could die if we can't heal them. I think it must be something else. Zacharius is in jail, so he can't be the one behind it.

"Maybe we missed something. He could have a helper," Abby said.

"That would make sense. He probably needed help all these years to keep the well poisoned. We should have thought of that," Richard said.

"How will we find this person?" I asked.

"I think we need to worry about healing all these people first," Abby said

"Abby's right. Let's go see the sick townspeople first." I created a bubble of air around everyone's head to be safe. I didn't know if whatever sickness this was could be passed on to us by breathing it in.

Abby nodded her thanks, and so did the others as we walked to the center of the town. Tristan led us to the sick area, and I stopped short when we came across it. So many of the townspeople were lying on blankets on the ground. Others ran between them carrying buckets of water to try to cool the fevers.

I walked through the aisles while Fiara talked to the healers. A young girl was lying on the cot crying as I walked up to it. I sat next to her and brushed the hair out of her face.

"Hi," I said. "Are you sick?"

"No, but my mommy is. Are you here to fix her?"

"I don't know what's wrong yet," I told her. "I am going to try to find out what caused everyone to get sick. Maybe you can help me. When did your mommy get sick?"

"After breakfast. She said her tummy didn't feel well, and she thought she would lay down for a while. She fell over before she made it to the bed, and I had to run out to the field to get my dad. He brought her to the healers."

"Did he get sick too?"

"No. He is helping check the town for anyone else who is sick that may need the healers. He told me to stay here."

"What did your mom do this morning? Anything different than usual?"

"No. She got me up and started doing chores. I had to do chores too.

She made me help dry the dishes," the girl pouted. "I didn't have to do them all though because someone dropped off fresh milk at the door, and I got to go get it while my mom finished washing the dishes. Mom was surprised because milk usually comes tomorrow. Mr. Sunn must have gotten his days mixed up, Mommy said."

"Wait, did your mom drink the milk?"

"Yes, she likes to put some in her coffee."

"What about you? Did you drink any?"

"Yes, I finished the milk from the other bottle. Mommy got the new milk. Do you think the milk made her sick? Mr. Sunn wouldn't give out bad milk. He loves to make milk for everyone."

"I don't know yet. I'm going to go talk to Fiara about this and see what other people remember."

I walked back over to Fiara and told her what the little girl said. The healers quickly talked to everyone capable of answering questions. Each one had received milk that morning and drank some. Fiara sent someone to go find Mr. Sunn.

While we waited, I walked back to the little girl and told her the milk may have made her mommy sick. Fiara came with me and sat next to her. She picked the girl up and held her on her lap while the girl sniffled.

"You are the queen, right?" the little girl asked.

"Yes, I am."

"Then you will help save my mommy, right?"

"Yes. We are going to try to save her. Can you tell me anything else about this morning when you went to get the milk off the front porch?" asked Fiara gently.

"No. I grabbed the bottle and went back inside."

"You didn't see anyone on the road?"

"Only the man delivering the milk."

"Mr. Sunn didn't deliver it?"

"No. Sometimes Mr. Sunn has someone help him when he is really busy."

"Do you remember what the man looked like?" I asked.

"Yeah. It was the guy that works in the woodshop for Mr. Guther. He's mean. He never waves at me when I walk by the shop. Mr. Guther always waves at me, and sometimes he even gives me a lollipop."

"What's the mean man's name?"

"I don't know. I call him the mean man."

"Thank you, little one," Fiara said, giving her another hug before placing her back on the cot. "We are going to talk to Mr. Sunn and find this man. We will see if he can tell us anything about the milk. Ok?"

The little girl nodded, and we walked back to the front of the room. Mr. Sunn was waiting for us and bowed when he saw Fiara. She told him what happened and asked why he sent milk out early. He told us he didn't know what she was talking about and that he didn't make any deliveries. Someone stole almost all of the bottles of milk stored in his barn during the night.

I asked if he hired the mean man that the little girl had told us about.

"I would never hire him. He is as mean as they come. He never talks to anyone and glares at everyone that comes near him. Mr. Guther is the only one he'll talk to, and he barely does that, but Mr. Guther says he is a good worker."

"We need to find him," I said. He had to be the one who poisoned the milk. One of the healers overheard us talking and told us where the man lived. It was on the outskirts of the town. He kept fences up around it to keep everyone out, so it would be easy to find. We thanked them and left, hurrying through the town.

As we neared the house, I crinkled my nose in disgust. An awful smell was coming from the side of the house, and a weird cloud of magic clung to the property. Fiara went to open the fence, but I stopped her.

"Something is wrong here. Can't you feel the dark magic?"

I walked around the side of the house, looking for any signs of a trap. I heard a noise near the back of the house and stopped, crouching down behind the bushes. Fiara crouched down too. We snuck further along the fence line until we could see the back of the house. The back door stood open, and so did the fence. A man was running toward the jungle with a bag slung over his shoulder. The magic from the house trailed after him.

"Fiara, that's him. We need to stop him."

We took off after the man. We wouldn't be able to catch him on foot. I used a burst of air to propel us forward, lifting us off the ground and setting us down twenty feet away. The man was almost to the jungle. I knew if he made it, we would never find him. Before I had a chance to use my magic again, Garuld fell out of the sky, diving for the man.

The man screamed and ran faster, trying to reach the safety of the jungle. He wasn't fast enough, and Garuld landed between him and the trees, cutting off his escape. Garuld's tail lashed out, hitting the man in the chest. He flew backward, landing on his back. He raised his hands to shoot magic at Garuld, but we ran up to him. I used ropes of air to tie his hands to his side and stop him from hurting Garuld. He struggled against the magic but couldn't escape. When Fiara stepped into view, the man cowered.

"What did you do to the townspeople?" she demanded.

"What needed to be done. They are standing in our way."

"Whose way and how?"

"They wanted to wake you all up. You can't be awake. The shadow king is going to kill us all."

"The shadow king isn't the one poisoning us, you are. And Zacharius. Did he tell you this?"

"The shadow king told him to make you sleep. He had to do what he was told. The shadow king is mad at you for protecting humans."

"The shadow king knew we were protecting you, fool. Do you think he is stupid? He knows everything we do. As long as you were all under our protection in the fire realm and didn't interact with regular humans, he wouldn't hurt any of us. Zacharius lied to you, and you fell for it."

"No, Zacharius wouldn't lie to me. He has taken care of me since the beginning. He is the one who told me to come into this realm, so I wouldn't be killed. He only wants to protect us all."

There was no way we would get through to this man. He really thought Zacharius was trying to help them. Fiara realized the same thing and changed her questioning.

"How did you poison the townspeople?"

"I can't tell you," he said.

"You will tell me," Fiara said, raising her hands. The man stared at her but refused to talk.

"If you don't tell her, I will send Garuld after Zacharius. You know we captured him, right?" I asked.

His eyes got big, and I could see his fear for the man he thought was his friend. I didn't like using his feelings against him, but we needed to save the people. I could feel bad later.

"Garuld," the queen raised her voice. The large dragon padded over to her, dropping his head so he could look at the man. "Go get Zacharius. Don't hurt him too bad carrying him here."

Garuld lifted one of his feet, clicking his claws together. They were only inches from the man's face. I saw him gulp.

"Fine, I'll tell you," he said as Garuld turned away, getting ready to take off. Garuld's head turned back to look at the queen.

"Wait. Let's see what he has to say." Garuld stepped back and lowered his wings.

"We made the poison as a failsafe in case the townspeople found out what was happening and tried to stop us. Zacharius used the bokal berry to create the poison. There is nothing you can do for them." He seemed pleased as he said this.

Garuld roared, and Fiara shook her head. "No, he couldn't." Garuld bumped Fiara's head as she stared at nothing. I saw a tear fall down her face.

"What's wrong? We know what the poison is made from. Let's go make the antidote."

"There isn't one," Fiara said sadly. "That is the most poisonous berry in the fire realm. Touching it causes sickness and occasionally death, but to ingest any part of it is fatal. There is no way to save them."

She turned to the man on the ground. "How could you be so hateful. You killed mothers, fathers, and even children. Whole families are dying because of you. They never hurt you. Why would you do this to them."

The man cowered again. "We did it to save everyone."

"No, you did it because you are a fool, and you believed a man who caused us to be sent to our own realms in the first place."

The man looked shocked when Fiara said this. I told him exactly who Zacharius was, but he refused to believe me, shaking his head and muttering no over and over. I felt bad for him until I remember the little girl asking me to save her mom.

"Garuld, please take him to the dungeons. We must go back to the town and tell them what has happened and that there is no hope of making a cure. The families will want to spend as much time together as possible before the end."

Garuld roared and grabbed the man with his front claws, jumping skyward and taking off toward the palace. I walked back to the town center with Fiara. She didn't talk, and I saw tears streaming down her face as we walked through the town. People stopped to watch her, and she called for them to follow her. In the center of the town, she turned to face everyone.

"I have bad news," her voice cracked, and she took a deep breath. "The milk everyone drank this morning was poisoned with the bokal berry." A gasp swept through the crowd. Many of the townspeople started to weep.

"Is there nothing you can do?" someone asked.

"No, you all know there is no antidote, and our magic can't heal them from this. The person responsible has been taken to the dungeons, and we will deal with him."

No one said anything else. I listened to the cries of the townspeople and felt my own heart break. Abby walked up to me and put her arm around my shoulders, trying to comfort me. She had tears in her eyes too.

"We can't let all these people die," I told her.

"There's nothing we can do to stop it. You heard Fiara. There is no antidote."

"There may not be an antidote, but we may be able to do something to save these people. I am supposed to have power over life and death. Isn't that what we read in one of the books on void?"

"Sally, no. It could destroy you. You still don't know enough about void magic. What if you are consumed by the darkness?"

"If the darkness takes me over, you will have to destroy me. I have no choice. I refuse to let these people die when there is a chance I can help them."

Fiara was listening to us, so were a few people in the front row of the crowd. I looked into their hopeful faces. People began to whisper and stop crying, waiting for me to say more.

"Bring all the sick people to the town center. I am going to try and save them. It might not work, but at least we can give them one more chance. Hurry. Check every building to make sure. You have one hour."

By the time all the houses were checked, Richard, Tider, and Adam were back in the town with us. So were all the other fighters. I told them what I had planned. The guys argued with me, but I wouldn't back down. I had to try. Once I was ready, I stood in front of all the sick people and raised my hands. I closed my eyes to concentrate and called on void.

The golden colors of void surrounded me, making me feel light and carefree. I let the magic spread out around me, keeping any dark threads of void from weaving their way into my magic. It didn't stop the dark magic from trying. It hovered close to the golden magic, wanting to get out and take over.

I felt the darkness trying to force its way into my mind. I could almost hear its whisper, begging me to use it, promising me it could help heal the people. The cost of the dark magic was too high though, and I ignored it, focusing on only the golden magic.

I was very careful to make sure the magic didn't get out of control. When I felt like the magic would burst out of me, I threw my hands up and asked it to heal all the people in the town. The golden magic swept through the town square, covering every living thing in a shower of love.

All the townspeople smiled as void magic touched their skin. I watched as it worked its way through the sick and injured. The magic flowed down into them before shooting back out, eradicating every piece of poison. When the magic finally came back to me, I was shaking. I hadn't noticed Richard put his arm around me, or my other friends come over and link hands, adding their power to mine.

I smiled as the magic left me with a calm, happy feeling. My knees buckled, and Richard and Adam lifted me. They helped slowly lower me to the ground, not breaking contact with me. Abby told Fiara what was going to happen when we let go of each other, and she called all the healers to come help us. Adam counted down, and on three, they let go of me. Immediately, I felt the loss of their energy, and my eyes slammed closed.

CHAPTER TWENTY-ONE

Everyone was still in the town center when I opened my eyes. "You were only out for a minute," the healer told me. "We gave you a small dose of energy to help you wake up." She held up a small vial. It was the same potion I used when I first came to the fire realm. I tried to tell her that I wasn't supposed to take any more of it.

"You will be fine, don't worry. I am the master healer here, and I made sure you would be able to handle it before giving it to you. As you can tell, you are still exhausted. You barely had a sip. Now come on, let's get you up. The people want to see their savior."

She helped me stand up. Fiara came to stand by my side. "Thank you for saving them, Sally. They would have died without you."

She turned to the people. "Sally is awake. She will be fine." Everyone cheered and celebrated. I was glad they were all so happy. Fiara helped me walk forward until a tug on my shirt stopped me. The little girl who had given us information stood next to me.

"Thank you," she said. "You saved my mommy." I looked at the woman standing near the little girl. She smiled at me and nodded her thanks. I smiled too. I really had saved these people. They were already up and moving around as if they had never been sick in the first place. The little girl gave me a hug and then ran back to her mom.

Tristan stepped in front of me, stopping me from following Fiara.

"Thank you for what you did," he said. "I know how hard it was to use that magic. You must try not to use it again. If the dark magic seeps into you, it will eventually consume you. It can take years for it to happen."

"How do you know this? How do you know about the dark and light magic?"

"I knew someone once who had void. She was a beautiful woman until the darkness got ahold of her. She told me all about void magic."

"Can you tell me?" I asked. "I barely have any clue what to do with void magic. There are only a handful of books that I have been able to read about it."

"Void users were very secretive and didn't write much down. They feared others would find the books and find a way to access void, plunging the world into darkness. Very few were able to control void. Those that could stayed away from most of the elementals. They thought it was safer that way."

"Was it?" I asked.

"No one really knows, but the woman I told you about didn't think so. She thought void users should tell the other elementals more about their power. Maybe if they understood exactly how dangerous void could be, they wouldn't want as much magic."

"So dark magic came from void users?"

"Dark magic can be used by any elemental, but yes, the first dark magic was taught to elementals by a void user. Thankfully they were stopped long before they became too powerful, but others followed in their path. Eventually, enough books on dark magic were written that any elemental trying to amass a lot of power could learn how to do dark magic, like Zacharius."

"Does every void user eventually get consumed by the darkness?"

"No, but most of them do. Usually, they realize what is happening, and many take their own lives. Some give in to the darkness and become dark magic users. Not all are equal in power though. Many void users are weak in void magic. It's a good thing, or no one would be able to stop them. You, on the other hand, are incredibly strong. You may be able to harness your void magic and never give in to the darkness."

"Do you really think I will be able to?"

"Maybe. If you continue to make the right choices. You will have to embrace your void magic at some point if you want to defeat what is coming for us. It might be too much for you. Only time will tell. Don't use it unless you have to. That's your best chance of not being corrupted."

"Do you know what is coming for us?"

"I know its name is Helerium but what that means I still haven't figured out. That is all I can tell you about void. I wish you safe travels, Sally," Tristan gave me a small bow and walked away. I wanted to chase after him and ask him more questions, but I knew that was all he could answer for me. I was happy to have gotten some more information on void.

Gavin stopped me next. It was getting hard to stand up, but I tried to pretend I wasn't exhausted. He thanked me for helping his people and gave me a quick hug. I told him how much we appreciated his help and that I hoped to see him again someday. He moved away to say goodbye to my other friends as I started walking.

I continued forward until we reached Garuld. Fiara helped me get on his back, and she climbed up behind me. My friends were already on other dragons. When I asked Fiara where we were going, she told me she was taking me to the castle to rest. That sounded fine with me. I waved and smiled to the people in the town as Garuld flew into the sky. As he wheeled around toward the castle, I felt a small disturbance coming from that area.

It was gone so fast I thought it must be my magic adjusting to using such a large amount of void. When we dismounted and headed into the castle, I thought I felt something off again, but when I tried to figure out what, the feeling disappeared. I let Fiara lead me to a room and fell into the bed. She laughed and slipped my shoes off. Pulling the covers over me, she told me she would send someone to wake me for dinner in a few hours.

It didn't feel like any time had passed when someone was shaking me awake. I opened my eyes to see Abby above me. She looked frantic.

"I can't find Adam."

"Did you ask Richard?" I asked groggily.

"Of course, I did. He can't find him either, and Tider hasn't seen him since they went to their rooms."

The panic in Abby's voice made me wake up. I reached out with my mind, looking for Adam. His mind was easy to find. I had been in it enough times to know exactly what it felt like, but it was far away. I could barely hear him when I connected our minds.

"Where are you?"

"Help, Sally. Zacharius escaped. He took me with him. I felt like something was wrong in the castle, and I went to investigate it. It was a trap, and Zacharius was able to overpower me. He is taking me to some secret house of his past the mountain. I think he is going to try to control me so I turn on you guys."

"Calm down, Adam. We are coming for you. I won't let him hurt you. Buy us some time. I'm going to get every one right now. Stay connected to me so you know what I'm doing, and I can track you. You feel far away. How did he get so far away this quickly?"

"Sally, I've been with him all night. He hasn't stopped to rest at all."

"All night?" I turned to Abby. "How long have I been asleep. I thought Fiara was going to wake me for dinner."

"We tried, but you didn't want to wake up. Finally, we decided to let you sleep until morning. Adam was with us at dinner, but I couldn't find him this morning. He was supposed to meet me before breakfast."

"We need to go," I said. We would need a dragon to make it to Adam's location before Zacharius did something to him.

I had been slipping my shoes on as I talked to Adam and Abby. I ran into the hallway, Abby following. I called out to Sievroth with my mind, screaming his name. I heard echoing roars all along the outside of the castle. I ran through the gates and directly into the dragons. Sievroth flew up to me and head-butted me, trying to calm me down.

After I assured her I wasn't hurt, we walked out of the forest and climbed back onto our waiting dragons. They dropped us in front of the castle. Fiara brought us to the main room.

"I think we are finally free of the evil Zacharius brought into our realm, thanks to you all. As the queen of the fire elementals, I want to give you something for all the help you have given us."

She stepped in front of us and looked us each in the eye. I wanted to tell her she didn't have to give us anything, but her look kept me silent.

"I can strengthen your magic. You will also have more energy," Fiara said. "Sally, we will fight with you when you are ready. All you have to do is call for me." She raised her arms and let her magic surround each of us. Her magic was a light orange glow. I felt my own magic reaching out for it. When they combined, I felt my energy level increase.

I heard Abby gasp and looked over. Her face was flushed, but she was smiling. She saw me watching her and laughed. "I feel so much stronger. I think I can even help in some of the fights now," she said.

"Abby, it's good you want to help your friends, but your healing power is your most important gift. Try to use offensive magic only when you have no choice. The more time you put into your healing, the stronger it will become," Fiara said.

"I will, Fiara," she said. She was still smiling, and I knew she was going to try to fight with us next time something happened. I would have to keep an eye on her to make sure she didn't get hurt. Tider was watching her, too, and nodded. He was thinking the same thing. We all thanked Fiara and talked for a few more minutes before saying our goodbyes.

Garuld was waiting for us. He was the only dragon big enough to carry all of us through the portal. Before I climbed up on him, Sievroth flew up to me and nudged me with his head. I put my arms around his neck, giving him a big hug. He was growing so fast now that we were in the fire realm. I couldn't imagine how he was going to stay with me.

"Sally," I heard his voice in my head. "I'm not going back with you. I am staying with my family, but I will be there when you call. Your little water sprite can get in contact with me if you need me." I felt my eyes well up as I gave him another big hug.

"I will miss you, but I'm glad you are with your family. Be safe." He flew back over to the other dragons. I heard a little yip coming from behind me. Fiara walked over, holding the little queen. I held her and gave her a few hugs before handing her back to Fiara. I climbed up on Garuld. As he took off, the dragons below us roared, and the fire elementals watching cheered. I waved to them as we circled higher and higher.

Garuld flew toward the mountain, gaining height the entire away. The air was thinner, the higher we got, and no one talked. We had to concentrate on breathing.

"Hang on," Garuld told us, and we grabbed his scales as hard as we could. He shot forward. At the top of the mountain, I saw a shimmer in the sky. We were headed directly for it. He flew through the shimmer, and I felt a tightness around my chest. It only lasted a second before it was gone, and we emerged over a different mountain. It was night time in the human realm, so Garuld flew further down the mountain, skimming the tops of the trees.

When he came to a clearing about halfway down the mountain, he landed, and we got off.

"Thank you, Garuld."

"It was my pleasure. Thank you for saving us. Be careful. We need you to save the world from the darkness." I grimaced. I still wasn't one hundred percent sure I was the right person to fight the darkness. I thought of the south wing and the paper we had found. *Be careful of the imposter. That could be me.*

I shook the thought away and focused on Garuld. I said goodbye to him, and he leaped into the sky, flying back up the mountain and to the portal to take him home.

CHAPTER TWENTY-TWO

After Garuld left, I fished my cell phone out of my pocket and pulled up my GPS. We were in the middle of nowhere. I sent a text to Mrs. Sullivan and Jordan. They both said not delivered. I looked at my phone again. I didn't have any service.

We started to hike down the mountain. Garuld hadn't been able to take us all the way down the mountain because people would have seen him. It's hard to hide a dragon, even in the dark. Their wings still create a giant breeze that moves the trees and bushes.

It wasn't worth the risk. We would find our way down, and Jordan would come to get us. We made a small camp and tried to get some rest until morning. I sat against a tree, watching the forest for any signs that the Pulhu found us. The tightness I felt when we came through the portal reminded me of when they tracked me through a portal before.

I stayed up the rest of the night while my friends slept. Every time I heard a noise, I jumped. By morning I was exhausted. I checked my phone, but the messages still wouldn't send. We hiked further down the mountain, careful not to make too much noise. If anyone was looking for us, we wanted to hear them coming.

After a few hours, we stopped at a stream to rest. We were sitting down, eating whatever we could find in our packs when Abby shushed us. She could hear someone talking further downstream. We left the stream and ducked behind the trees. We moved silently between the tree trunks making our way toward the voices. When we were close enough to hear them clearly, I smiled. It was a couple of kids skipping school to play in the river. They were talking about the drive back into town.

I took my phone out. If they were coming here to skip school, we had to be getting close to a town, and if there was a town nearby, there should be cell service. I had two bars. I pressed the send button. This time it sent.

Almost immediately, the delivered tag changed to read. Mrs. Sullivan was texting back, and I showed my friends quietly.

We waited impatiently for her response. When it came, Tider jumped up, startling the kids at the river. I could hear them grabbing their stuff and asking each other if maybe a bear was in the trees. They took off downstream pretty quickly, and I laughed.

"Jordan is going to come and get us. I need to send her our GPS."

"Wait," Richard said. "What if that isn't Mrs. Sullivan. What if the Pulhu have her phone?"

I stopped writing the text. "What should we do? How am I supposed to know if it's her or not?"

"We need to ask her something that only she would know."

We all thought for a minute. "I know. I will ask her what my brother's name is."

"You don't have a brother."

"Exactly," I said, smiling.

"The Pulhu will know you don't have a brother too, Sally," Richard said, looking confused.

"Mrs. Sullivan will know I mean Tider. She knows he is like a brother to me. No one else but my parents would know what I was talking about."

"That's a great idea, Sally," Tider said. "Send it. Let's see if we can get off this mountain. I need a shower and some food." I grinned and sent the message. It only took a few seconds to get the response.

"She said Tider. It's definitely her." I sent her our location as my friends cheered quietly. Within minutes Jordan appeared.

"Hi, guys. Did you do what you needed to do?"

"We did."

"I figured. You must have stirred a hornet's nest. The Pulhu went crazy on the mountain for a few days. They were everywhere. They kept bringing more in, but the other day it stopped. All the Pulhu disappeared from the mountain except for a handful. I only saw about half of them leave, so I'm not sure where they went." He arched a brow, silently asking me what happened.

"We don't have to worry about those Pulhu. They are being taken care of." I was sure all the Pulhu who had made it through the portal would be sent to the dungeons.

He laughed. "I'm glad to hear it. Things have gotten a little crazy over here lately. The Pulhu have almost completely taken over the council. Mr. Merrem and Mr. Connor were taken in for questioning. The council thought they were hiding you, but they were let go as soon someone said they saw you on Mount Etna."

"What about Mrs. Sullivan? Why wasn't she at the school?"

"She was. Someone put a sleeping spell on her, and then hid her in one of the unused rooms. Mrs. Chanley found her and broke the spell. Mrs.

Sullivan has been in hiding with the others. That's where we are going. Adam's grandfather has a safe place for all of us. The Pulhu are hunting everyone who has helped you, Sally. They are saying you attacked Mr. Mitchel for no reason."

"That's not true."

"We know that, but Mr. Mitchel is very persuasive. Not all the council believe him, and many of the schools are shutting their doors to the council. Too many of the schools have dealt with Mr. Mitchel. A lot of the teachers won't believe a word of what he says. They are trying to protect their students, but Mr. Mitchel is already trying to get the council to give him full authority over the elementals. He made them believe the elemental community is in turmoil because of our school not following the rules, and now the other schools don't want to follow the rules either."

"How can he do this? How can any of them believe him?"

"We think he has some sort of charm that helps force multiple people to believe his lies. It is powerful to be able to work on so many people at once. Usually, charms like that are only good for one or two people at the most. Mr. Mitchel has gotten his hands on some very powerful magic recently."

We nodded in agreement. Whatever magic Mr. Mitchel was using wasn't regular elemental magic. He was using something he shouldn't be messing with. I was sure it was some form of dark magic, but where he was learning it was still a mystery.

Jordan had us grab our stuff and hold hands. He transported us into a dark room. I couldn't see anything in front of me and started to panic. A light flashed on as I began to hyperventilate, and I realized we were in a rectangular room. The door opened, and my parents ran in to hug me. I threw my arms around them, thankful they were ok. Abby's dad and even Richard's family came running over too.

Of course, Tider's family wasn't here. They were part of the Pulhu and didn't care about Tider at all unless he was helping them. My parents grabbed Tider and gave him a big hug. I watched the smile cross his face as he hugged them back.

Adam walked over to Chet and gave him a hug. Everyone was talking at once, and Chet raised his hand for silence. He told us we would be staying there from now on. The place was magically blocked, so no one could track it. The only way to transport in was to have a special charm that could move people through the magic. Jordan reached into his shirt and pulled out the necklace he was wearing to show us.

We walked through the door and into a large room filled with tables and chairs. Mr. Connor and Mr. Merrem were there, and I saw many other faces I knew. There were a lot of people I didn't know too, and I asked Mrs. Sullivan who they were.

"These are all the people the Pulhu are after." I looked around again.

There were a lot of people hiding from the Pulhu, not only me.

"You will have to stay down here now unless you have a very good reason to go out." She winked at me, knowing I would need to leave the safety of this place if I wanted to defeat the darkness. I didn't know how I would find the dryads. The prophecy said they were bad, but I could figure out how to deal with that tomorrow. Today I wanted to spend time with my family and friends over a nice meal.

ABOUT THE AUTHOR

H.M. Sandlin is a stay at home mom of two daughters. She loves to read, garden, and run. She lives in South Carolina and enjoys the heat of the long summers. She spends most of her time writing but likes going to the park with her kids when they get home from school. She also enjoys taking coffee breaks with her friends.

Every day is an adventure for H.M. Sandlin. She has many stories waiting to be told and is trying to get them all out on paper to share. Her kids are always giving her ideas for new stories, and she has multiple small books that she writes for them to read. To stay up to date, visit her website, and join her newsletter at hmsandlin.com or follow her on twitter @SandlinHm.

Other Books by H.M. Sandlin

Sneak peek of book four in Elemental Seekers

Chapter One

Everyone turned to stare as we walked farther into the room. Mr. Connor and Mr. Merrem, teachers from my school, stood up and started clapping. The rest of the large room stood up and did the same. I glanced behind me to see why they were clapping, but no one else was there. My parents started clapping too, and I looked at my friends to see what was going on. They were as confused as I was.

I felt the connection in my mind to Richard form. "Sally, I think they all know who you really are. Why else would they be clapping?" I was able to talk to all of my friends without speaking. It was an awesome power we had figured out how to use. It came in handy in situations like these where we didn't know what was going on.

I could also track them if the Pulhu took one of them, or any crazy elementals, I thought, thinking about how Adam was kidnapped by a man who was poisoning the true fire elementals. He had been keeping them in a stupor, and when we woke them, he tried to turn Adam into a mindless follower. I felt a wave of sadness as I thought about Richard and Tider killing him. He was an evil man, but I hated seeing anyone die. Hopefully, no one else would be killed.

"Sally, pay attention," Abby hissed in my ear.

I tuned back in and heard Chet talking.

"These kids managed to stop the Pulhu from getting their hands on whatever they were after," he was saying. The people in the room cheered. "The Pulhu are going to be sending as many as they can after this group right here. We must protect them at all costs. If they get ahold of them, it could turn the tide of the battle in their favor."

"Is one of these kids the chosen?" someone yelled.

"We don't know who the chosen is, but these kids have managed to put a stop to many of the Pulhu's plans. They are also the ones who hurt Mr. Mitchel at the school."

The crowd gasped, and another person yelled, "How? I've heard no one defeats him."

"He can be defeated, and he underestimated this group. He won't make that mistake again. We all know what's at stake. The Pulhu are getting more and more people on their side every day."

Chet continued talking while I let the breath I had been holding out. They didn't know I was the chosen. Or the imposter. I still wasn't sure which one I was. Everyone thought I was the chosen, but until we met the other chosen or imposter, I wouldn't know for sure. Right now, I was trying to do as the prophecy said and get all the true elementals on our side. We were going to need them to defeat the darkness.

We learned it had a name. It was called Helerium, but we still didn't know what that meant. I wanted to ask Chet. He was an archaeologist and spent all of his life researching the true elementals and their origins. Maybe he would be able to tell me what Helerium was. We sat at one of the large tables after Chet finished talking.

My parents wanted to know if I was ok after the fight with Mr. Mitchel. After I reassured them I was fine, they calmed down. I didn't tell them about the multiple times I was in danger this past week when I was in the fire elemental realm. They wouldn't let me out of their sight, and I needed to finish finding the true elementals. I found the water, air, and fire elementals so far. Next was the earth elementals, but I didn't have any idea how to find them.

The prophecy said that the dryads were bad, but that didn't mean the true earth elementals were bad. Each elemental group had come to earth with an elemental creature. The water elementals had water sprites, air elementals had sylphs, the fire elementals had dragons, and the earth elementals had dryads. No one knew if the void elementals had anything special with them. The true elementals didn't consider void an element. They thought they were part of the earth long before they came seeking refuge from the shadow king who created earth.

The shadow king hadn't been seen since he destroyed all the human elementals after they started fighting between themselves, causing massive destruction on earth. The shadow king created realms for each element and sent the elementals to live there. They weren't allowed to let humans know they existed.

Void users had been rare before the banishment, but afterward, only a handful of human void users existed. If there were any others, they kept themselves hidden. It was the most dangerous magic, and it could consume the user if they allowed any of the dark magic of void to be used while they were using the light magic of void. So far, I had been careful, and no dark magic had seeped into my golden magic, but I used it as little as possible to be safe.

I had to use it last week to save an entire town of human fire elementals after they were poisoned by the bokal berry in the fire realm. I was pretty sure I hadn't let any dark magic in, but I passed out at the end of the healing. I was too scared to think about what would happen if I messed up. Supposedly, almost all void users eventually go crazy with a lust for power.

Abby grabbed my arm and pulled me out of my thoughts. "Come on, Mrs. Sullivan is going to take us to our rooms."

Mrs. Sullivan, our headmistress at the school, led us down a long hallway.

"You girls will stay together here. Your parents are right up the hall if you need anything. You should be safe. Chet knows people on our side that were able to enchant the whole place to keep the Pulhu from being able to track anyone in here. From the outside, it looks like an ordinary warehouse."

"Why aren't there any windows?" I asked. I noticed the lack of windows right away. I didn't like being underground or in tight places.

"We are on the basement level. It is the safest. The levels above us house more people who are fighting the Pulhu, but we don't want them knowing about you or what you have been doing. Most of the people in the upper level still need to go out in public and could be caught by the Pulhu. We don't want them to break into their minds and find you. The people upstairs don't even know there is a basement level."

"How many people are going to fight the Pulhu?"

"So far, only about one hundred people are here."

"That's not a lot."

"No, but it will grow as things get worse."

"What do you mean, as they get worse."

"I forgot, you have been in the fire realm and don't know what has been happening. The darkness is getting closer. Ordinary humans are now starting wars with each other over nothing. There have been nonstop terrorist attacks, and all the major powers are gearing up to fight each other. There is even a mandatory draft in many countries."

"We need to stop them," I said in horror. "They will destroy the world."

"We have been trying, but no one can get through to them. The regular humans think they are doing the right thing. Everyone is being manipulated by the darkness, or maybe by the Pulhu."

I thought back to what the air elemental had told me. We only had until the end of summer before the darkness arrived. I easily used half of that time dealing with the fire elementals. I needed to find the earth elementals right away. When I asked Mrs. Sullivan she told me not to worry, Chet had an idea about where they were, and he would tell us after we got some rest.

She left us in our room, and we both rested for a few hours. I couldn't sleep any longer, so I snuck out of the room, careful not to wake Abby. She had done a lot in the fire realm and needed her sleep.

I made my way back down the hallway, first stopping to see if my parents were around. I met them in the main room. They called it the meeting room since everyone met there. The rooms were too small in the rest of the place for big meetings.

I talked to my parents for a while, letting them know a little bit about what I needed to do next. They weren't pleased, but they knew I had to, or the whole world could potentially be destroyed. They let me know they supported me and asked if there was anything they could do to help. I gave them the task of finding anything they could on void, but I warned them not to let anyone know they were researching it unless they fully trusted them. When my dad asked how dangerous it was to go into each realm, I sidestepped the question. I couldn't lie to them, but I didn't want to tell the truth either.

Giving them something to do would keep them from worrying so much about me, and I really did need more information on void. I saw Chet walk down a different hallway while I was talking to my parents and followed after saying goodbye. I promised to meet them for dinner. I was surprised they weren't trying to follow me around. Before I learned I was an elemental, my parents wouldn't have allowed me to do half of the things I was doing lately. Maybe they realized I could take care of myself. I was almost an adult, after all.

I strode down the hallway like I knew where I was going. I didn't see anyone familiar, but the few people I passed didn't try to stop me. I continued until I heard Mrs. Sullivan and Chet talking. They mentioned my name, and I stopped. It wasn't right to eavesdrop, so I started forward until I heard Chet say something about the imposter. I stopped again and looked up and down the hallway. When I didn't see anyone, I put an invisibility shield up and crept closer to the open door.

"We don't know which one is the imposter," Mrs. Sullivan was saying.

"What if we got it wrong. We can't let her sit in their jail. She could be the chosen."

"What if she is the imposter and we break her out of the Pulhu jail? She could destroy everything."

"I think we need to tell Sally," a new voice chimed in. It was Mr. Merrem. I heard Mr. Connor agree.

"If we tell her, she will try to save the girl no matter what. She could be captured too."

"We can't tell her. We can't take that chance," Mr. Burwel spoke up. I was surprised he was here. I didn't think Mrs. Sullivan would trust him since he was from the council. He was part of the reason Mrs. Sullivan was suspended from the school. That was before Mr. Mitchel had shown his true allegiance to the Pulhu in front of Mr. Burwel. I knew Mr. Burwel was a good teacher, and if everyone decided to trust him, so would I. I could still learn a lot from him.

I listened to them argue with a few other voices I didn't recognize. When they finally agreed not to tell me, I slipped back down the hallway to find my friends. We needed to break this girl out of the Pulhu prison. She could be the key to saving the world from the darkness, and the adults weren't saving her.

I used my connection to call my friends to the main room. I picked a table in the corner and waited for everyone else to show up. Once we were all seated, I put up a silence bubble. No one would be able to hear us talk. I wished we could all talk in our heads, but I was only able to connect with them. They couldn't hear each other, and I didn't want to relay all the information to everyone.

I told them what I heard the adults saying.

"I can't believe they didn't tell us," Richard said.

"I can," Tider replied. "They are trying to protect Sally and keep the world from being ruled by the darkness. They think Sally is the chosen."

"We all think Sally is the chosen, don't we?" Abby asked.

"I don't," I said. "I told you guys I wasn't sure. I think we need to find this girl. Until we know for sure which of us is the chosen, we need her with us."

"And what if she is the imposter. Remember the note we read, beware the imposter?"

"If she's the imposter, it's better for her to be with us than with the Pulhu. I'm sure they are trying to corrupt her. If they think she could be the chosen they will want her to embrace the darkness. If she is the imposter, she can destroy the world by trying to fight the darkness. Either way, in the hands of the Pulhu, she is dangerous. With us, she might not turn to the darkness at all."

"Let's break her out then," Adam said.

"I agree. Even if she is the imposter, we can't let her be a prisoner of the Pulhu any longer."

Tider was the only one who wasn't sure we should save the girl, but after a little more arguing, he finally agreed. We talked about ways to find out where the Pulhu could be hiding her. We wouldn't be able to ask anyone, or they would know what we were up to.

We saw Chet heading toward us, and I lifted the silence bubble as he walked up. We started talking about random things, and he looked at us strangely.

"What are you up to?"

"Nothing," we all said.

"I'm sure you're up to something."

"We are trying to find out where the entrance to the earth elemental realm is," Tider said in a quiet voice. He was the best at lying, and we all nodded. Technically it wasn't a lie. We were trying to figure that out, we just had to deal with the imprisoned girl too now.

"I can help you with that," Chet said. "Why don't you follow me. We have a room set up down the hall where we all can put our knowledge together to try to figure out what to do next. I have a map in there of the locations I think they might be in."

Chet led us to the room he had been in with all the other adults, discussing the other girl. I looked around as we walked in, amazed at how big it was and all the different maps taped to the walls. Chet explained that each map was a different part of the world. He showed us the red pins sticking out of the maps. They indicated a strong Pulhu presence. I noticed many areas where a group of red pins was surrounding a black pin. Chet explained the black pins were for us, those not in the Pulhu, and actively fighting back.

There weren't many black pins compared to red pins. Seeing the maps reminded me how far the darkness was already spreading. Too many people were becoming corrupt, and more would follow.

Chet led us to a few maps on the back wall. They were of each continent. Blue pins were placed sporadically on the maps. I watched as Chet took one of the blue pins out and replaced it with a green pin.

"What are you doing?" I asked.

"Each blue pin is a location that could be the entrance to the earth elemental realm. We have someone going and checking those places out. If they aren't viable options, we change the pin to green, so we know it's not the right spot."

"How do you know if it's not the entrance?"

"We don't always, that's why there are a couple of yellow pins. Those are for unsure areas. If an area has become populated and is teeming with people, we know it isn't an entrance and mark it off. The entrances to the realms are set in areas that humans can't live in or get to easily."

"That makes sense. So how will we figure out which of these places is the right place." I looked at the maps. There were at least fifteen different places marked with a blue pin and a few yellows. "This is going to take a lot of time."

"Don't worry. We have a plan for that. Jordan is going to start transporting you to these spots. He will only take you and Abby, so he doesn't get tired too fast. He should be able to take you to at least three to four spots each day. We also have another transporter who can help if we need her."

"I don't even know what I'm looking for."

Chet walked across the room and grabbed a pile of books. "These are the best books on earth elementals. I've read them, and they talk about a symbol carved into a tree that opens the portal."

He walked over to a set of drawers and pulled out a yellowed piece of paper. "This was inside one of the books I unearthed during one of my digs. It's the only thing I've found that resembles the symbol I've read about."

He handed the paper to me. I spread it out on the table in front of me. A triangle surrounded by an oval with lines that could be wings crossing the center was drawn on the paper. It looked familiar. I had seen this symbol before. I tried to remember where, but the memory was too blurry. Hopefully, it would come back to me. I asked my friends if they had seen the symbol, but none of them remembered it.

I asked Chet for a copy, which he handed to me from another pile of papers. He said he had been giving them out for people to keep an eye out for it. He hadn't heard anything back from anyone yet though. We moved back to the map.

We made plans for which sites we wanted to go to first. I used my connection to Richard and asked him to keep Chet occupied while I looked around the room. I wanted to see if there were any areas Chet didn't want me looking.

Richard asked Chet a question about one of the areas with red pins, and I slowly walked around the room, looking at the different maps on the walls and glancing down at the desks. I didn't see anything that talked about a Pulhu prison, but there were a lot of papers on different businesses the Pulhu owned.

As I rounded one of the desks on the far side of the room, Chet abruptly stopped his conversation with Richard and walked over to me.

"What are you looking at, Sally?" he asked.

"Nothing really. There is so much information on the Pulhu here. It must have taken years to gather it all."

He laughed nervously. "It did, but it's mostly boring paperwork." He led me back to the map. "This is the most important part, finding the earth elemental portal."

"Can we start now? I want to find it soon."

Chet relaxed as I talked about the map and seemingly forgot about the rest of the room. "No, tomorrow is soon enough. You need to read those books and get some rest. You just got here after all."

Chet talked for a few more minutes and then shooed us out of the room, telling us he had some work to do. We headed to the main room. We had our own work to do.

Made in the USA
Columbia, SC
02 August 2022